KV-372-657

PART ONE

THE SURVIVORS

ADAPT

By Don Thomas

Copyright © 2015 Donald L. Thomas
All rights reserved.
ISBN: 1519683383
ISBN-13:978-1519683380

CHAPTER 1

Jeffrey left the seminar at 1:40 P.M. He thought he had better not stop for lunch it was too late and he wanted to check his instruments at the office. The seminar had been on global warming. However, the primary conversations involved the recent sighting of a huge asteroid, 7736 Ru8, streaming toward earth. It was scheduled to be its closest, about 40,000 miles, that afternoon, which astrologically is a very near miss. He was anxious to check his instruments for the latest info and see what effect its proximity had to them.

He crossed the plaza leading to his office building. He went around the central fountain which blew a fine spray on him from the slight breeze of this late summer day. What a glorious day he thought. Mid 70's, a gentle breeze rustling the trees and flowers. He was ambivalent about global warming in spite of the lecturers foreboding. I need more proof he thought.

He arrived at the steps leading to his office building just as his colleague Jennifer did.

"Hi Jen, just getting back from lunch? Lucky you, I didn't have time."

"Oh that's too bad Jeff. Here, I've got a half of a chicken pita you can have,"

"I'll take it but you'll probably want a dinner for it."

"Of course. Flowers would be nice too."

They ascended the steps into the building, crossed the lobby, waved to Harry, the guard, and entered the elevator. Jeff pressed the Down button and said his usual "to the catacombs" remark. At that instant there was a huge explosion outside of the steel walls of the elevator. Both he and Jen were pushed forcibly into the back wall of the elevator. Both struck their heads on the wall and were knocked unconscious and fell to the floor.

Jeff was the first to awaken. He felt the back of his head and found a large, very tender bump. Re-gaining his senses somewhat, he looked over at Jen. He was afraid to touch her or move her until he was certain she didn't have a broken arm or leg or worse.

He called to her; "Jen, Jen, wake up, wake up. Are you alright? Jen?"

She moaned and shook her head slightly. Her eyes opened a bit, she blinked twice and said "What happened? What happened, Jeff? I remember getting in the elevator and then what happened?"

"I don't know, Jen. But are you alright? Can you move? You don't have any broken bones or anything do you?"

"I think I'm alright, Jeff. Where are we? Did we make it downstairs to the office?"

"I don't know but I doubt it. That explosion or whatever it was happened just when I pressed the button."

"Do you think pressing the button caused it?'

"No, I don't think so. If the elevator exploded, we wouldn't be here. I'm going to try to get the door open so we can see what's going on."

Jeff looked at the control panel of the elevator. He wondered if the electricity was still on. He thought it was until he noticed that the only light in the car was coming from the battery back-up emergency lights. He saw a small door above the control panel that said "manual controls". The inside surface of the door had a sign saying "move lever to the right – caution – open door slowly". Jeff moved the lever slowly, nervous about what he would find. Would they be in the basement? Would they be halfway between floors? What would he find?

He was not prepared for what he did find.

CHAPTER 2

The lobby was destroyed. All the windows were shattered. There was broken glass and debris everywhere. Well, he thought, at least that answers the question of which floor we're on. But that's the only question that's answered. He still didn't know what happened. He looked up and there was no ceiling above him. All the upper floors of the building were gone. He looked out through the broken windows and saw that it was dark and wondered how long they had been unconscious. He saw no movement outside except the flickering flames of fires he could see in the remains of the surrounding buildings. A pall of smoke hung over everything outside. We've been attacked he thought. The nuclear war has started. The radiation, what about the radiation? He knew that if there was radiation it was already too late for him. He was already exposed. He carefully walked over to the guard station avoiding the debris that was everywhere. Harry wasn't there. No-one was there.

Jen followed him out of the elevator and to the guard station. The only light was coming from some very dim emergency lights. Jeff decided not to mention the radiation until he could check the readings.

"Brr, I'm cold, Jeff. Why is it so cold in here?"

"You're right. I hadn't noticed, but it's freezing in here. That's strange. It was a beautiful day when we got here. It's like that explosion or whatever it was sucked all the warmth out of the air. Let's see if we can get downstairs to the office. Maybe they know what happened."

They walked around the useless elevator to the stairs. They had to clear the debris away from the door before they could open it. However, that steel fire-door had kept the debris off of the stairs. They walked down the stairs to the hall. They opened the door to their offices and lab. They called out but no-one answered. Apparently their co-workers were gone. Jeff thought of course they are. After the explosion and its aftermath they had probably gone home. It is dark outside. Jeff wondered what time it was. He pulled out his cell phone. His phone was on military time because of his work as a climatologist. It read 1433 hours, 2:33 P.M. Jeff thought that's odd, it's dark outside. The emergency lights were the only illumination. Jeff went to the mechanical room and started the standby gas generator. Thank god he thought we had this installed in case the power service was interrupted.

"Is that going to get any heat in here, Jeff? It's still really cold."

"Not much. I've got a portable electric heater in my office. I'll get it. It will help. I wonder where Stan and the crew are. It seems nobody's here. Maybe they had to evacuate and didn't realize we were in the elevator. I'll try Stan's cell phone."

Jeff punched in Stan's number; "Jeffrey, I'm so glad to here from you. Have you seen Jennifer?"

"She's here with me, Stan. We're alright. We were trapped in the elevator. What the hell happened?"

"Where are you, Jeff?"

"I'm at the office."

"That's good, Jeff. When it happened the only thing that saved us was being in the basement. Maybe you can give us some readings on how dangerous the conditions are outside."

"When what happened, Stan? Jen and I got in the elevator to come in to work and Bam, that's all I remember."

"From what they're saying, from the few resources they still have available, that asteroid that was supposed to fly by, for some unknown reason exploded instead. They say the force of the explosion altered the earth's orbit, pushed us into the shadow of Venus. It all sounds so fantastic it's hard to believe. Maybe with your instruments you can give us more information. I have to hang up. It's hard to find a place to re-charge this phone. Thank God it didn't destroy all the cell towers. Text me. It takes less juice. See what you can find out. Bye"

Jeff told Jen what Stan had said and they agreed they should check all their instruments to see if they could get more information. They set to work.

11

CHAPTER 3

"Well, Jen I've checked the outside air quality readings and they're not bad. No radiation to speak of and no harmful gasses. It may be rather smoky but I think we should go outside and see just what the hell happened. It seemed to be cold outside, it is in here. I've a couple jackets in my office that I use to check the roof-top equipment. I'll get them. I was getting really tired of having to go all the way up there from here while they remodeled our offices, but now I'm glad it's taking them so long. If we had been up there instead of in the elevator when the explosion hit we could have died."

They put the jackets on and made their way back up the stairs. They crossed the glass strewn lobby and exited through what used to be the doors. They looked up and down the street. All the buildings were heavily damaged. Most of them were just a pile of rubble with very few walls left standing. Jeff shuddered to think of all the people that must have been in those buildings. They must have perished in the explosion. He thought how lucky he and Jen were. If they had been ten seconds later, they wouldn't be here. They descended the steps. The same steps on which he had encountered Jen on her way back to work about an hour and a half ago. He thought it was about an hour and a half as he had checked the time not long ago. It seemed so long ago now. They saw the fountain on the plaza was off. They looked into the reflecting pool and saw a thin film of ice covering it.

"It must be colder than I thought. I'll check the temperature readings when we get back to the office." He said.

They looked around. There was devastation everywhere. They saw no-one.

"This is really strange. Where are all the people? How did they get everyone out of here so fast? No police, no fire trucks, no emergency vehicles." Jeff was thoroughly puzzled.

It was spooky out there so they headed back to the office that was also spooky but less spooky. Jeff sat at his climate computer and typed in a request for historical readings. Thank goodness the computers had battery back-ups. The current reading of the outdoor temperature was 31 degrees. Checking the hour by hour history Jeff found the temperature one hour ago was 34 degrees. The hour previous to that it was 36 degrees. He continued checking and found the temperature had not been higher than 42 degrees for four days. But that's impossible he thought. When I came back from my seminar this afternoon it was about 75 degrees.

"Jen, Jen, come here. You have to see this. This computer says it hasn't been more than 42 degrees for four days. Just how long were we unconscious? I'm calling Stan again. I want to know what's going on. What day is it and where is he?"

He punched in Stan's number; "Stan, I'm sorry I have to use up your cell battery but I have to know what's going on. Where are you? What day is this? Where are all the people?"

"Jeff, I was so happy to here from you earlier that I forgot you didn't know any of the details. When the asteroid exploded, the force of the explosion caused a severe increase in air pressure and most people that were outside disintegrated and were swept away by the cosmic wind that forced us into our new orbit. That's the theory anyway. No-one that was outside can confirm it. There are a lot of distraught families. Since those folks were shall we say "gone with the wind." The remaining authorities were unsure as to what to expect next.

They ordered everyone to take temporary shelter underground. Tunnels, caves, or deep basements they said. Thank God you missed all that. It was traumatic. I'm thinking that you and Jen must have been affected by the cosmic wind to be unconscious for four days. I think it's four days as I believe today is Tuesday although it's hard to know when you're living in a cave and it never really gets to be daylight outside. The rest of the crew and I are in what they call the Jerseyville Caverns."

"What do you mean it never gets to be daylight outside?"

"I mentioned to you that we are in the shadow of Venus. We have been since the cosmic wind blew us into a different orbit. It's a good thing we are living in a cave as sometimes the temperature falls close to zero outside but the earth so far has maintained its underground temperature of 54 degrees. We don't know how long that will last and then what will we do?"

"Thanks for the info, Stan. Next time I'll text you, but this time I just had to talk to you. I'll get back on my equipment and see what I can find out."

Jeff went back to work. After a couple of hours of diligent effort he discovered what he thought was the new orbit pattern. According to his calculations the earth was now three million miles closer to Venus, not that much as cosmic space goes, but to be pushed that far in four days they would have had to been pushed at least 30,000 miles an hour by the force of the explosion. The new orbit matched the orbit of Venus for about 120 days a year. Venus revolves around the sun in 220 days. The new orbit of the earth would be 345 days, not the 365 plus it had before. Comparing it to the orbit of Venus, he concluded the earth would be in the full shadow of Venus for 90 days each year with 15 days getting into the full shadow and 15 days getting out. Since they would not be warmed by the sun for those 90 days, it would get very cold.

Conversely, their shorter orbit would put them closer to the sun than previously, which would make that time of year very warm if not downright hot. He re-checked his calculations and was disheartened when he found them to be correct.

"Jen, come here please. I want you to check my work here and see if I missed anything."

Jen spent some time reviewing his calculations and said; "They look correct to me but then you know a lot more about these things than I do. Besides, I'm hungry. What are we going to do for food?"

"Now that you mention it, I never did get to eat that chicken pita you gave me. I must have dropped it in the elevator. Oh well, it's four days old now."

"Just because you dropped it and never ate it doesn't mean you can weasel out of buying me dinner if we ever get out of this mess. I will forgo the flowers. The cold weather has probably killed them all anyway."

"I will gladly buy you dinner and flowers if we ever get out of this mess. In the meantime, let's see if we can find something to eat. If the evacuation was as quick as Stan said, there is going to be food left in refrigerators and cupboards. Put on your jacket and let's go find some."

CHAPTER 4

They made their way up the stairs and through the lobby. They wandered from office to office searching for food. The fifth door they tried opened to a lounge area with cabinets and a refrigerator. They found four cans of soda, two bottles of water, a bag of potato chips and an apple. After raiding all the other offices and finding nothing, they decided to go outside and see if they would have better luck in what was left of another building. Upon exiting their building they thought it had gotten even colder. They descended the steps and made their way to the building next to them. Flipping on the flashlight he had retrieved from his office, Jeff pushed through the mangled door, Jennifer right behind him, and reviewed another scene of debris and destruction. They moved cautiously into the building and through what surely was the reception area which was now a jumble of smashed chairs, tables and desks. They went down the hall to their right and through the first open door. The flashlight illuminated an overturned desk and what appeared to be a mini-bar with a small refrigerator. Hallelujah Jeff said and moved around the desk toward the fridge.

“Stay there, Jen, you don’t need to see this.”

But she was already by his side looking at what used to be a person. The body was mangled and disfigured as if it was being devoured by an animal.

“My God, Jeff, let’s get out of here. What could have done that? I’m not hungry enough to stay here any longer.”

"It looks like some animal did that. If they haven't eaten in four days and no-one's taking care of them it could be. I just hope the poor guy was already dead when it happened."

"Yuck, Jeff, you didn't have to say that. I'm going back to the office. You can continue your scavenger hunt by yourself."

He watched her go into their building and then continued his search. After three more buildings he had found some bagged snacks and some canned goods He wondered how he would heat them if he could get them opened. He headed back toward his office and thought he saw some movement out of the corner of his eye. He shone his light in that direction but saw nothing. He moved toward his office again, heard a growl and turned to face a crouched dog. The dog was of medium size and appeared to be a terrier mix. When he shone his light on it he saw it had a collar and tags and was probably some very hungry abandoned pet. He dug in his bag and found some snacks and laid them on the ground. The dog didn't move so Jeff backed away. When he was some twenty feet away the dog approached and started eating. He turned back to his office.

"I'm back, Jen. I found enough that I don't think we'll starve but it won't be gourmet dining."

"I'm so glad you're back. After what we saw, I didn't know what you would find out there."

"It was fairly uneventful but I did have one nervous incident. I heard a growl and turned around to see a dog crouched behind me. He didn't look like he was ready to spring so I laid some food on the ground and backed away."

"Wonder if you were wrong and that was the animal that did that thing we saw before."

"He didn't look like a killer. He had a collar and tags. I'm sure he's an abandoned or lost pet."

Jeff and Jen went through the food Jeff had gotten and had something to eat. Not delicious but life-sustaining.

CHAPTER 5

Jeff called Stan and after first apologizing for calling instead of texting told him his theory of the new earth orbit. He asked Stan if he knew anyone that could corroborate his theory. Stan replied that he should try to contact Dr. Hollis Blackmore, chief astrophysicist, at the National Meteorological Bureau. He said to give Holly a call, gave him the number and wished him good luck. Jeff hung up and tried the number. After several rings it was answered.

A deep male voice said; "Hello, this is Dr. Blackmore"

Jeff stammered and said; "Dr. Blackmore, this is Jeffrey Lawrence, Stan Patterson said I should call you about a theory I have about our current situation. I'm a climatologist and I work with Stan."

"You sounded surprised Jeff. You were expecting a woman. I get that a lot. Well, Jeff, may I call you Jeff, you can call me Holly, everybody does. We need some new theories. As you can imagine this place has been a madhouse the past few days."

Jeff outlined his findings to him and waited for his reply.

"You're on the right track, Jeff. However, we've discovered a few things recently you should be aware of.

No.1 Although we endured a tremendous and deadly, punishing explosive force the earth is still revolving at the same rate as before. So a day is still a day.

No.2. That means that as it revolves it will all be in Venus shadow. Asia, Europe, South America, Africa and everywhere will have twenty-four hours of darkness every day for about three months a year. We are hoping, so far it is true, that since the sun is so large, everyday it will be like a total solar eclipse and some light and heat will leak out around the circumference.

No.3. We are unsure how deep the frost will penetrate in such a prolonged period of cold. Perhaps you would have a better idea of that being an earth person and not a space person like us.

No.4. Snowfall, rainfall, wind. We don't know at this time how they are affected. We do know that this is the fifth day since the explosion and no one on earth has had rain since then. Not even the rainforests. This of course is disastrous as it affects the growing season, the food supply, the water supply, everything. If you come up with anything else Jeff, let me know. I'll do the same. We, and all other agencies, are working on getting the infrastructure up and running as quickly as possible. Thank you for your help."

Jeff called Stan; "I talked to Dr. Blackmore. He said they are still searching for answers and will call when he has news. Should we get together now? Where is Jerseyville Cavern and how do I get there?"

"They wouldn't let you in if you did find it as we are at maximum occupancy. I found a charging station I can use so you don't need to apologize for phoning. I would have to get permission for you and Jen to get in here. I can do that but it will take a day. As to how you find it, you need to know that twice a day the military shuttle drives through the neighborhoods picking up approved stragglers. It is always about 12 hours apart. They drive a big armored vehicle, a JLTV they call it, with a revolving top light and a siren. When you're ready to come here, watch for them 12 hours since their last pass through and hurry out and get aboard. I'll give them a thumbs up about your location. Be careful, I don't know if you've been out but I hear there are some survivors out there called stragglers, who are very dangerous."

"Okay, Stan I'll be in touch."

CHAPTER 6

Jeff decided to check the outside to see if anything had changed. He climbed the stairs, rounded the corner of the elevator and found the dog he had seen curled up in front of it. The dog opened its eyes and arose when it saw Jeff. Jeff was slightly apprehensive until it wagged its tail and approached him. He petted its head and said he was sorry but he didn't have anything for it to eat. He moved toward the exit door and the dog followed. They stepped outside. The dog stopped, raised its hackles and emitted a low growl. Jeff looked up and saw a group of four or five people 200 yards down the street. He thought they can't be good if the dog is wary of them. He turned to go back into the building just as one of them looked up. At that instant a siren went off and the rescue vehicle rounded the corner with its lights flashing. The group of stragglers turned and ran.

Jeff went out to meet the vehicle. They stopped and the driver rolled down his window. He had a .45 pointed at Jeff.

"May I have your name sir, and some I.D.?"

Jeff fumbled in his pocket for his wallet with his driver's license. Handed it to the officer and asked if they could take him and his colleague to Jerseyville Cavern.

The officer replied; "I'm from Jerseyville Cavern but I can't take you there until I get the proper paperwork. If you can arrange that, we'll be back in about 12 hours, sorry sir."

With that, he gave Jeff his wallet, closed his window and they drove away.

Jeff went back into the building, the dog following him. He told Jen about seeing the stragglers and about his conversation with the rescue vehicle.

"Is that the dog you gave the snack to? You're right. I don't think he was that scavenger dog. He's probably an abandoned or lost pet. Poor thing."

"I thought you'd feel that way once you saw him Jen. However, we have bigger problems. I don't know if that straggler saw me or looked up because of the rescue truck. Anyway, we can't take the chance. Stan said they are very dangerous. I'd better call him and have him get the paperwork so we can get out of here ASAP."

Jeff contacted Stan, told him what happened and asked him to expedite the paperwork.

Stan called back shortly thereafter; "Jeff, I went to the headquarters office. The only one there was the night clerk, a civilian, Albert Boyd. I told him what I wanted and he said I would have to come back in the morning and see the military commandant who is in charge of the facility. That would be Colonel Alexander Burden. Colonel Burden was not available. He is making his nightly inspection of the guards at the cell phone tower. The cell towers supply our only means of communication at this time. Radios and televisions have been affected by the cosmic wind or something and are useless right now."

Disappointed, Jeff told Jen the news and his hope that the paperwork could be completed within the 12 hour window before the truck returned. Hopefully the stragglers had not seen him. They were marauding and looking for anything that would help them survive so they would probably be coming here sometime. Jeff hoped it was after they had been rescued. Jen disconsolately leaned against the wall and slid down to a sitting position with her back against the wall. Jeff knew her feeling because his was the same. He slid down the wall and sat next to her. He took her hand and held it hoping she would feel that they were in this together and she was not alone. Several minutes passed. The dog, which had been sleeping on the floor, arose, padded over and licked Jen on the cheek. She smiled and petted his head. She wondered what his name is but it was not on the tags.

"Thanks for the kiss boy, now I feel better. We should give you a name. It's like you were blown in by the big bang. We'll call you "Banger." Is that alright with you, Jeff?"

"Sure. That's a good name for him."

The dog curled up on the floor and slept.

CHAPTER 7

The night passed slowly and nervously for them. The dog being there was comforting. He would be able to hear trouble long before them. After nine and a half hours Jeff could not stand it anymore.

He called Stan. "Any good news on the paperwork?"

"Well, I filled out the application and it is in Colonel Burden's hands but no word yet. I'm in his office waiting to speak to him. Hopefully soon."

The phone rang. The clerk answered and said "Yes, sir" turned to Stan and said; "Colonel Burden will see you now"

Stan rolled into Colonel Burden's office. It was austere. A desk, two straight-backed chairs, a map of the district and a picture of the President. At the front of the desk was a nameplate reading "Col. Alexander M. Burden"

He addressed Stan; "Why is it so important that Mr. Lawrence and Miss Quigley be admitted to Jerseyville Cavern? You know we are presently at maximum capacity"

"Yes, sir, I understand that. Mr. Lawrence and Miss Quigley are climatologists and are working with Dr. Hollis Blackmore of the National Meteorological Bureau to arrive at survival parameters. They are in a very dangerous location at present. They also have much equipment in their office that would be a tremendous scientific help if we could get it here."

"I'm going to reluctantly approve this and have the rescue truck crew help with getting the equipment. However, I wish to meet with Mr. Lawrence and Miss Quigley as soon as they arrive. That's all." He turned back to the paperwork on his desk.

Stan, though happy he got the approval for Jeff and Jen and the equipment, was very put off by the Colonel's arrogant attitude. He left the Colonel's office. Boyd the clerk was gone.

A military man was now at the desk. A Sergeant Riley according to his name tag.

"What happens now that I got the approval, Sergeant?"

"I'll fill out the paperwork for the Colonel's signature and get it to the rescue truck crew. You need to tell your people it's been approved and they should get ready to evacuate."

"Thank you, Sergeant. Is the Colonel always that brusque?"

"He's very military, sir. Very much by the book. I have never known anyone that has as much a sense of duty and love of country as he though."

Stan called Jeff and told him his evacuation had been approved. The truck crew would help with loading the equipment. Stan also voiced his concern that the approval would not reach the crew prior to their leaving for their rounds.

"Thanks, Stan, That's a relief. I certainly hope the paperwork gets there in time. We don't want to spend another minute here, much less another 12 hours."

Jeff told Jen their evacuation had been approved. They immediately set about deciding which equipment they should take and readying it for removal and transport. After a half hour, Jeff decided he would go to look for the truck as it was almost time for it to arrive. Jen stayed to finish packing. Jeff made his way up the stairs to the lobby. The emergency lights were getting increasingly dimmer. The temperature had fallen another few degrees and his light jacket was barely enough to prevent his being incapacitated by the cold. He wondered how they were going to survive the constant cold. He reached the door, looked out into the darkness and did not see the comforting lights of the rescue truck. However, he could make out some moving shadows down the street and knew instinctively it was a group of stragglers. He didn't think they had noticed him, but they would present a problem if the rescue truck arrived. He waited quietly inside the lobby for the truck to arrive, not even stamping his feet as any noise may alert the stragglers. The minutes dragged by slowly and still no truck. He waited, shivering uncontrollably, for thirty minutes past the time the truck should have been there.

Then, disappointedly, went down and told Jen the bad news that it would be another twelve hours before they could leave. It was slightly warmer in the basement because of the heater and he stopped shivering. They decided they would have to be very quiet and turn out the lights so as not to alert the stragglers. With the lights out, they could barely see each other by the dim glow from the dials of the equipment still hooked-up. Time dragged slowly by as it always does if there is no stimulating activity. Eventually they began to tell each other the events of their lives. Their schooling, their families their hopes for what is now a dubious future. Though Jen had only been at the climatology office for less than four months, she and Jeff had instantly made a friendly connection. Jeff, though interested, had not asked her out because it can be very uncomfortable if things go awry. Now everything has gone awry and their conversation and predicament led to a new feeling in their relationship. As the night passed, the time went increasingly fast as they were more and more comfortable with each other as individuals and not just co-workers. That comfort led to a hug, which led to a kiss, which led to several more kisses, which was stopped by a low growl from Banger and the sound of voices outside their door. Their joy immediately turned to fear. They remained deathly quiet, their hearts pounding. Not in desire, but in fear.

Then a voice called; "Mr. Lawrence, Miss Quigley, this is Lieutenant Edwards from the truck. Sorry we're late. We got a call from Sergeant Riley, Colonel Burden's clerk, telling us to delay our departure as he had an emergency evacuation order for us. You're that order. Are you in there?"

Jeff extricated himself from Jen's arms and went to the door.

He said; "We are so glad you're here." Even though part of him wished they weren't right at this moment.

"If you'll tell us what equipment needs moved, we'll get right on it. I don't want to be out of the truck for too long. It can be dangerous as some of these stragglers are merciless. Some are alright but it's hard to tell the good from the bad. I figure as soon as they start shooting at me, they're the bad ones."

There were two men with Edwards. All were armed with rifles and handguns. When told what equipment to take they immediately started removing it. Edwards told Jeff and Jen if they had any extra rations or personal items, take those also as both were in short supply at the Cavern. When all items were removed from the office, the four of them, Jeff, Jen, Edwards and one of his men, left the office. The dog followed. The men were carrying the last of the equipment. They ascended the stairs and crossed the lobby. Jeff saw that the truck was parked at the street, about 75 feet away. As they crossed the concourse and passed the now frozen fountain, a roar rang out from their left and a group of stragglers charged towards them. One, brandishing a pistol, fired several shots at them. All missed luckily but that didn't mean the next volley would. Edwards and his man immediately reached for their handguns as they were carrying the equipment and their rifles were on their shoulders. They would have had to put the equipment down and there wasn't time for that as the stragglers were getting closer. They fired and one of the stragglers staggered and stopped running. The others kept coming and were now just 100 feet away. "Head for the truck" Edwards said. "We'll hold them off" Jeff and Jen immediately sprinted toward the truck. Just as they got there, Jeff heard a bullet ping off the steel side of the truck. He turned to see where the two soldiers were and saw that they were retreating toward the truck, firing repeatedly at the ten or twelve stragglers closing on them. Their movements were impeded by the equipment they were carrying. Jeff was concerned that they would run out of ammunition before they could stop the stragglers charge. The cargo door of the truck opened and the third soldier of the squad told them to hurry and get in. He didn't have to tell them twice. As Jeff and Jen and Banger entered, he exited with his rifle on his shoulder and immediately started firing. With his appearance the stragglers decided to find someone less well defended and fled.

The crew got into the vehicle; luckily none had been hit in the exchange of gunfire. Edwards instructed the driver, through the intercom, to take them to Jerseyville Cavern. The driver had been left in the cab to defend it. Stragglers would love to capture one of these vehicles.

"Thank you, Lieutenant for coming for us. We were afraid to spend too much more time there. It was getting nerve-wracking."

"I'm glad we made it on time. Not only for your sake but for ours. Colonel Burden does not like his orders to go unfulfilled. Speaking of Colonel Burden, I have orders to escort the two of you to his office as soon as we arrive. I hope the dog won't be a problem."

"Good, maybe he can update us on the current situation. How long will it take to get to Jerseyville Cavern?"

"About three-quarters of an hour. That's why they called and delayed our departure. They knew we wouldn't get the Colonel's order before we had already left."

"What is this Jerseyville Cavern? I've never heard of it."

"Jerseyville Cavern has been a secret installation up to this time. It was first developed during the late 1940's or early 1950's as a gigantic bomb shelter from a nuclear attack. It was stocked, and has been periodically updated, with provisions, generators, furniture, fuel, water, building supplies and thousands of other items to sustain life for a finite number of people for a certain period of time. The number of people and the length of time is classified Top Secret. I don't have that classification. Colonel Burden does. That's why he is very strict in admitting new residents. That increases the amount of people to support with no increase in provisions. Jerseyville Cavern itself is about 100 feet under ground. The entrance is guarded 24/7 and all vehicles entering, including this one, must have proper paperwork and undergo a physical inspection both outside and inside. The Colonel doesn't want any Trojan Horses infiltrating his command. We will proceed slowly in getting there. We'll look for people wanting to be rescued and initiate the procedure if we find any. We normally don't as the stragglers have already found them."

"Who are the stragglers Lieutenant and why are they not rescued?"

"There are different kinds of stragglers. When the explosion came, some of the only buildings able to withstand the shock were the prisons. They had massive reinforced walls unlike other structures. Not all of those walls withstood the force, some crumbled. The prisoners were inside those walls that for the most part stayed intact. They escaped through the holes and began marauding, seeking clothing, food, and weapons, anything they could find. They are the most dangerous. Another group of stragglers are those people who have a huge distrust of the government. When the government told them they must go to an underground shelter, they balked. They said I don't trust the government. They're going to put us some place they can watch us. Who knows what will come next. Slave labor? They wouldn't go. Now, several days later, the shelters are full. They have to contend with the ex-cons. The weather is cold and it's always dark.

Then there are stragglers such as you two. You were at a place where you were spared in the explosion. Now you are prey for the marauders, hungry, tired, cold, and mystified as to how it happened. That's the group these rescue trucks are sent to help. We find fewer and fewer of them as the days pass."

CHAPTER 8

The truck arrived at the location of the Cavern. There was no sign identifying it. They stopped in front of a pair of steel doors set in about 25 feet from the face of the hill. An armed guard walked out of a guard outpost set discreetly into the side of the hill. A second armed guard stood at the ready at the entrance to the guard station. The guard approached the truck and asked for his authorization. The driver handed him the paperwork. He looked it over then told the driver to exit the truck and face the wall. The second guard trained his weapon on the driver while the first examined the cab. He exited the cab, went to the crew door, knocked and stood aside as the door opened. He said; "Exit the cab one at a time, state your name and move over beside the driver at my command." The passengers filed out as told. As the guard examined the papers, the dog sneaked out of the truck and crawled under it as if he knew he wasn't supposed to be there. The guard entered the crew cab and inspected it. He looked in all parcels and containers and inspected all the equipment. Upon completion of his inspection he said; "Okay, Lieutenant, you're clear to go."

They re-entered the truck, the gates swung open and they proceeded across the entrance way to a massive elevator, another guard next to it said Okay into the phone he was holding and pressed the button which opened the elevator gate. They drove onto the elevator. The gate closed and they began their descent. They arrived at the Cavern floor and exited the truck. The Cavern was probably 150 feet wide and maybe 30 feet high. They could not see the far end of it from where they were.

Edwards said; “If you’ll follow me, I’ll take you to Colonel Burden’s office.”

Jeff and Jen fell in step behind him. Banger followed. They went past another guard station that the driver headed toward. Just beyond that was a small building with a door and window on the left and a larger window on the right. They entered. They made the dog stay outside.

“Sergeant Riley, I have Mr. Lawrence and Miss Quigley here. The Colonel wanted to see them as soon as we arrived.”

“Thank you, sir. I’ll take it from here.”

Jeff and Jen threw a “Thank you, Lieutenant” over their shoulder as he left.

The Sergeant over the phone; “Sir, Mr. Lawrence and Miss Quigley are here. Yes, sir.”

The sergeant went to the door and they followed. They entered and he closed the door.

They approached the desk where Colonel Burden was seated. A few seconds passed. He did not look at them. Nor did he tell them to be seated.

He looked up and said; “Mr. Lawrence and Miss Quigley. This is a military establishment. I am the Officer in Charge. Everyone and everything in this establishment is my responsibility. I take my responsibilities very seriously. You are here because perhaps you may be of help in the country’s current situation. I hope the equipment you brought is of use. We are in short supply of everything and do not need any useless equipment. Mr. Lawrence, what is the electrical load, in amps, of this equipment? We have limited generational capacity.”

“At full load, sir, it is about 80 amps.”

"When you say "about 80 amps" I don't expect it to be 90 or 100, understand?"

"Yes, sir."

"And you Miss Quigley, what do you do?"

"I'm a climatologist in training. I have the proper college degree but must intern before I am permitted to take the exam for licensing."

"Sergeant Riley will have someone show you to your quarters and provide you with the booklet of the rules and regulations of this location. That's all."

He turned back to his desk and they left his office.

Sergeant Riley said he had called for an escort for them. He handed each a booklet of about four pages.

He said; "Read these thoroughly and carefully. The Colonel does not like anyone disobeying the rules. He is the ultimate authority and can banish you from this facility."

CHAPTER 9

The escort arrived. She was a Corporal. Her name is Lolene she said.

Jen said; "Lolene, that's an unusual name. Is it a family name? Your name tag says "Gomez."

"Gomez is my last name. My father's name is Lorenz and my mother's is Arlene so I became Lolene. I'm taking you to the compound where your colleagues are located. Your equipment should already be there. How did you get permission to get the dog in here?"

"He's a rescue too."

They got in an expanded and military version of an electric golf cart. It had a driver's seat up front and two additional seats behind. Each a bench seat for two persons. The driver's seat had a raised area beside it, so only one person, the driver, could sit up front. The raised area had a tray top and that is where Banger jumped up and sat as if it was designed specifically for him. They drove away. Other vehicles similar to theirs were going in both directions. Lolene gave them a running commentary just like a tour guide.

The first set of buildings they drove by were the barracks, mess halls and offices of the staff and guards. They were closest to the entrance in case of unwanted visitors. She said that the Colonel had lost seventy-five or eighty percent of his command in the initial explosion. They were now making do with support personnel pressed into service as guards, drivers, etc. That is one reason the Colonel is so strict. He must instill discipline in those troops immediately as they are not used to it.

They passed mostly two-story buildings which were on each side of the central driveway. The buildings were of a modular construction consisting of multi-color panels about 4 feet wide separated by vertical strips of what looked like stainless steel. They reminded Jeff of the sound abatement walls along highways although much more colorful. The panels were in a rainbow of colors, no two buildings being alike. The narrow end of the buildings faced the central driveway and it appeared as if the buildings extended all the way back to the cavern walls.

"Lolene." Jen said. "These buildings are very colorful. It looks like someone has an artistic bent."

"They're colorful for a reason. When you are living in a cave, you need something to buoy your spirits. The color relieves the monotony of the drab earth walls. Besides, all the buildings panel colors are different to help in identifying the buildings. It will be much easier to know which building is yours. And speaking of that, here we are at yours. It is not yours exclusively. People other than your co-workers will be here. All these facilities are very crowded. People will do most anything to get into this Cavern and escape the conditions outside. Try to be patient with others. People have been under extremely difficult circumstances the past few days. Most have lost everything, including their families, and they're being forced to adapt to this new lifestyle by those circumstances."

They made their way into the building and entered into a large open area at the front that served as the living room. Jeff saw that his equipment had arrived and been placed in that room. The door at the rear of the room opened and Stan came rolling out in his wheelchair. The other three members of the office, Tom, Amos and Amanda immediately followed. Hugs and "Thank God you're here's" were exchanged.

"It's great to be here." Jeff said. "The outside was getting very scary with all the marauding stragglers. I'm so glad all of you made it. Tell me, Stan, how did you get out of our building? We had to remove the debris in front of the door before we could go down to the office."

"The freight elevator at the rear of the building. The elevator you were on wasn't working of course."

"I'd forgotten about that. Thankfully the stragglers hadn't found it."

"Tell us, did you have a run-in with the stragglers? What's it like outside? We've been here four days now and know nothing of what's going on outside."

Jeff and Jen filled them in with what they knew of the situation. They told them that no solutions had been arrived at and unless something equally as drastic as the explosion took place they had to adapt to this as their new life style.

Jeff said; "What about this place? What about food? How do we spend our days? Are there work details? The Colonel said it's a military establishment. Do we have inspections?"

"Did you get one of the booklets? You need to read it. There is a mess hall the third building down. Our chow time is 6:00 A.M. to 6:30 A.M. also 11:30 A.M. to Noon and from 5:30 P.M. to 6:00 P.M. An orderly comes around every evening and gives each person three meal tickets good for the following day. They are a different color every day and have a letter on then; A, B, C, etc. You can only get in the mess hall if you have the proper ticket. You have 15 minutes after your appointed time to finish eating. Then they clean up the place for the next shift. I don't know if you've noticed, but there is a string of lights down the middle of the driveway. Those lights are dimmed from 10: 00 P.M. to 6:00 A.M. The street is patrolled overnight. All persons are double bunked. There are no private rooms. Lights out inside the buildings at 11:00 P.M. There is no radio or TV yet. Hopefully soon. Every thing is in short supply and most things are rationed. Theft is punishable by banishment to the outside. Other infractions incur similar harsh treatment. Welcome to your new world."

Jeff and Jen were surprised at the severity of the rules. Then their thoughts turned to their meeting with Colonel Burden, and they were not nearly as surprised. One of their first tasks would be to read the booklet. Thoroughly. After a discussion among the staff, it was decided that Jen would share a room with Amanda and Jeff would share a room with Stan who said; "There goes my privacy, do you snore?" "You'll find out" The other two members, both guys, Tom and Amos, would share a room as the few things they had were already there. By that time it was almost 5:30 so they freshened up for dinner.

As Jeff rolled Stan to the mess hall the conversation resumed. "You know, Jeff; one nice thing about this place for me is it has no handicap ramps. There is no rain or snow so they don't have to worry about those things. The floor of the buildings is on solid rock so shimmed strips are used to level it and plywood laid over them forms the floor."

"I'm glad you found something positive about this place

They arrived at the mess hall. It was cafeteria style. Others were there ahead of them so they waited in line for a few minutes. Jeff handed the door attendant their tickets. He grabbed two trays and headed through the line. There was a limited selection. If you selected something you got one portion. He helped Stan through the line and headed for one of the tables that could accommodate Stan's chair. The others of their group followed them and took adjoining seats. The food tasted very good to Jeff as he had had very little for days. None of the food was from fresh ingredients. All was from canned, condensed, concentrated or frozen items. Jeff thought that is what they could expect from now on.

Upon arriving back at their quarters they spent some time arranging and hooking up their equipment. There was a minimal amount of electrical outlets so equipment was scattered about the room. They were then ready to get it operational in the morning. There were many questions of which they hoped to find answers.

The orderly arrived with their meal tickets for the following day. Because of that they met the other six people who shared their floor of the building. Both floors of the building had six bedrooms which accommodated twelve people. The other three bedrooms on their floor were occupied by people with sad or fortunate stories of survival.

A weary-looking mother named Myra and her traumatized daughter Angie, a ten year old that cried all the time and clung to her mother. They had been in the basement doing laundry when the explosion occurred she said. The father was not so lucky. He was asleep in a second floor bedroom. When mother and daughter were able to get out of the basement they found the entire second story of the house was gone. They were rescued two days later.

There was a pair of older men that said nothing, took their meal tickets and went back to their room. They simply nodded when Jeff said hello, not even saying their names. They shuffled along to their room as if in a dream. Or a nightmare.

Boris and his wife Cassandra were the other duo. Boris was very happy to get his meal tickets and looked it. He looked as if he wanted everyone else's too. Cassandra said they were going through a tunnel when the explosion occurred. They were lucky the tunnel entrance they had just come through had collapsed. They could have been there except Boris was driving so fast they were through it. "Shut up Cass. You know that guy cut me off and it made me mad." Cass shut up. They took their tickets and left.

The others retired to their quarters. Jeff and Stan did the same. Jeff started to read the rules booklet. He discussed it with Stan and they agreed it was not going to be a desirable vacation spot. All residents would have to participate in some of the necessary labor details. A schedule would be established and they would be required to do their part.

Jeff said; "I'm tired, Stan. I'm going to hit the hay. We don't have to worry about bedclothes as no one has anything other than what they're wearing. I wonder if that is something the powers that be are going to address? Can I help you with anything Stan before a lay down?"

"No thanks, Jeff. I've been doing this by myself for a long time. Goodnight."

Jeff lay down, closed his eyes and thought of the previous night and his closeness to Jen. He smiled contentedly and drifted off to sleep.

CHAPTER 10

Jeff slept soundly. Exhausted from the events of the past few days. When he awoke he checked his watch. Five o'clock. Hopefully in the morning. It was impossible to tell. They were in a cave. There was neither dawn nor twilight. He arose and went to the front and looked out. The "street" lights were still on so it must be morning. They were on until 6:00 a.m. He refreshed himself in the tiny bathroom. Thought of Stan and his wheelchair and how difficult it will be for him. He checked the equipment to make sure it was operational. He went to arouse everyone as they were due in the mess hall at 6:00. If you missed a meal you were out of luck. There were no snacks to hold you over.

At 5:55 they headed toward the mess hall. There was a line already. Boris and Cassandra were in it. Eventually they were admitted and had their breakfast. Jen wrapped some of her Spam and part of a biscuit in a napkin to give to Banger.

When they returned to their quarters, Boris was waiting for them. He asked what all the equipment was for and how long it was going to be there. Jeff described it and what they were trying to do. Boris said he hoped they could do it fast as it was occupying everyone's living room space. Jeff told him that if they could find the answer to some of the problems it would help everyone. Boris said it sure would help him because right now he was with Cass twenty-four hours a day. Jeff thought it would be even more of a help to Cass but he didn't say it.

Jeff, Stan and the crew turned on the equipment and researched their memories to find a clue about the possibility of rain falling. Their initial search was fruitless. They tried several other possibilities but none of them resulted in a solution. The time passed quickly and they realized it was almost time for lunch. They refreshed themselves and headed toward the mess hall.

Upon returning to their quarters, they did get to meet the people staying on the second floor. Those people said they hoped they weren't too noisy and disturbing them. Jeff told them truthfully they hadn't realized anyone was up there.

Back to the equipment, they spent another two hours searching for answers. Being frustrated upon their failure, they decided they would have to go outside the Cavern to continue their search. They knew they would have to get the Colonel's permission to go out. They would also need some warm clothes, flashlights, transportation and an armed escort. Jeff and Jen set out for the Colonel's office. They resolved to get his office phone number for next time as it was a long walk and perhaps transportation would be available.

Jeff however, thought this was a prime opportunity to talk to Jen and was secretly glad they had this long walk, just the two of them.

"I hope you don't think I've been too cold and impersonal since our rescue." Jeff said. "So much has happened and I don't want you to think that I would take advantage of that situation. I think we should be careful so no-one gets the rumor mill going. I think too much of you for that to happen."

"I appreciate that, Jeff. I understand and know you're trying to protect us from problems we don't need at this time. Perhaps when things get stabilized somewhat…." She let that comment trail off into the future.

"I hope that's a positive perhaps."

"It is, Jeff. It is."

He took her hand and they walked to the Colonel's office. As they walked they went by many buildings. All were the same as theirs except for the streetscape fronts were of different color arrangements. They passed one building whose front panels formed a red cross. They were sure that was the Infirmary. The sides of all the buildings were of an off-white hue. Probably done to offset the drabness of the surroundings. All had an outside stair going to the second floor except the Infirmary.

They arrived at the Colonel's office and approached Sergeant Riley, stated why they were there, and wished to see the Colonel.

The Sergeant picked up his intercom and told the Colonel they were there and what they wanted. He hung up. He said to have a seat; the Colonel would see them shortly. Fifteen minutes passed. Then twenty. Then the intercom rang.

"Yes, sir. I will, sir. The Colonel will see you now."

They arose slowly and nervously made their way to the Colonel's door. Jeff tried to collect his thoughts so he could conduct persuasive reasons for their request. He felt somewhat like the Christians must have felt approaching the lions. They entered the office and approached the desk. Once again the Colonel did not offer them a seat. They stood in front of his desk and waited.

The Colonel looked up. He had a stern expression. He said; "Mr. Lawrence, Miss Quigley, what situation do you find yourselves in that you need my help?"

Jeff told him of their unsuccessful attempts to arrive at satisfactory answers to the precipitation question. They wished to conduct further experiments outside but to do so they would need warm clothing, flashlights, transportation and an armed escort.

"Mr. Lawrence, if I approve your request, how long would this take? Half a day? A day? More than a day? My facilities, supplies and personnel are very limited. You want warm clothing. This situation started in the summer and the only warm clothing available is what was here because the temperature is a constant 54 degrees. My rescue crew says it is about twenty degrees outside. I will do what I can with what I have. Exchange phone numbers with Sergeant Riley so we may contact you. You have not answered my question of how long this would take."

"Well, sir, I think we can get what we need in one day."

"I'll hold you to that. That is all. We'll contact you."

They turned and left his office with a sigh of relief that that was over. They stopped at Sergeant Riley's desk and exchanged phone numbers.

Then Jeff said; "Any chance of us getting a ride back to our compound?"

The Sergeant said he would see if anyone was available and they should wait outside. They did. Fifteen minutes later Lolene pulled up in her vehicle. They got in.

"How's your crew doing here in the cave?"

"We're surviving" Jen said "That's something we wouldn't have done outside. However, I'm getting tired of wearing these same clothes. They've been through explosions, abandonment, rescue, new housing arrangements, etc.,etc. and they are filthy dirty. Is there any way to get different clothes? The Colonel said the supplies are limited?"

"There are some army fatigues that I may be able to scrounge up for you. I know the Quartermaster Sergeant and I'll see what I can do. No promises however. Everyone's in the same predicament."

"Thanks, Lolene. I'd appreciate your trying."

They had arrived at their compound. The others wanted to know what had happened and whether they had gotten permission to go outside. Jeff told them he thought they had but the Colonel had to make the arrangements and then they would call. They were momentarily disappointed but then realized it was not a "no". Someone said this has been a long afternoon and I think its chow time. They headed to the mess hall.

The evening passed slowly. Boris, with Cassandra following, passed through the living room. Boris scowled at them. Myra and Angie came out too. They took seats with Angie sitting as close to her mother as possible. They didn't stay long.

They left and Stan said; "Did you hear that girl? She sobbed the whole night. I could hear her through the wall."

"No, I didn't hear her Stan. I was dead tired. Your bed is next to the wall so the sound carried. Sound is a powerful thing."

"Yes, it can be very powerful."

Jen said; "Without being able to do any more work right now, I wish we had a deck of cards or a chess set or something, just to pass the time."

"Oh Jen, you don't want to play chess against Stan. I tried it once. It was embarrassing."

"You play a good game, Jeff. You give me too much credit. Good night. I'm calling it quits for today."

"Thanks Stan, but I've had enough of chess with you for now. However, some time in the future when things are better I'd like to play you again. Goodnight. I'll be in very shortly. I'll try not to disturb you."

He paused, turned to Jen and said; "Do you play chess, Jen?"

"Yes I do. But I don't play games if you know what I mean."

"Yes, I know and I don't either. Good night, Jen. I look forward to seeing you in the morning."

"Me too. Goodnight

He wanted to kiss her goodnight but Tom, Amanda and Amos were still there. He bade them goodnight and walked disappointedly to his room.

CHAPTER 11

Jeff's phone rang as they were on their way to the mess hall for breakfast. "Yes, sir. That's just great. We're on our way to breakfast. Give us an hour for that and to gather what is necessary. OK, we'll be waiting. Thank you, sir."

They ate breakfast excitedly and hurriedly. They went back to their quarters and gathered the equipment.they thought they would need. They had ten minutes to spare and waited nervously. At 6:58 Lolene pulled up to their compound. She called to them to help unload as she had camo fatigues and flashlights. Jeff, Jen and Amos quickly changed.

They loaded the equipment and had no room to spare. Jeff wished Tom could go but there simply was not enough room. Lolene drove to the guard shack at the elevator and gave the guard the authorization papers. He got on the phone and said "They're here."

Lieutenant Edwards and one other man walked out of the adjacent guard quarters. Both were armed with rifles and handguns. They got into one of the golf cart vehicles parked at the guard house. They drove over to Lolene's vehicle. "Good morning." Edwards said addressing Jeff and party. He turned to Lolene and said; "Thanks, Corporal, we'll take it from here." Lolene exited the vehicle and the trooper with Edwards took her place. Jeff got in the vehicle Edwards was driving They headed toward the elevator.

"This is Sergeant Emmons. He'll be your driver. It's nice to see you again. I hope you've been as comfortable as possible considering the situation. I'm told you want to go outside to correctly determine atmospheric conditions. With hope of finding a way to produce rain. If you're successful today it will be snow or ice. It's 22 degrees outside."

They arrived at the elevator, got aboard and ascended. When it reached the entry level the gate opened and the guard at that station examined their paperwork. Being satisfied he picked up the phone and within ten seconds the massive steel doors swung open. The cold rushed in. They couldn't tell if it was windy or just the cold air. Regardless, they shivered. They put on their gloves and lifted their collars hoping to find some protection.

Edwards stopped and they pulled alongside. "Is there any particular area you need to find or can you get your readings anywhere?'

Jeff replied; "I would like to be as high up as possible. I think the chances would be better"

"We're on a mountain. We'll try to climb a little higher but I don't think these electric carts have enough power to go very far."

He drove around the mound of the entrance and headed up the hill. After ascending about 200 feet he stopped. He asked if this would be alright. Jeff's first thought was "Brr, it's cold" but he said it would be alright. He turned to Jen and Amos, nodded and they began to unload the equipment. The equipment had built-in batteries but how long they would last in this cold he didn't know. Edwards and the trooper exited their vehicles and stood alongside with their rifles unslung. While Jen and Amos were setting up the equipment Jeff looked around. Though it was dark, there was still some light emanating from the ring of the sun that shone around the globe of Venus. Jeff noticed in the distance some structures that looked like cupolas. He asked Edwards what they were.

"Those are the air intakes for the Cavern. The Cavern is huge and on a constantly changing schedule those intakes are opened to refresh the air. Whenever the intakes are opened we supply a well armed guard detail. If the stragglers could gain access when the intakes were opened, they would have direct access into the cavern. That would be disastrous. They would take the few things we have and think nothing of killing all the inhabitants."

"How many air intakes are there?" Jeff inquired.

"There are ten. That makes it very difficult to man the guard detail. The cavern is so big that if we open just one it refreshes the air in just 10 percent of the Cavern. We try to alternate and give everyone some fresh air. The stragglers know the intakes are there. They also know that they have no chance of getting into the Cavern when the intakes are closed. When they get hungry enough and desperate enough I'm sure they will try to overpower the guard detail and gain access. They roam this area all the time. That's why Emmons and I are here."

"Thanks Lieutenant. We'll try to get our readings as quickly as possible and review the results when we get back. Are you all set up Jen?"

"They're set up and running. They're running slowly. Must be the cold."

"As soon as they're finished with that exercise, run No.41. Jen."

"OK Jeff will do."

It did not get any warmer as they proceeded with their work. After an hour and a half they were finishing.

Emmons said "Lieutenant, I think I detected movement at about eight o'clock."

Edwards looked but saw no movement. Regardless, he knew Emmons was not the type to be spooked. If he thinks he saw movement there probably was some.

"Can you finish quickly Mr. Lawrence? We can't be sure we're still alone."

"Jen, are you about finished?"

“We’re wrapping it up now Jeff.”

“Good, get it packed up and into the vehicle.”

“Lieutenant.” Emmons said. “I see four bad guys at about 150 feet at eight o’clock.”

“Put a shot over their heads. Maybe it will scare them off.”

“We’ll know if they shoot back. Won’t we.”

Emmons fired. They fired back.

“Hurry up. Let’s get out of here.”

They threw the equipment in and climbed in themselves. Edwards took the drivers seat in their vehicle while Emmons got in the other. Two shots rang out. They missed. Edwards turned the key to start the vehicle and it went “rrrrrrrrrrrr” “Come on baby, start.” He tried again and it started. He pressed on the accelerator and they started moving. Two more shots rang out and Amos cried in pain. He grabbed his leg and said; “I’ve been hit.” Emmons was in his vehicle and moving. He had his handgun out and fired four quick rounds at their attackers. Both vehicles moved down the hill as quickly as possible over the rock strewn path. When they reached the Cavern entrance the guard was standing outside looking up the mountain.

He said; “I heard the shots but I couldn’t leave this Post. I thought if they followed you down the hill maybe I could help.”

“Thanks for the thought but I think they’re gone. We have a casualty so we need to get him to the Infirmary ASAP.”

“Right I’ll open the doors and make sure the elevator is there and the Infirmary is notified.”

They drove through the doors and onto the elevator and down. When they reached the Cavern floor, Edwards drove as fast as possible to the Infirmary. The emergency personnel were waiting for them and immediately took Amos in to treat his wound. They inquired how long he would be in the emergency room. They were told if it wasn’t too serious and no bones were shattered it would be about an hour. They asked Lieutenant Edwards if he could take the equipment to their compound, inform the others of what happened and have the equipment unloaded so Stan could start the analysis. He said he would be happy to do that as there was nothing he could do here. He left.

Jeff and Jen stayed at the emergency room. Jeff felt guilty that Amos had to get injured so that he could have some alone time with Jen.

"I hope it's not too serious. Hopefully no bones were broken." She said.

"I don't think they were, Jen. We'll know very shortly. I know it's an unkind thing to say, but if it had to happen, I'm glad it was Amos and not you."

"Oh, Jeff, I think it's only natural to want people we like not to be hurt."

"Nor the people we love."

"Perhaps, we'll see."

They fell silent. Jeff wondered if he had been too bold, assumed too much, and should not have rushed things. Probably, he thought. After all they had spent one night together under very harrowing circumstances. That one night should not be a basis for a permanent committed relationship. It should not be but he wanted it to be.

The doctor emerged. "I'm Doctor Linquist. Amos is resting comfortably. No bones were broken. We cleaned it, applied an antibiotic ointment and bandaged it. Would you like to see him? Fine. The nurse will show you to his room. We will keep him overnight to make sure there is no infection or complications. If everything is alright, we'll release him tomorrow. With the incidents of the past few days we have a shortage of beds. He will be on crutches for a few days."

"Thank you, Doctor. We're so glad it's not too serious."

The nurse took them to Amos' room. It was a semi-private room. The other bed was occupied. The Doctor said they were crowded. Amos was awake but drowsy. They wished him well, apologized that he was injured, told him to get well soon and everyone would be thinking of him. Then they left.

CHAPTER 12

Lieutenant Edwards arrived at the compound with the equipment. He went to the door and knocked. Amanda opened the door.

"Hello" he said. He had her hooked with that first hello.

"Yes" she said, that was a portent of things to come.

"I'm Lieutenant Edwards. I have your equipment and can someone help me unload it. There was an injury. I don't think it's too serious. Amos, I think that's his name, was shot."

"Oh my God. Where is he? What about the others? What about Jeff and Jen? Where are they?"

By that time Stan and Tom had come to the door and were listening.

"Come in Lieutenant. We'll help unload in a minute. Tell us what happened."

Edwards filled them in on the details. He told them that Jeff wanted to get the equipment to them so Stan could start on the analysis. Jeff and Jen were at the emergency room and would be until they knew Amos condition. Amanda, Tom and Edwards went to unload the equipment. They carried it in, hooked it up and Stan started reviewing the results of their exercises.

"Thank you, Lieutenant, I'm Amanda Burgess, we do appreciate all you've done. I'd like to offer you some refreshment or something, but of course we have nothing."

"I appreciate the thought, Amanda. It's Phillip. Phillip Edwards. My good friends call me Phil."

"I'll call you Phil. I hope you'll consider me one of your good friends."

"I already do, Amanda. I had better get going. With any activity outside the Cavern we have to write a detailed report. See you later."

"I hope so, Phil."

She watched him get in his vehicle and drive away. He waved goodbye to her. That's a good sign she thought.

CHAPTER 13

Edwards went back to the Infirmary to check on Amos and to see if Jeff and Jen needed a ride. He arrived at the Infirmary just as they were leaving.

"I thought you may want a ride to your place. How's Amos?"

"Thanks for thinking of us. It would have been a long walk. Amos is doing fine. No broken bones. He'll be on crutches for a while. He's resting now."

Edwards took them to the compound. He said; "I'll see if everything is alright before I leave."

They went to the door and as soon as they opened it they heard Boris voice complaining.

Upon entering Amanda said; "Hello, Phil, I'm glad you came back."

"Well I'm glad I did too. Is everything alright?"

He looked directly at Boris. Boris looked directly at him and then diverted his eyes, turned and walked down the hall to his room.

"Thanks, Lieutenant." Stan said. "You showed up just in time. He was getting surly."

"We're all under a lot of pressure, so people are going to be on edge. The Colonel wants us to be on the lookout for the troublemakers. They can make it more unpleasant than it already is. Call me if he gives you too much trouble and we'll try to change his attitude. He won't like it."

He gave them his phone number. Handing it to Amanda he said; “Nice to see you again so soon, Amanda.”

“Yes it is nice. Goodbye, Phil.”

He turned and left. Immediately Jeff and Jen said in unison; “Phil, not Lieutenant Edwards, but Phil, what happened while we were not here?”

They were told what happened and Jeff gave them an update on Amos condition. Jeff asked Stan if he had any success with the results of their morning’s work. Stan said he had not but he would continue reviewing it this afternoon. Jeff realized at that instant that it was still morning. He looked at his watch and saw that they had only about five minutes to get to the mess hall for their assigned lunch time. They had all been busy so none of them realized it was lunch time. They hustled out the door. Jeff pushing Stan, almost at a run. They made it with two minutes to spare. That only gave them about fifteen minutes to eat. That did not bother them as they were anxious to get back to work and find answers. Besides, the meals were not large enough to take more than fifteen minutes to eat.

On the trip back Stan said; “I think Boris was on his way back from lunch when he came in and started complaining to us. If he’s that nasty on a full stomach, I wonder what he’s like when he’s hungry.”

“Cassandra probably knows. I guess she went to lunch earlier unless she gave him her ticket so she could be rid of for a few minutes. From the looks of his stomach and considering how thin she is that’s a possibility.”

“It’s a good thing that Lieutenant brought you back. Things could have gotten nasty. I don’t think Boris wants to tangle with a fit young man like that. But just maybe Amanda would like that sort of entanglement.”

“I’m glad Amanda showed an interest. She’s been working very hard long before this happened. I think her social life has been on hold for a while. Besides, everyone could use a diversion from the realities of our current situation."

They went inside and immediately set to work. Hours passed with no positive results. They took a break occasionally to get their eyes away from the computer screen. At one time the two old men shuffled through the room and out the door. Not a word was said. The object of their mission known only to them. It was a mystery as the Cavern had no unusual features or attractions. Monotony ruled.

Myra and Angie made an appearance for a short time at about 5:00 P.M. They sat in a corner of the room together. Jeff thought that if they ever get out of here and back to some sort of civilization, Angie would need therapy. At 5:15 Boris, with Cassandra this time, walked through and out the door. Dinnertime I guess. The line always formed 15 minutes before the assigned meal time. Boris was always at the front or near the front of the line. The climate crew washed up for dinner and went over as a group.

They returned and continued discussing the exercise results. The orderly came with their meal tickets, called everyone together and told them that a limited supply of clothing had been secured from the stores demolished in the explosion. They are to fill out the form he would give them with their clothing sizes, shoe size and their most urgent need. They are to put their name on the form. He will affix a sticker with their location. He will gather them tomorrow when he brings the meal tickets. Are there any questions? There were none.

They went back to reviewing their work. They still found nothing useful. Jen and Amanda left to go to their room. Jen wanted more details about Amanda and "Phil".

Frustrated and tired Jeff said; "This has been a long day. Up early, left early, cold weather, got shot at, got a man injured and so far, all for naught. I'm turning in. Good night."

He left Stan and Tom still working. He wished them luck and went down the hall toward his room. He faintly heard Angie crying. The noise from Boris and Cass room was not faint at all. They seemed to be having some kind of disagreement, but Boris was doing all the talking. Loudly. Jeff entered his bedroom and shut the door and fell onto the bed. He racked his brain to see if he knew anything that may help find answers. He found nothing and dozed off.

Jeff awoke early. His watch read 4:30. He knew he was frustrated with the work. He thought he had been so absorbed in the work he had not even asked Jen how she was doing. He'll have to apologize. He thought this was a terrible place to be. It didn't even have a moon that he and Jen could take long, romantic walks in the moonlight. With that thought he realized that there was a moon. He had seen it on the horizon as they went up the mountain. The moon was shining through some high thin clouds. Not rain clouds, but clouds. If there were clouds it may be possible to induce rain. Excitedly he went back to the bedroom and roused Stan.

"Stan, Stan, wake up come out to the living room I have something I have to ask you."

Stan rolled into the living room and Jeff told him that years of seeing the moon in the heavens made him so accustomed to it he took it for granted. But in their current situation nothing could be taken for granted. He had seen the moon on the horizon when they were out. The moon let him see a cloud. If there are clouds maybe there will be rain.

Stan said; "You may be right. Let's call Holly Blackmore in the morning and see what he can tell us."

CHAPTER 14

"This is Dr. Blackmore."

"Holly, Stan Patterson. Jeff Lawrence and I have been working on trying to get a handle on what the weather is going to be in our current situation and beyond. We were unsure of the likelihood of rain, snow or any precipitation. Without those things mankind has no hope of surviving. Jeff was outside this Cavern doing some experiments and saw the moon. The moon was partially obscured by some thin clouds. We believe that if there are clouds we have a chance of getting rain. We didn't even know that the earth still had its moon."

"Good to hear from you Stan. Yes, we still have a moon, and remarkably it is in orbit with us. It is just beyond Venus' shadow which affords us a bit of reflected light. Since the earth is still spinning, we have some hours that are a bit brighter than others. Consequently, we have turned our nights and days on end. We consider the times the moon is out days since they are brighter. We are trying to determine how much longer we will be in the Shadow of Venus. We have a longer orbit so we will come in and out of it as a year passes. Our latest calculations indicate that we will be in the full shadow for sixteen more days and then coming out of it for fifteen days. Luckily, we started about in the middle of the four month period of Venus shadow. Any suggestion as to how we proceed with your theory?"

"I don't know if we should just wait a while to see if it's going to rain naturally or if there's another sort of approach we should take."

"Alright, Stan. Let's give it a couple more days and see if we get lucky. If not there is one other thing we can try."

The next afternoon Lolene brought Amos back. He was on crutches.

Stan said; "Welcome to the club."

After that they spent three very boring, monotonous days. The reports they received were negative. No rain anywhere. On the fourth day the monotony was relieved somewhat when the orderly showed up in the afternoon with some clothes for them. They immediately changed. It felt good. The fifth day passed and still no reports of rain anywhere. Stan and Jeff decided they would call Dr. Blackmore the following day.

CHAPTER 15

It was very cold for the four guards at Air Intakes No. 9 and No. 10 at the far side of the mountain. The Intakes were about 300 feet apart. The guards, to a man, were thinking only 55 more minutes and the Sergeant will come to get them. They were too cold to talk much so they made their circular forays around the structure. The intakes had been opened when they started their shift 65 minutes ago. They would remain open for another hour and be closed five minutes before the Sergeant came to get them. There was very little light emanating from the eclipse and no heat at all.

Simultaneously four shots rang out and the four guards crumpled to the ground. A horde of ragged stragglers ran to each of the Intakes, destroyed the cupolas, secured ropes to the tattered remains and one by one started to descend toward the Cavern. When they reached the screening just above the Cavern ceiling they disabled the door mechanism so that the doors couldn't be closed, cut through the screening and descended into the Cavern. It was 11:00 p.m. The street lights were on. There was very little other light.

Four stragglers had dropped onto the floor under No. 9 Intake. They hid between two of the buildings and awaited the patrol. The patrol vehicle's headlights could be seen 300 feet away. It closed the gap slowly and when abreast of the stragglers, they fired. The driver fell dead and the vehicle stopped when his foot left the accelerator. The invasion had begun.

As more stragglers dropped to the Cavern floor from Intake No. 9, the ones already on the Cavern floor began bursting through the buildings doors and rousting the residents into a pack in the middle of the street. Those that resisted were clubbed with rifles or shot. As more stragglers dropped to the floor, the capture of the residents expanded toward the Air Intakes No. 8 and No. 10. Meanwhile, the stragglers that had dropped from Intake No. 10 raced toward the far end of the Cavern which contained all of the supplies for the Cavern. They quickly over powered the guards and seized control of the supply depot as well as the fuel and water supply.

The Communication Specialist of the night watch informed the Officer-in-Charge that she was unable to contact the guards at the Air Intakes. They did not report at 11:00 P.M. She said she was also unable to contact the patrol vehicle. Then the shots that were fired reverberated throughout the Cavern. The sound bounced off the Cavern walls and immediately notified the military that the invasion had begun. The Officer –in-Charge sounded the alarm. The shrill sound of the alarm awoke the troopers and the residents.

The troopers mobilized outside their barracks; fully armed, knowing something very serious had occurred. Colonel Burden appeared, fully dressed as if he had still been awake, he had. He ordered Lieutenant Edwards and Sergeant Emmons to take two squads in the JLTV's in the direction of Intakes No. 9 and No. 10. to investigate and report.

As Edwards and Emmons neared No. 9 they saw a large amount of people standing in the middle of the street. At that moment the street lights came on to their day time brightness. They saw some stragglers were surrounding the group of residents. They stopped about 100 feet away from the group and Edwards spoke through the external speaker system.

"Who's in charge of this unlawful invasion?"

A tall, thin man with a narrow face and a small beard stepped to the center of the group. “I am” he said “My name is Felix Murchison. Perhaps you’ve heard of me.”

Edwards had heard of him. Most everyone had heard of him. He was a rabble-rousing opponent of government. An anarchist. The only government he wanted was a dictatorship with him as the dictator. He had been instrumental in fomenting civil unrest and disobedience for two decades. He had been incarcerated for masterminding the bombing of a federal communication station. Apparently he had been freed as a result of the explosion. It did not take him long to organize a group to carry out his wishes.

“You and your men have invaded a military establishment Mr. Murchison. What do you want?”

“The first thing I want is for you to exit that vehicle so that I know who I’m talking to.”

Edwards knew there was some danger in exiting the vehicle but until he did he could not listen to what Murchison wanted. He exited the vehicle.

“I’m Lieutenant Edwards”

“Lieutenant Edwards, don’t take this personally but I don’t want to talk to you. I want to talk to Colonel Alexander M. Burden. The man in charge.”

“Anything you have to say to Colonel Burden you can say to me.”

“No, no I can’t, Lieutenant. I will give you one minute to call the Colonel. If you don’t, and he doesn’t come, I will have one or more of these poor residents shot.”

Edwards got on the phone to the Command Post. “Let me talk to the Colonel” pause “Sir, we’re dealing with Felix Murchison. I’m sure you know of him. He says he won’t talk to anyone but you and is threatening to shoot one or more of the residents he captured.”

“Alright, Lieutenant, tell him I’ll come but tell him it will take a while as I am not dressed and we only have the electric vehicles and they are slow. Meanwhile I'll try to form a plan."

Edwards relayed the information to Murchison.

Murchison snarled; "I'll give him a half hour. Tell him."

Edwards did.

Colonel Burden tried to assess the situation. He met with the remainder of his officer Corp. By that time they knew that the stragglers had captured the supply depot. That was a very damaging realization as they now controlled the water supply, the fuel supply and the food. The electrical supply and substation were still in their control. When the half hour had passed he called Edwards and told him to tell Murchison he was on his way.

The Colonel knew Murchison's promise to shoot someone was not an idle threat. He would do that. Shortly thereafter Burden got into one of the electric vehicles and left. Lolene drove.

Lolene pulled into the space between the two JLTV's. The Colonel got out and approached Murchison. He appraised the situation. There were about fifty residents herded into the middle of the street. They were surrounded by maybe ten stragglers as guards. There were another fifteen or twenty stragglers behind the residents. They were pointing and snickering especially about the women.

"Well, well, good morning, Colonel. It was nice of you to come. These people behind me should be very grateful."

"You know Murchison, now that you're here, the only way to leave is through the front door. What do you want Murchison?"

"You don't sound very hospitable, Colonel. We want to join your little community here. Although your inhospitable attitude does present a problem"

"That's impossible, Murchison. We are already at maximum capacity for this facility."

"There's a very easy solution to that problem, Colonel. If you and all your men and some of these residents would leave there would be plenty of room for us."

"You can't be serious, Murchison. If we had to go outside most of us would be dead within days."

"Colonel, oh Colonel, you don't understand. If you and your men go, and maybe twenty of your residents, there would be plenty of room for us. The only other way is if we, shall we say do away with, a significant number of residents. Two of them for each one of my men seems about right."

"I'm responsible for all these people. I have to think about this."

"Take all the time you want. After two hours we eliminate one resident the first hour, two residents the second hour, etc."

By the time that confrontation ended, some of the Colonel's troops had arrived on the scene. They took positions in the street to prevent the stragglers from advancing any farther. The Colonel called Edwards and they got in the vehicle and Lolene drove back to their headquarters.

CHAPTER 16

The shrill sound of the emergency alarm awoke the residents of the Cavern. The building housing the climatological crew hurried to the front door to see what was happening. They of course saw nothing as the events were occurring some distance away from them. Jeff looked at his watch. It was 11.10. He thought perhaps it was a fire. That could be disastrous in the Cavern as smoke could fill it and asphyxiate them. The information booklet they had received mentioned it. Seeing nothing amiss, he went back to his room and told Stan.

Jen and Amanda remained outside. Curious as to what happened that was serious enough that the alarm sounded. A few minutes passed and they saw the two JLTV's speeding down the street. Even more curious, they waited. After some time had passed they saw Lolene in her vehicle.

"That's Colonel Burden with Lolene." Jen said. "I wonder what's going on."

"Whatever it is, it can't be good" Amanda said.

They stayed outside. They were there when Lolene drove past in the opposite direction. Lieutenant Edwards was in the vehicle along with Colonel Burden.

"I would love to know what's happening" Amanda said "But I don't dare call Phil while he's with the Colonel. I'll wait a while."

CHAPTER 17

The Colonel and Edwards arrived at their headquarters. They knew they had a short time to decide a course of action; they were sure Murchison would carry out his threat. The Colonel updated them on what had transpired and asked for input from his staff. No ideas were forthcoming until the Sergeant in charge of electronic monitoring said that the stragglers had disabled the mechanism that closed the Intakes. So they did have a way to escape.

"That's it" said the Colonel; "They made a mistake. If they can get out that way, we can get in that way. Edwards, pick twenty men, go around the mountain and use the Intake shafts to attack them from the rear. They probably have guards posted at the shafts, so take care of them quietly. We don't want them to alert Murchison. Their ropes are still there. Call me when you're in position. We'll attack them from the front."

"Yes, sir" and he left immediately.

Burden knew it would take Edwards about an hour to get in position. He would have to approach stealthily assuming Murchison had left guards up top. He would have to scout the situation to determine the number of guards. They would have to approach the guards from the rear and dispose of them before they could sound the alarm. Then descend the shafts and await the attack signal.

Edwards got his men together, twenty plus Sergeant Emmons. They all volunteered. They loaded into the electric vehicles, no motor noise, drove to the elevator and were taken to ground level. He had Sergeant Emmons command the group attacking the stragglers at Intake No.10. That meant Emmons squad would take out the group at the supply depot. He relished the idea.

Both squads skirted the mountain beyond the sight line of the stragglers. Edwards gave Emmons five minutes to go the further distance to Intake No. 10. Emmons called and said he was in position. They cautiously ascended the mountain side. They saw there were two stragglers standing guard. Standing guard is incorrect as they were sitting on the ground. Edwards and one of his men crept around to attack them from behind. As they were ready to attack, Edwards's phone rang. Edwards, his man and the guards were equally surprised.

Edwards and his man recovered first. They jumped, clasped their hands over the guard's mouths and drove their knives through their throats before they could make a sound or fire a shot. Edwards checked his phone. Amanda.

He answered and said in a whisper; "Not now, I'll call later" and hung up. He silenced his phone.

The other men approached the shaft and they began to descend one by one. When they reached the bottom of the shaft they stopped and waited for the attack signal. The shaft was very crowded with all eleven of them in it ready to attack. They hoped it wouldn't be too long before they got the signal.

Colonel Burden waited just less than an hour. He told Lolene this trip may be dangerous and if she wanted him to get another driver he would. She said; "Sir, I'm a soldier; this is what I get paid for." He smiled for once. They left for the vicinity of Intake No. 9. The Colonel told Lolene of the plan of attack. He said he needed her to alert the troops that they had left there so they would be ready. They pulled up to the troops. She got out and stretched and moved over to the troops. The Colonel got out and moved to the middle of the street. He was moving toward Murchison when his phone started vibrating in his pocket. Edwards was in position. Then the phone vibrated again. Emmons was in position.

"Close, Colonel, you had another three minutes before you lose one of your residents. Now, if you'll step aside my men will take those men's weapons as they will have no further use of them."

"Wait, Murchison. We're not going to do that until you let these poor people go back to their quarters."

"You are not in a position to put conditions on your surrender."

"And you are not in a position to start shooting them because my men will start shooting yours. And you will be the first to die." The Colonel said.

Murchison said; "Have your men lay down their weapons and I will let the residents go."

"I will have half of them lay down their weapons until you release the residents. I don't trust you, Murchison."

"Colonel, how can you say such a cruel thing?" He told his men to start releasing the residents.

The Colonel turned to his troops and said; "Every other man is to lay down his weapon. Count off starting at each end. Even numbers lay down your weapon. That's an order."

The troops started laying down their weapons. That's when Murchison made his second mistake. They did not confiscate them immediately. The stragglers stood aside and the residents ran back to the safety of their quarters.

As the last one disappeared the Colonel said "Now, Corporal"

Lolene laid on the horn of the vehicle. The attack signal.

Edwards, Emmons and their men rappelled into the Cavern, shooting at stragglers as they descended. The troops with Burden snatched up their weapons and began firing at the stragglers that had been guarding the residents. Colonel Burden pulled out his pistol and aimed at Murchison.

Murchison whirled around, brought his rifle up and shot the Colonel. The Colonel staggered and fired at Murchison. He missed and Murchison disappeared into the melee.

Edwards and his men were all on the ground now and maintaining a steady volley of fire into the stragglers. The forward troops were firing also and soon the remaining stragglers held up their hands in surrender.

Meanwhile Emmons squad was engaged in a firefight with the stragglers at the supply depot. There was not much cover for the troops so it was touch and go picking off one straggler then another. The firing was intense. Emmons called Edwards to ask for reinforcements. Edwards, who had rushed over to help the Colonel, said he would send some. Then a stray bullet hit the fuel storage tank. It exploded with a tremendous roar. Burning fuel sprayed everywhere. The stragglers were closest to the tank when it exploded and several of them were screaming in pain as the burning fuel ignited their clothing. That seemed to take the fight out of the remainder and they raised their hands in surrender. Emmons called Edwards and told him what happened.

Edwards told him to round up the prisoners and start walking them toward the front of the Cavern. He told him to leave two men at the Air Intake, as it was still open and he didn't want any more surprise visitors. He did the same at his location. He told Emmons the Colonel had been hit and he was taking him to the Infirmary. He made a mental note to get a repairman to fix the operating mechanisms. He called the squad leaders over and asked them if Murchison had been captured. They told him he had not. In fact he has not been seen since he shot the Colonel. They searched all the way to Air Intake No. 8 but no sign of him. Maybe, somehow he had been able to use the ropes to climb up the air shaft and escape. He told the men that Sergeant Emmons was on his way and would be in charge.

Edwards called Lolene over with her vehicle and they got the Colonel, who was shot in the shoulder, into it. He got in the vehicle and told Lolene to get them to the Infirmary. Fast.

Emmons got there and took charge. They herded the prisoners together and started walking them toward the front of the Cavern. There were about twenty of them. Emmons called for and got more vehicles and the wounded were given rides to the Infirmary.

CHAPTER 18

While the previous was happening;

Some time had passed and Jen and Amanda were still outside. Amanda said; "I wonder if I can get Phil now and see what's happening."

She punched in his number. It only rang once before Phil answered. She paused. Then she told Jen he said; "Not now, Amanda, I'll call later." and hung up. I hope I didn't get him in trouble."

"You better let it go until he calls." Jen replied; "Something drastic is happening."

A few minutes later they heard all the gunfire.

"Oh, I hope I didn't cause him trouble. I would never forgive myself." Amanda said.

Shortly after the gunfire ended they saw three vehicles headed the way Lolene and the Colonel had gone. After fifteen minutes one of the electric carts went by the other way. Colonel Burden was slumped over in the seat and Lieutenant Edwards was with him.

"Oh no, I hope I didn't cause that with my phone call. Why did I have to call?" Amanda said remorsefully.

"It may have had nothing to do with your call, Amanda. Let's wait until we know more." Jen said trying to console her.

Jeff, the other men and other occupants checked periodically with Jen and Amanda for any updates on the activity. They gave them a running commentary whenever they were asked. The whole incident had taken less than four hours so it was still only 3:00 a.m. or so. Boris wondered if this was going to interfere with the preparation of breakfast. No one replied.

About 5 o'clock Amanda's phone rang. It was Phil; "Amanda, I'm sorry I had to be so short when you called. We had a very dangerous situation we were trying to resolve. We were invaded by a group of stragglers led by Felix Murchison. I'm sure you've heard of him. A real bad dude. We finally overcame them but the Colonel got hurt in the fight. They had to do surgery on his shoulder. It went alright and he's resting now. I'll go see him in the morning. Now I'm going to try to get some sleep myself. I'll talk to you in the morning. Goodnight, Amanda."

"Goodnight, Phil. I'm so glad you weren't hurt."

They saw the three vehicles carrying the wounded men headed to the Infirmary. An hour later they saw the twenty prisoners, under armed guard, being marched to the front of the Cavern. It was 6:00. They headed to the mess hall. They had plenty to talk about.

They returned from the mess hall and debated as to whether it was too early to call Blackmore. They decided to take the chance and place the call. He answered.

"Holly, this is Stan. We're anxious. We couldn't wait any longer. Still no rain and we were wondering if you had anything new or any suggestions."

"No, Stan, nothing new. The only thing I could think of that may work is a new device called the Sonic Precipitation Accelerator, SPA for short. The problem is the only one on staff that knew how to operate it, Bertram Hornsby, was lost in the explosion."

"Bert's dead? What a shame. I'd known him for years. I last saw him at a seminar last July. He told me about the SPA then. He was really excited about it. He gave me some fundamental facts about its purpose and operation."

"You know how to operate the SPA?"

"I just know what he told me. I've never seen the machine."

"We have it here. Why don't you come and give it a try? We know nothing about it."

"I'd love to try. We've exhausted all the ideas we had. However, it is 175 miles to your lab. Not to mention the straggler problem. We don't know the condition of the roads and my condition would make it very difficult."

"Think about it and see what you can come up with. Let me know."

Stan hung up and told the others about his conversation and about the SPA.

"I'll go talk to Lieutenant Edwards. I'll see if we can have one of their JLTV's take us there." Jeff said.

"That's a good idea, Jeff. See if we can. It is very important that this old earth has rain."

Jeff called Edwards headquarters and was told the Lieutenant was not there but would be back shortly. He waited a short time then anxiety got the best of him and he walked to Edwards headquarters.

CHAPTER 19

After leaving the Infirmary Edwards arrived at headquarters and informed the Officer-in-Charge that the prisoners would be arriving. He said to keep them herded together and under guard. He would confer with the Colonel regarding what to do with them. Then he went to his quarters to sleep.

He awoke four hours later. He dressed and got one of the vehicles at H.Q. and told the clerk he was going to see the Colonel and would be back in an hour. He drove to the Infirmary.

The Colonel was awake.

"How are you feeling, sir?

"Alright, Lieutenant. They have me on pain medicine but I don't think I need it. Update me on the incident yesterday. Did we capture Murchison?"

"No, sir, we did not. We think he managed to climb up the air shaft and escape."

"Damn, that means we'll see him again. Sergeant Riley was in earlier and said we have twenty prisoners. He was wondering what to do with them. I told him I would talk to you about it. I want you to take charge of the camp while I'm here. I'm giving you a temporary promotion to Captain. We'll talk about making it permanent when I get out. Now, what about the prisoners?"

"It's a big problem, sir. We don't have the facilities, manpower or supplies to keep them incarcerated. We can't just round them up and shoot them. I wouldn't do that and I won't ask my men to do that. If we turn them loose, I'm sure some, if not all, of them would rejoin Murchison. I think, though I hate to do it, we have to turn them loose. Banish them from the Cavern and tell them if they are seen again within 200 yards of it they will be shot."

"Releasing them is a disappointing thing to do but I think we have to do it, Captain."

Edwards said; "I will take care of it, sir." He wished the Colonel a speedy recovery and left.

He arrived back at his headquarters and told Albert Boyd, the clerk, that he was temporary commander. Albert congratulated him and said he was sure he would do the job well. Edwards called the squad leaders together and told them to muster the troops in front of headquarters in 15 minutes. When the troops were in place he addressed them;

"At ease. I have been given the responsibility of commanding this establishment while Colonel Burden recovers. The Colonel is doing well. I have been given the temporary rank of Captain. I want to thank you for your actions in the recent skirmish here within these earthen walls. A job well done. I know there are tremendous challenges yet to come. Supplies are limited and no word on when or if they will be replenished. We are trying to find answers to those questions. Thank you for your service. Dismissed."

Edwards thought his first duty as Commandant was to resolve the problem of the prisoners. They were being held under guard in a temporary enclosure. He went to the enclosure and spoke to them.

"Is there any one in charge of you men?"

No answer. No one stepped forth.

"You were captured while participating in an armed invasion of this facility. As such you are prisoners of war and can be held until the war is over. Our facilities are limited and we can not support you. Therefore, the alternatives are to execute you or free you. We have decided to…….free you. You will be released and ushered out. I have ordered my troops to shoot you if you come within 200 yards of the facility after being released. Corporal of the guard, usher these prisoners out."

The guard detail opened the enclosure and escorted them to the elevator. They went up and out through the steel doors. All the guards thought they would see them again.

Edwards went back to his office to find Jeff Lawrence waiting for him.

"Hello, Mr. Lawrence. May I help you?'

"Yes, and call me Jeff. We have a lead on a device called the Sonic Precipitation Accelerator, SPA for short, that could cause rain. The problem is it is at a lab 175 miles away. We would like to be able to use one of your trucks, the JLTV, to go there."

"I'd really like to help, Jeff, call me Phil, but there's a problem. Our fuel dump was destroyed last night and the only fuel left is what is in the trucks or what we need for the electrical generators. We are still making our rescue runs and will do that as long as we can."

Jeff dejectedly thanked him for listening and left to tell the others the bad news.

He started walking toward their quarters when Lolene pulled up and said she was headed that way and did he want a ride. He did. Jeff suddenly had an idea.

"Lolene, how far can these things go on a charge?"

"They're good for about six hours. Top speed is 20 MPH. However far that would take you."

"That's not far enough. I need to go 175 miles."

"That would take two of these."

"Thanks, Lolene, for the ride and the info."

CHAPTER 20

He walked into their quarters and told the crew the bad news about his meeting with Edwards. He told them Lolene had given him a ride and the idea he had to take one of the electric vehicles. They didn't have the range to go that far. It would take two. They sat in stony silence.

Then Jen said; "Why can't we take two? We could tow one and drive one. We could run the first one until the batteries die and then take the second one for the rest of the trip."

"I don't' know if Edwards would let us take two of them." Jeff said.

Jen said; "He probably would if Amanda asked. Would it be big enough for all of us?"

"There are two bench seats and the driver's seat. That would be enough for you, Stan, me and Stan's chair" Jeff said.

They agreed to try to get permission. Jeff and Amanda went to talk to Edwards. They entered the office and told his clerk it was very important they talk to the Lieutenant for a few minutes. He asked why and went into Edwards's office after they told him. The clerk came out and said the Lieutenant was very busy but he would see them. They went in. Edwards offered them a chair.

"Hello, Jeff. Hello, Amanda. How may I help you?"

"Phil, oh I know I shouldn't call you Phil when we're here?" Amanda said. "We know we can't have one of your big trucks, but can we have two of your electric carts?"

“They‘re military vehicles and not to be operated by civilians. Besides it’s dangerous out there. You’d have to have an escort. Also, the electric vehicles don’t have the range to go 175 miles.”

“We’d drive one and tow one until the first ran out of juice.”

“Then what would you do with it?” Phil said. “You can’t simply abandon it.”

“We’d hide it and pick it up on the way back.”

“But the one you’d be in wouldn’t have enough range to get you back.”

“I’m sure they have trucks at the lab that could bring us and the carts back.”

“Make the call and see if that’s true. If you can arrange it, I’ll see what I can do on this end.”

They called Dr. Blackmore. He said no. He didn’t have a truck to take them back. He said that they had the same kind of electric vehicles and he could give them some spare batteries and recharge the vehicle they came in. They told Edwards.

He said; “When do you want to do this?”

“We would like to leave tomorrow morning if you can arrange it.” Jeff said.

Phil said; “I’ll see about an escort and if vehicles are available.”

“Thanks, Phil.” Jeff said. “Call me and let me know.”

“I will, Jeff. Amanda may I talk to you before you leave?”

Jeff left to go make their plans. Amanda stayed in Phil’s office.

“I don’t want you going on this trip Amanda. It’s dangerous and I want you to stay here.”

“Is the only reason you want me to stay is because the trip is dangerous?”

"No, I like it when you're around. The dangerous part of it is secondary."

"But it might be dangerous if I stay here."

"That's the kind of danger I like to face."

"Me too, Phil. Bye now. Call me later." She left.

CHAPTER 21

The arrangements were made. Stan, Jeff and Jen would be going. Phil had Lolene and Sergeant Emmons volunteer to drive and be the escort. Emmons and Lolene would pick them up at 7:00 a.m. They were traveling light. The trip would take less than a day. They were hoping they could make the journey in less than 9 hours. The transport arrived at 6:55. The second vehicle was being towed. Lolene and Jen got in it. They assisted Stan into the first cart along with his collapsible chair. Emmons laid his rifle on the floor in front of the bench seat. He had a sidearm as did Lolene. Jeff got in and they waved goodbye to Amanda, Tom and Amos. “Goodbye, good luck.” they said in unison.

They went up the elevator and through the steel doors. They were on their way. It was cold. Though they had layered their clothes it was still cold. The road leading from the Cavern was just barely passable. As they descended the mountain the area became more and more forested. There were huge trees that had been toppled by the explosion. There was a winding path through them. The rescue vehicle came this way and it had to make a path. Eventually they would be past the rescue vehicles path. Maybe there would not be as many downed trees then. Conversation was at a minimum. They were too cold to talk and they wanted to be alert for any sign of trouble. Murchison and his men may be lurking in these woods.

It seemed to get slightly warmer as they descended the mountain. They thought that strange as there was no wind and they were still in Venus' shadow. They were willing to accept that small victory without question. When they arrived at the foot of the mountain they paused. They surveyed the map they had brought. There was no GPS as all the satellites of that system had either been destroyed in the explosion or were left behind when the earth was moved to a different orbit. All the familiar landmarks were gone. As they rode through the town at the foot of the mountain all the street signs were gone. The streets they could see were littered with debris. The fires they had seen shortly after the explosion had burned themselves out. Even though there was a distinct, though faint smell of acrid smoke. After some time they agreed on which direction to go. Jeff wondered if the entire trip would be this puzzling. Stan had been to Blackmore's lab previously but now he was totally confused about how they should get out of this town, their own. And they still had several towns and rural areas to go before arriving at Blackmore's. They saw no one. The streets were deserted.

They had decided on their route and immediately set out. Any time spent while they were stopped, the batteries were still working. They agreed they would make minimal stops to preserve the batteries.

As they passed what used to be a city park they saw a crude shack with four people gathered around a small fire in front of it. The four stragglers looked up and saw them and immediately started running toward them. You could hear them yelling "get them" as they ran.

Emmons floored the accelerator and said; "I hope none of them are world class sprinters or we're in trouble."

Jeff looked around and saw the stragglers narrowing the gap. The top speed of the cart was reduced because of the tow. However, a world class sprinter can run 25 MPH for a short distance. The stragglers were not world class sprinters and started slowing down. Soon they stopped and knew it useless.

"If their camp had been closer to the road we would have been in trouble." Emmons said.

Lolene said; "I guess they didn't have guns or it would have been even more trouble."

After avoiding the pursuit of the stragglers, the trip went smoothly for quite a few miles. They were sure they were on the right road. They had left the developed areas of the town behind. They were headed toward the bridge over the Chiraco River. When they got to the River they saw that the constant cold had frozen all the water for ten or fifteen feet from both shores. The center was still open and flowing. That was because they had only been in Venus shadow for two weeks or so. Wait till next year Jeff thought. They found the bridge but the whole center section was gone. Extremely disappointed, they were not expecting this obstacle to their plans. They looked at the map for an alternate route. There was another bridge about a mile and a half downstream around the bend in the river.

Jeff asked; "That's fine, but how do we know it's passable? We can't drive down there without knowing and use all our battery power."

"I could run down there and check" Lolene said "I used to be a jogger before I was forced to live in a cave. I don't think I'd have to go all the way. Just around the bend so I could check it out. Probably 20 or 25 minutes tops."

"Good Lolene, if you can do that we'll hide our little convoy here." Jeff said.

Lolene shed her Jacket and set off on her run. She didn't think she would need the jacket. The run would keep her warm and it would also be easier access to her handgun. She hoped she wouldn't need it. She rounded the bend and saw that the bridge was still intact. She noticed some smoke atop the brush piles beyond the bridge. Straggler campfires she thought. I'll have to tell the group. She ran back to the others, told them the bridge was alright but she had seen the smoke. They unfolded the map to see if there was another bridge. The next one was ten miles downriver. Too far and they would have to pass the area Lolene saw the smoke. They had to take the chance of crossing the one Lolene had scouted. They were thankful for the noiseless engines. Perhaps the stragglers wouldn't hear them or notice them. They headed toward the bridge.

They got onto the bridge and were a third of the way across when they heard a shout. They turned and saw a straggler behind them pointing at them. He was shouting and was soon joined by three others and they started running toward them. Emmons floored the accelerator again. The cart picked up speed but not fast enough, they were gaining. Then they heard two shots.

Emmons said "This group has guns. Return fire, Lolene"

She unholstered her handgun, turned around and fired three quick shots. All missed but ricocheted off the concrete railing of the bridge. That was enough to scare the hell out of the stragglers and they stopped. She kept her gun in her hand until they were across the bridge.

After that incident they drove for miles through open country. There were no houses or barns, just piles of rubble where they had been. All the trees were down. The fields had plants in them that were yellowing and wilted from lack of rain and the cold. That fact put a new earnestness and energy into their quest. They passed several places that had been small towns, now flattened by the explosion. Jen felt sorry for the poor people. Without warning their lives were over. She wondered if the survivors, if there were any, had a problem with stragglers or if that was primarily in the cities. They were still in the country when the motor started slowing down. Soon it stopped. The first cart was out of power. They unhooked it and hooked up the other. There was a stand of fallen trees 50 feet from the road. They pushed the cart behind them.

Jen asked; "How will we ever find it on the way back? There are hundreds of these fallen trees."

Emmons said;" I'll take some of these branches and lay them in a straight line from the trees to the road. We'll look for that unnatural straight line. Let's get back in the cart and go."

They got into the cart. It was crowded now with all four in the bench seats plus Stan's chair. Maybe the closeness would keep them warmer. The miles went rolling by at maybe 16 MPH. No buildings. No people. No animals. Cell towers were still standing. Their open web construction must have saved them. The debris piles got larger as they approached Blackmore's city. His lab was in the basement level of the science building at the University. Stan hoped he could find it with the absence of familiar landmarks. They drove down the streets that Stan thought looked familiar. They came to a set of wide concrete steps with a low, wide masonry wall at both ends. The end of the walls facing the street were embossed with a bas-relief of the earth.

"Stop, this is it" Stan said; "I'll call Holly and tell him we're here."

CHAPTER 22

"Stan, glad you made it. You need to go around to your right. There's a handicap ramp that will take you down to this level. As you can see the building is virtually destroyed and the elevators are inoperable. I'll send someone to guide you."

Jeff, Jen and Lolene exited the vehicle. Stan stayed as Emmons thought the cart would be able to traverse the ramp. As they were half way down the ramp a lady approached and said "I'm Joan. I'll show you the way." The ramp descended to the deep basement level. Looming above them were the remaining walls that had surrounded the University's football stadium. They helped Stan into his chair, wheeled him in and were greeted by a large, black man with a short gray beard. This had to be Dr. Hollis Blackmore. It was. He greeted Stan heartily. Introductions were made and they entered his lab space.

"How did you survive the explosion, Holly?" Jeff asked.

Holly replied; "As you can see, we are in the basement level. The same as you were. This lab is on this level because we have equipment that has to be able to see into space. When the football Stadium was built it had walls that extended 100 feet high. Local regulations said 80 feet was the highest they could build. So they sunk the remaining 20 feet into the ground. They constructed a tunnel from my lab to the field level of the stadium. Now we take our equipment through the tunnel and onto the field for an unobstructed view of the sky.

It's a good thing that happened. The SPA is a large piece of equipment."

"Where is the SPA? I'm anxious to see it." Stan said.

"It's in the tunnel. Come on." Holly said and motioned for them to follow him.

They went to a set of double doors. Through the doors was a long tunnel. Sitting at the far end, which was a hundred feet away, was a large wheeled platform containing what looked like a large radar dome with four smaller radar domes inside it. The four smaller domes had a wand extending about five feet out of their center. The wands had a coil of glass surrounding them. The platform had what must have been the control console, all dials and switches.

"There it is. The Sonic Precipitation Accelerator." Holly said proudly.

"Looks daunting. Hope I can figure it out." Stan replied.

"I'm sure you will. You people have been on the road a long time today. Let's have something to eat."

After they ate, Stan went out to familiarize himself with the SPA. They helped him onto the platform. He told them to give him some time to look at the controls and try to remember what Bert had told him. They left him to his work. Jeff and Jen went in to talk to Holly.

"Dr. Blackmore, Holly, what's your opinion of what the earth can expect from its new orbit?" Jen asked.

"We'll know more when it gets out of Venus shadow. I think we will have temperate days for a while. Then as we approach closer to the sun the days will get hotter and hotter. We could have temperatures around 120 degrees or more for days on end. I hope I'm wrong. We have to find a way to survive that. We will have another temperate period as we move away from the sun's intensity. With that in mind, we have to plan our agriculture very carefully. We have to plant and harvest in the temperate times to prepare ourselves for the extremes of heat and cold we will have. It's not a pleasant scenario to consider."

"If we succeed in making it rain with the SPA, will that help us all year long, Holly?"

"Definitely, we may be able to store excess water or fill the lakes and reservoirs for use later. The timing is crucial as it may be impossible to generate rain in the extreme hot or cold periods."

"But if we can only generate rain in the temperate times, how can we plant and harvest with a lot of rain? The fields will be muddy and unworkable."

"That's why I said timing is crucial. We will have the fifteen days going in and out of the shadow. We need to concentrate our rain-making to those times. I hope it will be enough."

They went to see if Stan had any success in figuring the workings of the SPA. He was positive he could but had not yet. They left him to his work. Emmons and Lolene were in the break room of the lab having coffee. Jeff and Jen joined them. The four agreed it had taken them just under 11 hours for their trip. They thought they were lucky the second cart didn't lose power before they arrived. The two run-ins with stragglers and the bridge being out cost them precious time. Finding the other cart on the way back could be a problem. They could run out of power before they found it. All four thought that hopefully it's a problem we won't have to face.

Stan continued working. They talked to Joan and the two other people in the lab. Arrangements were made and accommodations supplied for them to spend the night.

Emmons and Lolene had gone to their rooms. Jen was still in the break room. Jeff joined her.

"Exciting day, huh?" He said.

"Almost too exciting. I'm glad we made it with no more trouble than we had."

"I'm not sure Stan can get the SPA operational in a day. Actually, we will be leaving Venus shadow in three days. It needs to be operational then."

"You're not thinking we need to stay that long are you, Jeff?"

"No, I'm not. We can't impose on Holly and his staff for that long. They have limited supplies too. Emmons and Lolene have to get back too. They have other duties. I'll talk to Stan about it. How are you, honey?"

"Don't call me honey." She said with a smile. "We're just co-workers, remember?"

"Oh, I forgot. I'll go talk to Stan. Goodnight Miss Co-worker."

"Goodnight, Jeff. Pleasant dreams."

"I'm sure they will be now."

Jeff went to get Stan. He was reluctant to leave the SPA because he thought he had it figured out. Jeff said it's too late today to try it. We'll try it tomorrow. He helped Stan in and they retired to their rooms.

CHAPTER 23

Felix Murchison had to struggle to climb up the rope in the Air Intake. When he got to the top he glanced at the two slain guards without pity. If they had done their job he would not be running away now. Instead, h e would be in charge of the entire Cavern and all of its supplies. He ran down the side of the mountain to the tree line. Now to get to my camp site and reorganize he thought. They have not seen the last of me. No, not at all. He wondered if the one shot he had taken at Burden had been fatal. If not, they would meet again. If so, there would be another in charge for him to defeat.

Later that day the steel doors opened and Murchison's men who were captured were released. Murchison signaled them and they rejoined his camp. They knew that he was their best hope of capturing the Cavern and its supplies. Murchison found it unbelievable that they had been released. He sneered; "The fools. If it had been me they would have been dead within minutes of surrendering. The compassionate fools. They'll regret this."

They surreptitiously watched the Cavern entrance. The morning of the second day they saw two electric carts leave. There were five people on board. They're electric, they run on batteries. They can't go that far. Then they'll come back. We'll be waiting. We'll take them and approach the Cavern as if we're those people returning. By the time the guards realize we are not the same, we'll overpower them and get access.

That plan was put on hold when the carts did not return that day.

"Those carts will have to come back sometime." Murchison said. "We'll be ready."

CHAPTER 24

The following day Edwards left the Infirmary after visiting the Colonel. He was mending nicely but would not be released yet.

He went to his headquarters and kept busy the remainder of the day writing and reviewing reports of the recent events. He went out to what served them as a motor pool and asked how many more rescue runs before they ran out of fuel. The Sergeant in charge told him another two would be stretching it. He said they did have to go on the next one as they had a pick-up of some one who had been approved by the Colonel. They are not finding any candidates anymore. The stragglers must have gotten to them.

"Make this pick-up run Sergeant. Then suspend the program. We may need the little fuel we have left." Edwards told Sergeant Riley.

Back at headquarters he punched in Amanda's number. "Hi, Amanda, did you here anything from the travelers?"

"No, Phil. Not a word. I hope everything is alright."

"I'm sure it is. Emmons would have called about anything disastrous."

"I'm worried about things troublesome too. Not only disastrous."

"They'll be alright, Amanda. Have you eaten? I thought I'd come over and we could have what passes for dinner together."

"I'd like that but hurry, it's 6:00 now, my assigned time. Besides you don't have a meal ticket."

"I don't need a meal ticket. Rank has its privileges."

"I'd love it if you came over. Jen's gone and I need some one to talk to."

"I don't think I'm the conversationalist Jen is, but I'll try not to bore you. Be right over."

CHAPTER 25

Phil arrived at Amanda's and she was waiting outside for him.

"I got here as quickly as I could. Have you been waiting for me long?"

"All my life. Shall we go?"

They walked to the mess hall. The other members of the crew and the other residents were just leaving. They got their food and found an empty table.

"I haven't had a chance to talk to you much the past couple days Amanda. Too busy with the invasion, The Colonel getting shot, your guys wanting to go and everything else."

"I know that Phil. I understand you have a lot of duties."

"Even more. The Colonel made me a temporary Captain and put me in charge of the camp."

"Congratulations. You deserve it."

"Thanks, how's things at your place? Is that big oaf still complaining?"

"Of course, but he doesn't bother me."

"He better not."

"Phil, I hate to get somber, but what's going to happen to us? I can't see us spending our lives underground like moles. We can't be holed up here forever. We'll run out of everything. What's being done to restore things? There are just so many questions."

"I know it Amanda. We have had to concentrate all our energies on establishing this camp and saving the people who survived the explosion to even think of what to do next. I may be able to find out what is going on outside now that I'm in charge. I want to know what's being done and if we, the survivors, can help and how can we be helped."

"Don't get me wrong Phil. I'm not complaining. I've always been a dedicated, hard-working individual and now to just sit around is horrible. Tom and Amos are great guys and I'm glad they're here with me. They do help take the edge off being with Myra and Angie who cries all the time, that loudmouth bully Boris and the two silent old men. See what you can find out."

"I'll see what I can do about finding some answers. Hang in there. You're not alone."

"I know that now. But it is depressing."

"I better get back to work. My girl wants answers."

"Bye Phil. Thanks."

CHAPTER 26

The following morning at Holly's lab, the travelers met for breakfast in the break room. Stan was anxious to get back to the SPA. Jeff asked him what his plans were when he got it operational. He said he would wait for a cloud to appear. Then he would bombard it with the sonic waves of the SPA to force it to expand and become a rain cloud. That's what the SPA is supposed to do. However, it has never been tested. The explosion happened just before Bert was going to test it. Jeff voiced his concerns about them imposing too long on Holly. Stan said he was concerned also but they of course couldn't move the SPA. The test had to be done there. Then it will be three or four days before they are out of Venus shadow to determine its efficiency.

Jeff said; "Stan, let's see if it would be alright with Holly if you stayed here and we went back. Would that be alright with you Stan?"

"Definitely alright. I need to get this thing going. The world will need it."

They went to Holly's office to talk to him. They told him what they wanted to do and asked him what he thought.

"It would be most definitely alright. Perhaps I could assist Stan and learn something about the SPA. No harm in having two people who know how to operate it."

They thought the day was still early and if they hurried they could leave right away. They asked about the spare batteries, given them and put them in the cart. Emmons made sure the cart was recharged as soon as they had gotten there. They said their goodbyes and thank you's and left, driving up the ramp and onto the street. It was 8:00 A.M.

Emmons reversed his entrance path and soon they were out of the city environment. They drove through the same demolished towns as before. No houses. No barns. No animals. No people. They were less crowded since Stan was left behind. Lolene sat in the last bench seat. She had the rifle and the extra batteries were on the floor. Jeff and Jen sat close together in the first bench seat. Ostensibly to keep warm. They talked, keeping their voices low. After several uneventful hours Emmons said to watch for the sticks he had laid out for the other cart. Since all the area looked the same, desolate, they didn't know exactly how close it was. Several miles went by before they saw them. Emmons said they would tow the one they retrieved until the one they were in lost power. That way they would have fresh batteries for the remainder of their journey.

They had only gone another eight or ten miles when the cart slowed down and stopped. They switched carts, put the fresh batteries in the new one and were on their way again. They were becoming concerned with the time. The moon overhead was shining on this their new daytime. They would have it for four or five more hours.

There were no mile posts or features to indicate how much farther they had to go. They were approaching the bridge over the Chiraco River. They had no alternative but to proceed. If the stragglers attacked they would have to drive like hell and fight them off.

They started across the bridge. No one was standing at the other end of it. They drove across and when they reached the end two stragglers jumped out from behind the railings and ran toward the vehicle. Emmons floored the accelerator and Lolene reached for her handgun. She shot at the one on the left and missed. She turned just as the one on the right was able to grab the cart being towed and scramble aboard. The cart was weaving back and forth as it was not carrying a load. Emmons saw what was happening and made quick left, right moves to dislodge the straggler. He held on. Lolene raised her gun and fired. She must have hit him for he let go and tumbled off. Other stragglers heard the shots and came running out of the woods. By that time the cart was off the bridge and running full bore down the road. The stragglers were falling behind. The travelers all breathed a sigh of relief.

They were approaching the park where the four stragglers had tried to stop them before. They drove past the park cautiously. That campsite looked abandoned now. They had moved on to what they hoped would be better pickings. Stragglers are nomadic and opportunistic.

They were approaching the tree line at the base of the mountain. It was getting late. The moon was waning and the light was fading. They headed up the mountain. A few more minutes and Jerseyville Cavern would be within sight. They were almost out of the forested area when Emmons saw a flash of light in the trees at the left. He knew it was trouble.

"Lolene, bandits at 10 o'clock." He said.

Lolene pulled out her gun. Emmons floored the accelerator and drew his weapon. As they came abreast of where he had seen the light, four men jumped out of the trees not ten feet away. Two were on each side of the cart. They grabbed at it and at the passengers to try to dislodge them from their seats and commandeer the cart. Lolene shot one of them and he fell off. Emmons concentrated on driving the cart which was swaying and bouncing over the rough roadway. Though his weapon was out he was too busy to shoot accurately. Lolene, who had gotten into the second cart, the one being towed, was being bounced around in her seat trying to fight off the other attackers using her gun as a club. One of them had reached into the cart and grabbed Jen by her coat and was trying to pull her out of the cart. Lolene clubbed at him.

She was afraid to shoot him as the cart was bouncing and swaying too much and she could accidentally hit Jen. Jeff was kicking at another on his side. One kick hit the straggler full in the face and he fell. As the cart gained speed the attackers could not hold on and the other two fell. Then a group of fifteen or twenty more led by Felix Murchison took up the chase. They raced after the cart. Trying to catch it before it could get to the Cavern. Murchison was yelling at his men; "Catch them. Don't let them get away." Some were shooting at the cart. Lolene kept up a steady stream of fire at them. She took aim at Murchison but it was very hard to score a hit with the cart bouncing and him weaving. Then click, click, click. Her gun was out of ammo.

Lolene turned and said; "I'm out of ammo."

Jeff and Jen had ducked and gotten as low as they could by that time because of the shots being fired at them. Jeff shouted at Emmons and he passed the gun back. She raised it and fired but the cart continued bouncing and it was hard to aim. The cart was laboring to go up the hill to the Cavern entrance. The climb caused the cart to become increasingly slower. Terror struck when they realized the battery may be failing.

The stragglers were gaining. The slower speed did let Lolene take better aim and three fell. Murchison had fallen behind and was no longer her target. She continued firing and saw one fall that she hadn't shot at. The guards at the entrance had joined the fight. They were the turning point. The stragglers ended their pursuit. The besieged occupants had reached the entrance.

"Thank you, guys. If you hadn't helped we would have been toast." Lolene said.

"Glad to be of service. We've wanted a crack at those guys anyway"

They opened the big steel doors and let them in. They phoned the elevator guard. They drove over to the elevator and descended.

"Home sweet home," Lolene said. "That got a little hairy there for a while."

Jeff said; "You and Sergeant Emmons were terrific, Lolene. Thank you very much."

Lolene smiled and said; "All part of the job"

CHAPTER 27

The following day Jeff went to report to Lieutenant Edwards. Edwards was not there, just the clerk. Jeff sat down to wait.

"Do you think he'll be a while?" Jeff asked.

"No, he should be here shortly."

"Did you move in here with the Colonel, Albert?"

"No sir, I was picked up by the rescue truck. I'm from Cedarville."

Edwards entered the office.

"Good morning Lieutenant Edwards."

"It's Captain Edwards now if you please. The Colonel gave me a temporary promotion."

"I'm sorry. I didn't know. But congratulations, Captain, you deserve it."

"Thank you. How was your trip?"

"Rather exciting. Four run-ins with stragglers. About six of them won't be bothering anyone anymore. Stan stayed behind to get the SPA operational."

"Tell me what it's like outside of this area. I've been here since shortly after the explosion except for those rescue runs."

"Desolate is the best way to describe it. No buildings. No people. From what we saw we are the only survivors other than the stragglers."

"Well that can't be. We received verbal orders to occupy this place. Somebody had to give those orders. I'll have to ask the Colonel." Phil said.

"Yes, of course. There must be others out there. They're probably holed up like we were, waiting for someone to tell them it's alright to go out. They wouldn't have the instruments I had telling them the air is okay."

Edwards said; "But once they get out, they'll be overwhelmed. Their civilization is gone. They'll have to adapt to a whole new world. We have to find someone who knows what is being done to establish some infrastructure and authority"

"Perhaps Dr. Blackmore has been in touch with someone. I didn't think to ask him. I'll call him."

"You do that and I'll talk to the Colonel and see what he can tell us."

CHAPTER 28

"Dr. Blackmore, this is Jeff. How's Stan doing with the SPA? Oh, he is. That's terrific. I have a question I should have asked before. Have you been talking to anyone about restoring utilities or services? Anyone in authority about what happens now? What we can expect."

"There is someone Jeff. Lidell Dix of the Department of Interior Affairs. He says the explosion caused immense damage and momentous loss of life. People are of course devastated. Not only have they lost loved ones but everything they had is gone. Lidell says they have the problem of identifying competent and knowledgeable people to restore the infrastructure. He could update you if you wish to call him. I'll give you his number. Call him. His name is Li-dell, That's L-I-D-E-L-L, not Liddle for obvious reasons. Please offer your assistance for he needs help."

Jeff made the call; "Mr. Dix, this is Jeff Lawrence of the Climatological Bureau. Dr. Hollis Blackmore suggested I call you. If I or my co-workers could be of assistance to you we would be glad to help. And can you give me any idea of the current situation and what is being done?"

"I appreciate the offer, Jeff. Where are you now and what is the status of that area?"

"We are in Jerseyville Cavern. It is a military establishment at maximum occupancy. Although we have ample supplies, except for fuel, at the moment, I don't know how long they'll last."

"I'm aware of Jerseyville Cavern. It was a secret installation but those secrets were revealed when we needed shelter after the explosion. I'll give you a brief up date on the situation as it is today as far as I know. The main explosive blast was in the middle of the Pacific Ocean just west of the Hawaiian Islands. The force of that blast caused a huge tidal wave, a tsunami, of gigantic proportions. It completely obliterated all the smaller islands in the Pacific. Midway, Wake, The Marianas, Guam, The Marshalls Etc. The West coast of the U.S. was badly damaged by the tsunami. It was felt up to the western slopes of the Rockies. Then the wind came. We don't know the maximum wind speed because none of the anemometers survived it and they could register to over 400 mile per hour. The wind spread in both directions, east and west, from the center of the blast. The wind continued across the U.S. and across Asia and Eastern Europe until the east and west blasts collided over Western Europe. Assessments are being made to determine what can be saved or restored. The Eastern hemisphere fared slightly better from what we've gathered from the limited contact we've had over the Transatlantic Cable. They were on the other side of the earth from the main blast and the wind had diminished somewhat.

There is horrendous loss of life everywhere in the world. Reports say 75 to 80 % died. The Asian nations were affected tremendously by the aftermath of the tidal wave. So was the northern portion of South America. All were bombarded with debris from the explosion. That debris became fiery meteorites when it entered earth's atmosphere causing fires wherever it landed.

All nations are cooperating in trying to get services restored. We are working diligently to restore electric power. When the explosion hit and all the buildings were destroyed it caused large electrical fires that destroyed much of the distribution system. Sewer and water utilities are inoperative. Speaking of water, it has not rained anywhere on earth since the explosion. Rain is an occurrence of low atmospheric pressure. We have had high pressure since the explosion. We don't know why nor if it is a permanent situation."

"We may be able to help with that problem Mr. Dix. Stan Patterson of our office is currently at Dr. Blackmore's lab endeavoring to start a new device called the Sonic Precipitation Accelerator, SPA, in an effort to induce the few wispy clouds we have to expand and grow into rain clouds. If this effort is successful, and I believe it will be, we will have the ability to produce rain and pinpoint it to any location."

"That is good news, Mr. Lawrence. When do you think it will be operational?"

"Within a week."

"Keep me informed of your progress. Thank you for your call. I must go. There are so many things to do." He disconnected.

CHAPTER 29

Edwards left for the Infirmary to talk to the Colonel. He was sitting up in bed.

"Help me into that chair, Captain. I get so tired of sitting in this bed."

"Certainly, sir. How are you feeling?"

"Better. They need to release me. I'm well enough to leave."

"Your command is waiting for you to recover, sir."

"How are things going, Captain? Have you released the prisoners? Are Lawrence and Quigley back?"

"Yes, sir. The prisoners were released. I'm sure the majority of them went to rejoin Murchison. Lawrence and Quigley are back. They had a couple of incidents with stragglers. Stan Patterson stayed to try to get that SPA machine operational. Jeff Lawrence and I were talking about what is going on outside. There must be survivors. How did you get orders to move into Jerseyville Cavern?"

"I received a call from General Elliot Arnold to evacuate my position and move my command and as much materiel as we could to Jerseyville Cavern. We were to occupy it no later than 6:00 p.m. the following day. He briefed me on what we could find there and its capacity. Considering the men I had left, most were on a field maneuver when the explosion took place, I had capacity for about 300 civilians. We loaded as quickly as possible and occupied this facility. That evening

I started the rescue truck rounds. The first three days we were able to gather almost 300 survivors."

"Have you had any further contact with General Arnold or anyone else?"

"I received a call the evening we moved wanting to know if the move was successful. I assured him it was and gave him a status report. He said he would call later with further orders but they were still assessing the situation. I've not heard from him since."

"Do you have his number? Should I call, sir?"

"No, Captain. Wait until I get back and I'll call."

Edwards said goodbye and left the Infirmary.

When he entered headquarters Albert Boyd was there. He asked where Sergeant Riley was and was told he had gone to the supply depot to take inventory.

"Has he been gone long?"

"No, sir. Maybe an hour."

"How long have you been here, Albert?"

"Do mean now or at the camp?"

"Both."

"Well, sir, I was picked up by the rescue truck two days after the explosion. I was lucky to be in the city when the explosion happened. I'm from Cedarville and it was obliterated."

"How did you get this job?"

"I was a civilian employee of the military. When the Colonel and Sergeant Riley found out, they asked me to help here as they were very busy."

"Good. Thanks, Albert. Were there any calls?"

"Yes, Mr. Lawrence called. He wants you to call him."

He punched in his number. "Jeff, Phil Edwards. Did you find out anything?'

"Yes. We need to get together."

"Okay. Why I don't I come out to your place and we can discuss it. It's about dinner time."

"I'll be waiting." Jeff said.

CHAPTER 30

Jeff, Jen, Amanda and Phil went to the mess hall for dinner and to talk about what they had discovered. Those facts did not ease their minds. Their future, if any, was still a mystery. They knew they were powerless to do anything more than what they were doing. Each of them was happy to be facing that uncertain future with someone they cherished.

They left the mess hall and went back to their building. Boris and Cass were in the living room.

"What's going on, Edwards? Boris growled. "I heard you were now running this place so you should have the answers."

"Yes, I've been given temporary command. We are trying to determine when we may leave here. Conditions on the outside are still in a state of flux and it's not safe yet."

"I've been patient till now but I'm damned tired of this place and you have to get me out of here. Now." Boris tone was demanding.

"I am certain I can accommodate you if that's really what you want. I will give you a ride to the elevator, up and out through the entrance. I must warn you things are not pleasant out there. There's the weather and the stragglers. It's a toss-up as to which one would get you first. Now, if you want to leave just go get in my cart and I'll take you. If not, sit down and shut up. Everyone else wants out of here too."

Boris glared at Edwards and sat down. Cass smiled. Boris sulked for a while then got up and left the room. Cass followed.

Banger got up and stared down the hall after them.

"Maybe Banger doesn't like him either." Jeff said.

Some minutes later they heard shouting coming from down the hall. Boris had been shamed and Cass was taking the brunt of his displeasure.

Edwards said; "If I hear what I think is physical abuse I will definitely interfere."

"We're behind you all the way, Phil." Jen said.

Things quieted down. Phil waited several minutes to see if any further incidents occurred.

"I had better get back to headquarters. I have to inspect the guard at the cell tower since the Colonel is unavailable. Let me know if any thing comes up."

Amanda said; "I'll walk out with you. Be careful on that inspection."

"I don't think they'll try to knock out the cell tower. Murchison realizes it's his only means of communication also."

"But there are other stragglers out there other than Murchison's."

"I'll take Sergeant Emmons with me if it will make you feel better."

"Oh it would, Phil. Thank you."

"I can't have your pretty little head worrying about me."

He kissed her on the cheek, got in his cart and left.

CHAPTER 31

The cell tower was high on the mountain on the opposite side from the Air Intakes. They were forced to take an electric cart now instead of the JLTV because of the fuel shortage. Edwards and Emmons waited until it was time to change the guard and had the new guards ride out with them for the inspection. There were three guards per shift. It was miserable duty for four hours. A very long time in those weather conditions. There was a small equipment shack at the base of the tower. The guards alternating in using it so there were always two guards outside and one in the relative comfort of the shack.

The trip up the mountain was slow. The electric cart was exerted to its maximum hauling the five of them up the slope. As they approached the cell tower they didn't see any guards. They moved forward cautiously.

As they got closer, a voice said; "That's close enough. Throw down your weapons. We have your guards."

Edwards said quietly: "Don't drop your weapons. Let's see what they want. A cell tower's not much use to them." Shouting. "What do you want? Release them now and you can walk away."

"We want food and clothing and won't let them go until we get it. If you shoot at us you'll hit your guards."

"Why are you doing this?"

"It's our only way to survive. There's no more food out here. No warmer clothing. Nothing."

"You should have come in when you had the opportunity."

"We never had the opportunity. The way we looked the truck would never stop for us. They thought we were convicts and thieves. Now we're willing to take your food to survive. Does that make us thieves?"

"That makes you survivors. I'm Captain Edwards. I'm commandant of this facility. If you surrender and release my guards I will listen to your story and decide if you can stay in this facility. We are at maximum capacity and supplies are short so it better be a good story."

"How do we know we can trust you?"

"You don't. You have to decide if this is your best chance to survive. Believe me, it is."

"Give us a few minutes."

"I'll give you two minutes. Then we will take action. I'm already on the phone calling for reinforcements."

Nearly two minutes pass; "We're coming out. Don't shoot."

They sent the guards out in front of themselves. That meant they were not 100% sure Edwards could be trusted. There were three of them. A man, a young woman and a young man. They were dressed in an assortment of mismatched clothing. Done for comfort from the cold, not for fashion. The men were holding rifles.

"Throw down your weapons" Edwards shouted.

The older man turned to the other two and said something and they put down their weapons. The new guards rushed up to take them into custody. Edwards told the prisoners to get into the cart.

He turned to the guards who had been captive and said; "You men have to walk down the hill. You should never have let this happen."

When they arrived at the Cavern entrance, he had the guards search them for weapons. They found none. Upon arriving at the Cavern floor he had Emmons take them to an indoctrination room they used for new resident indoctrination. He went to his office and asked Albert Boyd if there were any vacant bedroom spaces.

"I'll have to check on that, Captain. How many did you want? Are you anticipated getting new residents?"

"We found three people we may want to accommodate. Two men and a woman."

"I'll see what is available, sir."

Edwards left for the indoctrination room. The three stragglers were sitting in chairs around the table. Emmons was standing at the door. Edwards took the last seat at the table.

"First I need your names. Then I want you to tell me why you are here and why I should let you stay?"

"Well, sir. I'm Elmer Bailey; this is my daughter, Annabelle and my boy, Billy. We wuz out huntin'. It started to rain some and we ducked into this cave. Next thing we know'ed is we woke up and it's dark. We figured somethin' happened and Ma is gonna be real mad at us for stayin' out past dark. We made our way back home but there was no home. The house was gone. The barn was gone. Poor Ma gone. The chickens gone. Everything gone. Old Buster wasn't with us when we ducked into the cave so I guess he's gone too."

"Old Buster was your hunting dog?"

"Yes, sir he was. We didn't know whut to do so we started walkin' hopin' to find somebody to tell us what happened. There weren't nobody. So we been walkin' ever since. We saw that truck and tried to get him to stop but he didn't. Maybe because we had rifles. We saw a couple of guys and thought I'd ask them. I had Annabelle and Billy stay in the woods. I went up to them and asked if they knew what was goin' on. They looked at each other and said "No, but Felix can tell you. Come with us." I didn't like the way they said it, so I said no. Then we saw that truck goin' past and we followed that truck to here and saw the guards at the entrance. We thought they'd shoot first and ask later. That's when we come up with the idea to ransom those tower guards for food. Now, here we are."

"Do you have any I.D., Elmer?"

"No, sir, we don't. Them squirrels don't ask for I.D. afore you shoot 'em."

"Alright, Elmer. I'm going along with your story for now. I'm checking to see if we can accommodate you. Sergeant Emmons will take you to the mess hall and see if they have anything left for you to eat. Then I'll meet you back here."

Edwards went back to the office; " Did you find anything, Albert?"

"There are three rooms that are now single occupied."

"Thank you, Albert. Give me three rules booklets."

He took them to Sergeant Emmons and had him take care of the Baileys with instructions to see him in the morning.

CHAPTER 32

Jeff was wondering if Stan had any success with the SPA. He was anxious to talk to him but did not want to disturb him. Stan will call, he thought. Meanwhile time dragged.

He and Amos were in the living room. Jeff said; "Do you think you're doing OK on those crutches? Do you think they should have kept you longer?"

"I'm OK. They want me to come back tomorrow for a check-up. Do you think we can get some transportation? They released me because they need the bed space. Some people are seriously injured. Like Mr. Barkley."

"Was that your room mate?"

"Yeah. Clem Barkley. He lived in Cedarville. Of course he lost his house and everything in the explosion. His wife had passed away two years ago. He was glad she wasn't here to see this."

"He was from Cedarville? The clerk in Edwards's office was from Cedarville. I'll have to ask him if he knows Mr. Barkley."

"He may. It wasn't very big."

"I'll call for transportation. You for sure can't walk there. What time do they want you?"

"They said anytime. They're so busy I'll probably have to wait anyway."

Jeff placed the call to the office. Albert Boyd answered.

"Albert, this is Jeff Lawrence. Amos has to go back to the Infirmary tomorrow for a check-up. Can you arrange transportation?" Pause. "They didn't give a specific time so whatever you can do."

Jeff told Amos they would call about the time.

CHAPTER 33

Murchison's band of stragglers was getting larger every day. He preached a belief that they could band together and take over. Small groups and lone wolves believed that was their best chance of survival. They had suffered enough at the hands of civilization and wanted revenge. They would take what they wanted and to hell with all the others.

Murchison was livid with the failure of his men to capture the electric carts. After their failure he gathered his men back at their camp. He ordered the three stragglers who had initiated the attack, the fourth had been shot by Lolene, brought before him. He addressed them scornfully; "I told you to jump in front of that cart and force them to stop. But NO, you tried to grab it from the side. I knew that wouldn't work AND IT DIDN'T."

One of them replied; "They would have run us down if we had done that Felix."

Murchison replied; "That may have been better than what happens to you now."

He turned to the rest of his band and said; "Take these worthless pieces of shit and tie them face down on three of these fallen logs. The logs that still have the bark on them. Strip them to the waist first. Then each of you grab a branch of thorn bush and give them three hits. Three hits for each of them. Any of you who refuse will join them. All of you should know that that or something equally bad is what happens if you don't do as I say."

Although he was angry and frustrated with that failure, now he was planning bigger objectives. With his larger force he had larger aspirations. He knew the Cavern had limited supplies and soon they would have to abandon it and move elsewhere. When that happened he planned to attack the convoy and take it over. He would know their planned objective and would use the same subterfuge to capture an even bigger facility with even more supplies. He called his most trusted men to tell them what he was planning.

“But how will you know where they’re going?’

“I have ways of knowing these things. That’s why I’m the boss.”

CHAPTER 34

Jeff got the call from Albert saying Lolene was on the way to pick up Amos.

Jeff said; "By the way, Amos room mate was from Cedarville. Perhaps you know him, Clem Barkley? Oh, you don't. Okay we'll be waiting for Lolene. Thanks."

Lolene arrived a few minutes later to take Amos for his check-up. Jeff went along. Lolene was to pick up the Colonel and take him to headquarters as he was being released. They arrived at the Infirmary and Lolene helped the Colonel into the cart. Amos and Jeff were told to wait for Doctor Linquist.

Amos said; "I'm going to see how Clem Barkley is doing." Jeff went with him.

"Clem, its Amos. Remember me?"

"Why sure I remember you, Amos. How you doing on those crutches?"

"Fine, Clem. How are you doing? This is Jeff Lawrence."

"How do you do, Mr. Barkley?"

"I'm doing better all the time thank you. Pleased to meet you."

They shook hands. Amos said; "Jeff says there's someone else from Cedarville here, Albert Boyd."

"Al Boyd is here? Al and I grew up together. Went to the same school. Our desks were right next to each other. They were in alphabetical order so Boyd was right next to Barkley. We used to drive Miss Tompkins crazy. How is Al?"

Amos and Jeff looked at each other. Clem was in his mid sixties. Albert, the clerk, in his thirties.

Jeff said; "Excuse me, I have to make a call."

Jeff called headquarters. Sergeant Riley answered. "Sergeant, Jeff Lawrence, is Captain Edwards there?"

"He's outside, sir. Helping Lolene get the Colonel in. They just got here."

"I need to talk to him right away. It's important. Is Albert Boyd still there?"

"No, Albert's gone. He left a few minutes ago when I got here. Here's the Captain."

"Phil, I think Albert Boyd's a spy." He told him what Clem had said.

"He left in a hurry just as we got here. He's the reason Murchison knew so much about our facilities. Do you think he knows we're on to him?"

"I think he does and he'll try to lie himself out of it. Do you think he may be going after Clem Barkley? Try to silence him so we don't find out more."

"I'll tell the Colonel and have him call Dr. Linquist and tell him not to allow Clem to have visitors until we get Boyd in custody. Lolene is still here. I'll have her bring me there."

The Colonel called for Dr. Linquist but was put on hold. After a short time the Dr. answered.

"Dr., this is Colonel Burden. Do not allow Clem Barkley to have visitors until I call back and tell you it's alright."

"A man just went back to see him. I'll have a nurse go tell him he has to leave."

Albert went into Clem's room. He was surprised to see Amos there. He recovered quickly.

"Hi, Clem. I'm Al Boyd, Jr. You knew my father. I heard there was another Cedarville resident here and thought I'd stop and say hello."

At that the nurse came in and told him he had to leave because Mr. Barkley couldn't have visitors. She told Amos he had to leave too.

Clem said; "What's going on? Who says I can't have visitors?"

The nurse said; "Sorry. That's my orders."

CHAPTER 35

Lolene and Phil were approaching the Infirmary just as Albert was leaving. They stopped him and told him he had to go back to headquarters with them.

"But I'm done for the day. Sergeant Riley took over."

Phil said; "We're not asking you. It's an order. You're going."

He got in the cart with them.

They took him into the Colonel's office and sat him in a chair. Edwards blocked the door.

The Colonel stood over him. "Who are you?"

"I'm Albert Boyd. You know that, sir."

"No, you're not. Who are you?"

"Actually I'm Albert Boyd, Jr."

"You're lying."

"No, I'm telling the truth, sir."

"I know you're lying. Mr. Barkley said Albert Boyd had no children."

"That's not true. Barkley's a senile old man. He doesn't remember things."

"I've talked to Mr. Barkley. He is not senile. Who are you?"

"I've told you. I'm Albert Boyd, Jr."

"I don't know why I ask. It doesn't matter who you are exactly. You're a spy and this is a military installation. According to Military rules you can be executed for spying."

"I'm not a spy."

"I think you are. You only have to be concerned with what I think. I'm the one who gives the order to have you shot. Now, one more time, who are you?"

"If I tell you, you'll have me shot anyway."

"On my word as an officer and a gentleman, I won't"

"I don't believe you."

"I'll give you five minutes to decide if you want to cooperate. Then I'll have you shot."

The Colonel left the room. He went to the phone and called General Arnold.

"General, I'm sending you a picture of a man we have in custody. We believe he is a spy. Can you identify him?"

"Oh my god, Colonel. That's Aaron Strang. He's Murchison's right hand man. Don't release him."

"Thank you, sir. We'll hold him."

The Colonel went back into the room. "I have confirmation that you are Aaron Strang and you are Felix Murchison's right hand man."

"But, sir. You don't understand. He said if I didn't do this he would kill me."

"You're lying again. You could have come here and told me and Murchison wouldn't have been able to touch you. Take him away Captain and lock him up."

CHAPTER 36

Stan called; "Jeff, I think I have the SPA figured out. We're going to wheel it out onto the old football field and try it. Wish me luck."

"I wish you some clouds to try it on. How long do you think it will take to get results?"

"Some time between a half hour and three hours. I can't know until I try it."

"I wish I could be there." Jeff said.

"I know you do but I'm not waiting."

"I know that, Stan. It's too important to wait for anything. This earth hasn't had rain anywhere since the explosion."

Holly's crew hooked up the SPA to one of the electric carts and wheeled it out. Stan was onboard. They looked at the sky searching for a cloud. Though it was dark the moon's reflected light gave hope of finding one. They saw one directly behind the way the SPA was pointed. They hurriedly turned the SPA around before the cloud disappeared. Stan immediately started adjusting the SPA to aim it at the cloud. He turned dials and switches to get it operational. When it was ready he said; "Here we go. Come on baby, do your thing."

The machine let out a whirring sound but no light beams or crackling sounds. "It's not working." Someone said.

"Yes, it is." Stan said; "This is sound waves, not electrical or light. We can't see them."

They waited. After thirty minutes they could see the cloud begin to swirl. It swirled faster and faster. As it swirled it got larger and darker with every revolution. Though the light was poor and the cloud far away they thought it was producing rain.

"I think its working." Stan said; "I think it's raining over there."

Everyone cheered and offered congratulations.

Stan said; "I'm going to turn it off. We need to go over there and make sure it rained."

They wheeled the SPA back into the tunnel. They unhooked the cart for the trip to see if it had rained. They helped Stan into the cart. Holly got in and Joan drove.

"How far away do you think it is?" Joan said

"It's really hard to tell. It could be one mile or ten miles. We can only head in that direction and hope its close."

"I hope we don't run in to any stragglers. Maybe we should take guns."

"Good idea." Holly said and went in and brought back a pistol.

They headed up the ramp and out in the direction of the rain. They went four or five miles with no sign of rain having fallen. They were getting increasingly disappointed and then they saw something glistening in the street from the moon's glow. Rain drops. As they got closer they found it was not rain but ice. Of course. It's cold. It would freeze. They drove a bit farther and the street became covered in ice. The light-weight cart started slipping and sliding on the ice and they started grinning with happiness. Joan made a slippery u-turn and they headed back to the lab.

Stan said; "It worked. The SPA worked. Now I have to figure out how to control the direction of the rain. I have a bit of time to do that. At least until we're out of Venus shadow or it will all be snow or ice."

They jubilantly made the trip back to the lab. Upon their arrival Stan said he was going to call Jeff and tell him the good news.

Holly said; "Wait a minute,Stan. This is a very important discovery and I don't want it known until we can tell the authorities."

"But Jeff is so involved with it he deserves to know it works."

"Let's wait until morning and I'll make some calls to some interested people. Some people who will know how to handle this."

"But I think Jeff and the team should know."

"Yes, Stan they should, and they will. Trust me on this."

"Alright, Holly. I'm so excited about it I want the whole world to know."

"They will, Stan. Oh, they will."

Stan left Holly's office. He went out the double doors, rolled down the tunnel to the SPA and just sat there and looked at it with a grin on his face.

CHAPTER 37

The Colonel placed a call to General Arnold.

He answered; “Colonel, did you arrest Strang?”

“Yes, sir he is in custody.”

“Good. Did you get my message? Any problems? Will you be ready in three days?”

“What message, sir. I just got released from the hospital. This is my first day back.” Pause. “Of course, sir. Captain Edwards was in charge, sir. What message? I haven’t received any message.”

“I called and left a message with a, I think his name was Boyd, that you should mobilize all your men and materiel, all residents and as much supplies as you have and be prepared to transfer to Fort Kelly the day after tomorrow. At least what’s left of Fort Kelly after that explosion.”

“I didn’t get the message, sir. Aaron Strang was Boyd. As I said, we have him in custody. I do have a problem mobilizing as we have no fuel for the trucks. We had an invasion, successfully repulsed, and our fuel supply was destroyed. I was injured in the attack and consequently in the hospital.”

“I will send a truck with fuel tomorrow. Even though that’s a precious commodity. Is there anything else preventing you from getting here?”

“Not that I can think of right now. Should we bring Strang? It’s either bring him or shoot him.”

"Yes, bring him. We'll handle it here. Be careful out there Colonel. There are bands of stragglers who would love to get their hands on your equipment."

"We will, General." They disconnected and the Colonel turned to Edwards. "We can be sure Murchison knows of those orders."

CHAPTER 38

Lolene drove down the street with a loudspeaker announcing they have been ordered to evacuate this place the day after tomorrow. They were moving to Fort Kelly, sixty miles from the Capital. All residents should be packed and ready to go immediately after breakfast the day after tomorrow.

Jeff and Jen and the climate crew were excited to leave Jerseyville Cavern. They didn't know what Fort Kelly was but they were tired of living in a cave. Jeff said he was going to call Stan and tell him and he also wanted to know if he was having any success with the SPA.

"Hello, Stan. I wanted you to know we're being relocated to Fort Kelly and I was also anxious to know how you were coming with the SPA."

"Hello, Jeff. It's good to hear from you. Glad for you to be getting out of the cave. I have some very good news. We got the SPA operational. It worked. We went out and checked. We found ice not rain but it's cold so it froze. I was going to call but Holly wanted to wait until he could notify someone in authority."

"Well I'm happy it works. Can you pinpoint where it is going to rain?"

"I'm working on that aspect of it."

"I'm happy for you, Stan. I wonder why Holly didn't want you to call me? I bet he has been working with someone in the government and it's all a secret project. Even then, I kind of resent him saying not to call me. It's not like I didn't know anything about it."

"I'll keep working, Jeff. Call me when you get moved."

CHAPTER 39

The fuel truck arrived, was unloaded and headed back to Fort Kelly. All of the military personnel were busy packing everything for shipment. The only things not packed were C-rations for lunch and some medical supplies.

Departure time was scheduled for 9:00 a.m. All the vehicles were in line by 8:30. The residents got into the two busses they had and the JLTV's. The soldiers were in trucks. The resident's vehicles were interspersed with the military vehicles. The electric carts were loaded onto trucks as they did not have enough battery for the entire trip. All vehicles were loaded to the maximum in occupants, space and weight. They had moved into the Cavern with only the number of vehicles they could salvage after the explosion and the military personnel. Now they had an additional three hundred people.

When everything was loaded, Captain Edwards got in the lead vehicle. Colonel Burden, along with a squad of men and a vehicle, were to be last out and lock the Cavern. It was time-consuming getting the vehicles up the elevator but by 10:00 the convoy was ready to move. All the military personnel were armed.

The convoy moved down the mountain until the entire convoy was into what used to be the tree line. The fallen trees and stumps and brush provided plenty of cover for an ambush. Edwards knew if Murchison was going to attack it would be here. No sooner had he thought that when they rounded a bend to see a massive log barricade in the road. They had to stop. Edwards told the men to arm their weapons.

A voice emanating from somewhere in the brush and trees said; “Good morning, Colonel Burden. As you can imagine you are totally surrounded. If all of you exit the vehicles now you will not be harmed. If you choose not to, we will open fire and many more of you will be killed than us. Or we can just wait and pick you off one by one as you exit. You see we have food, water and everything while you have nothing. We can wait.” Shouting; “BUT WE WON’T. EXIT NOW.”

Captain Edwards answered; “Murchison, this is not exactly a surprise. We knew you’d try something like this. We will not exit these vehicles simply because I don’t trust you to keep your word.”

“Is that you, Lieutenant Edwards? I was hoping to talk to the Colonel.”

“It’s Captain Edwards now and the Colonel is not here. He left for Fort Kelly already.”

“Captain Edwards, huh. You’ve been a good little boy and gotten a promotion, how nice. However, we’ve been watching and didn’t see any vehicles. So don’t lie to me.”

“He was in the fuel truck when it went back.”

“You’re wasting my time, Edwards. You have two minutes to exit the vehicles or we start shooting.”

Edwards got on the phone with the Colonel telling him their situation. The Colonel told him to sit tight and stall until they could approach from the rear.

Edwards said; “If I let these residents come out, what are you going to do with them.”

“They can walk away and become stragglers. Let’s see how they like it.” Murchison said.

“Then what about my military personnel?”

“They will become prisoners of war.”

"And where would you keep them? You have no facilities for that."

"You're stalling, Edwards. You have no way out. Give up NOW."

"I'm going to send the residents out. If you shoot we'll know where you're hidden and we'll open fire."

He passed the word that the residents were to leave and get as far away from there as possible. They began to file out and run away. Jeff, Jen, Amanda, Tom and Amos, though they hurried, were the last to the door. Amos, still on crutches, fell down on exiting. Jeff and Tom bent over to lend him a hand. Jen and Amanda ran towards the woods. Then the shooting started. Amos had gotten upright but now all three fell on the ground getting as low as possible to avoid the hail of bullets.

Colonel Burden and his men left their vehicle and double-timed the last 100 yards to the rear of the convoy. As they approached, the stragglers at the rear saw them and opened fire. At the first sound of the gunfire, Edwards men had opened fire spraying the logs and brush with a cascade of bullets. As any straggler raised his head to fire he was met with several well placed shots.

The Colonel's men kept advancing through the brush, eliminating Murchison's men as they advanced. It was not easy as the tangled brush gave ample opportunity for concealment. Twice they passed by a hidden straggler who then rose and shot a man in the back. The Colonel gunned them down. He was everywhere, shouting and yelling orders. He was flushing stragglers out of their hiding places and causing them to run to get away from this military maniac.

Jen and Amanda were running through the brush and the fallen trees trying to avoid the jagged splinters of the trunks. They were part of a mass of running residents now being joined by some scared stragglers trying to get away from the murderous gunfire. Jen and Amanda were grabbed by two of the stragglers who saw Colonel Burden bearing down on them. Using the girls as shields they backed away from the Colonel. “Let them go and I’ll let you run away.” He said. They kept the girls in front of them. The one holding Amanda reached around her and fired a shot at the Colonel. It went screaming past his head. Amanda jerked to the side at the sound of the shot. The Colonel shot and hit the straggler right between the eyes. The Colonel fired a shot over the other one’s head and said; “Last chance.” He let go of Jen, turned and ran.

The Colonel left the girls to continue his war. He searched through the brush but the stragglers were running away. Firing was sporadic now. He saw that his men were not encountering much opposition. He lowered his weapon and stepped around a large brush pile to rejoin his men. He was startled to come face to face with Murchison. Murchison raised his gun and fired twice. Both rounds hit the Colonel. He fell backwards while raising his pistol and firing one shot that went wild. Then he collapsed to the ground.

Murchison immediately turned and ran. Burden‘s men shot after him but missed. One of the men ran to get the Captain while the others remained with the Colonel.

The Colonel was breathing in short gasps when Edwards arrived. Edwards told the men to go alert Dr. Linquist that the Colonel was injured and to get a stretcher. He knelt down to the Colonel.

The Colonel, in short gasping breaths said; “I think it’s too late for the good Doctor, Captain. I want you to get Murchison. You have to get Murchison. None of you are safe while he’s out there. Get Murchison, that’s an order. I have no doubt you will.”

That was his last order. They came back with both the stretcher and the Doctor. They only needed one of them now.

CHAPTER 40

Aside from the Colonel, they lost four other men. The two that were shot in the back and two others. They wrapped the bodies in body bags to take then to the Fort for a proper military burial. They had several wounded and the doctor was treating them. Murchison's losses were much greater. Though he escaped they knew they had not seen the last of him. The residents were rounded up, the barricade cleared away and the sad convoy was again on its way.

Actions such as that occupy a few terrifying minutes. The talking before lasted longer than the gunfire. Men who are alive one moment are dead the next. Those were some of the somber thoughts Edwards had as he knew that all the responsibility was now his.

Some of the vehicles were pock-marked with bullet holes. It was fortunate that the residents had been able to leave before the firing started. The deaths and injuries would have been much greater. The residents were starting to re-settle in their seats and talk about the fire-fight. Word had spread of the Colonel's death and although some were not sympathetic, most were sad knowing he was given a tremendous amount of responsibility in a very trying time.

Jeff, Tom and Amos had remained on the ground during the fight. Bullets were flying all around them and try as they might they could not get any lower in the ground. Jen and Amanda rejoined them when they were permitted back in their vehicle. They told of their run-in with the two stragglers and the action of Colonel Burden.

"Colonel Burden was a hero. If he hadn't been there I don't know what would've happened." Jen said.

"That's right." Amanda chimed in. "They could have kidnapped us."

Tom said; "Stan said Sergeant Riley told him the Colonel was one of the most honorable men he ever knew."

"Speaking of Stan I'm still puzzled about what he told me." Jeff said. He had told them as they were packing.

"Let's get this trip over and get settled and then we'll call him."

"You're right Jen, let's do that."

Jeff wanted to sit next to Jen so they could talk. However, Amanda slid in before he could do that. He sat next to Tom, leaving one whole seat for Amos, his bad leg and his crutch. At 1: 00 they came around distributing C-rations. The C-rations had probably been stored in the cavern no later than 1965 and tasted like.

CHAPTER 41

Murchison was angry. Very angry. Why didn't his barricade work? Someone would have to pay for this. He gathered the remainder of his men and told them he intended to make someone pay for the failure. They looked at each other in trepidation hoping it was the other guy, not them. They had seen examples of Murchison's wrath the last time things didn't go as he had planned. Those three men were left tied to those logs throughout the day and into the night. The cuts from the thorn bushes were not treated and they had no food or water all night. The following day, when they were released, all three hobbled out of Murchison's camp. They thought they would be better off on their own than with that madman.

Murchison watched them go. After they had gone about 200 yards through the open field he grabbed an AK47, took careful aim and shot them in the back. He mowed them down like a scythe through wheat. He turned to his men and said; "That's what deserters get. 200 yards away. That's good. That's very good. Now I won't have to smell their stinking, rotten corpses." He laughed as if he had told a joke. It was. It was the macabre joke of a sick mind.

He was still angry about their failure to capture the convoy. He addressed his men;

"Someone is going to pay for what happened yesterday. And the one who is going to pay for this is" he paused and they all shuddered "Edwards and his men. Since I got the Colonel, he is now number one on the list" Sigh of relief from his men." We'll follow them to Fort Kelly. Sooner or later I'll find a way to get him. I'll get all of them and the Fort will be mine."

CHAPTER 42

Stan was about to go to work on the SPA when Holly called him; “Stan, I’ve been in touch with the government and a Mr. Michael Murphy will be out later today to talk to us.”

“Okay, Holly, until then I’ll keep working.”

“Let me wheel you out there and help you get started.”

Holly helped Stan to the SPA and watched over his shoulder as Stan worked the dials and switches. He paid close attention. After three hours they quit for lunch. Then Stan went to his quarters to rest.

Later, Holly called; “Stan, can you come here? Mr. Murphy is here.”

Stan came out and was introduced to Murphy. Murphy was a rather dark-skinned Mid-east looking man with black hair and a black mustache. Not at all what Stan expected with the Irish name. Then Stan thought with the mingling of the races and ethnicity nowadays looks are no indication of heritage.

Holly said; “Let’s go look at the SPA. I think you’ll be impressed.”

“This machine can do everything you told me, Dr. Blackmore?”

“Yes, sir. Stan is working on arriving at a directional program to be able to cause rain in any part of the world.”

“And how is that program coming? Are you able to do that yet?”

"I'm close to having that program operational Mr. Murphy."

"Good, very good. My government would be very interested in acquiring it if that is done."

Holly said; "You keep working Stan and I'll go talk to Mr. Murphy."

Holly helped Stan onto the platform then he and Murphy left. Stan set to work although a thought kept nagging at him. Why did Murphy say "my government" instead of "the government"? I'll have to ask Holly about that.

PART TWO

THE FORAGERS

CHAPTER 43

The trip to the Fort was surprising for many. The ones who had not been outside since rescue were aghast at the destruction. The buildings were flattened. The trees were felled. Even in the dim light they could see the devastation.

Fort Kelly was about 15 miles past Holly's lab. The Capital was to the right of Fort Kelly. They had to pass through what was left of Holly's city to get to Fort Kelly. The three formed a triangle. As they passed through Holly's city Jeff said; "I think Holly's lab is down that street. I wish we could stop and I could talk to Stan."

Tom said; "I know. We'll call as soon as we get settled."

They arrived at Fort Kelly or what was left of it. The gaps in what was left of the fencing had been filled in with logs and rock so that it looked more like a restricted area. There were tents but very few buildings. The ones that were there were constructed hastily. Some were log cabins. Logs were available because of the felled trees. Others were built of whatever materials could be found from the debris after the explosion. All had been built since the explosion.

Jeff said; "I wish we could have dismantled the buildings at the cavern and hauled them here."

Tom said; "They had no roofs."

"It doesn't matter. It's not going to rain anyway."

A bullhorn broke the murmur of conversation and said; "Please exit your vehicles and stand next to them." They exited the vehicles. They saw that the bullhorn was in the hands of an officer who said; “I’m Major Lenhart. Welcome to Fort Kelly, is Colonel Burden on board?”

Edwards approached the Major, saluted and said; “Sir, we had a fire fight with stragglers on the way and unfortunately Colonel Burden was killed. I’m Captain Edwards. I was given command.”

“Sorry to hear of the Colonel’s death. Come with me, Captain. General Arnold wants to see you. These non-coms will take care of the remainder of your group.”

Lenhart took Edwards to one of the hastily constructed buildings. The Fort‘s headquarters and General Arnold’s office. They were shown into the General’s office.

Lenhart said; “Sir, this is Captain Edwards. He is in command of the Jerseyville Cavern arrivals.”

“Thank you, Major. Where is Colonel Burden, Captain?”

“Sir, we had a skirmish with some stragglers headed by Felix Murchison and unfortunately the Colonel was killed. I was given command.”

“I am so sorry to hear of the Colonel. He was a good man and a fine soldier. You say you were attacked by Murchison? I wondered when he would try to take over.”

“Yes, sir. This was our second run-in with him. He had invaded the Cavern a few days ago.”

“I remember Burden told me about that.”

“I don’t think it’s the last we’ve seen of him. I hope he followed us here. I have a score to settle with him.”

“Knowing Murchison, I’m sure you’ll get your chance. Glad you made it to Fort Kelly, Captain. Major Lenhart will familiarize you with the protocol of the camp.”

Edwards saluted and he and Lenhart left the office.

“Do you have quarters for all my people, Major?

“You can’t exactly call them quarters. We are a tent city you might say. I’ve had my men erecting tents since we knew you were coming. We found the tents in the cavern in which we initially took refuge. There was only about sixty of them so I hope we have enough. The only buildings erected are for the headquarters, the mess halls and the Infirmary. All of your people will be in the same general area. I think there will be work details coming from headquarters for both military and civilian personnel. We must rebuild this camp infrastructure. We have very limited supplies and must start being self-sufficient."

"I understand, Major. We brought everything we could and I think the civilians may be happy to have something to occupy their time. They had nothing to do at Jerseyville Cavern."

"The government had stockpiled many underground bunkers and caverns in the 1950's and 60's because of the nuclear war threat. Similar to Jerseyville Cavern. They had tents, cots, generators, fuel, food, water, and medical supplies, everything needed for a short time to sustain life. We are very fortunate they did that. However, our supplies are limited and we have no way to replenish them. We need to concentrate on food, water, fuel, power, everything needed to sustain life. Everything is rationed but we will run out too soon."

They got into a vehicle and went to the Jerseyville area. The area had a main access street with the headquarters tent and the mess hall on the left. There were three intersecting streets on the right. The streets were dirt with a bit if gravel. The intersecting streets had tents on both sides. One side was men's tents; the other side was women's. They were arranged so that back to back tents were of the same gender. There were washrooms at the end of each row of tents. Six washrooms total. The people were assembled in the main street and were being assigned quarters and instructed in the rules of the camp. Edwards was shown the tent that would be his headquarters until a more substantial structure could be built. He found Sergeant Riley and told him to set it up as best he could.

Edwards went to see where Amanda was quartered. He found her tent and the tent of the others. He excused himself then as he had to go to the other end of the camp to make sure his command was being taken care of. He told Amanda he would be back later. He never made it back before "lights out."

CHAPTER 44

Jen and Amanda were assigned a tent with Cassandra, Annabelle, Myra and Angie. Jeff, Tom and Amos were in a tent with Boris and Elmer and Billy Bailey. Boris was not happy with the arrangement. Cassandra was not unhappy.

Jeff called Stan as soon as they were settled; "Stan, we're at Fort Kelly. We had a fight with Murchison and his men on the way. Sadly, Colonel Burden was killed. Edwards was put in charge. Fort Kelly is not a dream vacation spot. We're living in unheated tents. I guess that's one step up from a cave. How are things going with you?"

"Hi, Jeff, things are going alright. I'm working on the directional program. I think I can have that soon. A Mr. Murphy was here from the government investigating the progress. He said they would be interested when I got the directional program working. It's strange; he said "my government" instead of "the government" I'll have to ask Holly about that."

"Yeah, Stan, that is strange. Well, keep in touch and we'll do the same."

Jeff told Tom and Amos that Stan was OK and working on the SPA. Jeff left to see how Jen and Amanda were doing. Especially Jen.

Elmer said; "Who's this Stan guy? Is he at a spa?"

"No, nothing that nice. He's working on a Sonic Precipitation Accelerator, SPA for short." Tom said.

"What's a sonic participation accelerator?"

"It's precipitation not participation. It's a machine that can make it rain anywhere in the world."

"Wow, we haven't had rain for weeks."

"Neither has anyone else in the world. That's why what Stan is doing is very important."

Boris was lying on his cot taking it all in.

CHAPTER 45

Jeff went to the girl's tent and called Jen out. He told her of his conversation with Stan.

"I wish I could go see Stan. He sounded concerned." Jeff said.

"You could ask Phil Edwards if someone could take you there."

"I'll do that tomorrow, Jen. He's very busy today getting his men settled. How are you doing? Is there anything I can do to help?"

"We're alright, Jeff. Amanda wishes she could spend more time with Phil. Cassandra is quiet, probably because she always had to be careful about what she said. Angie doesn't cry as much anymore. I think Banger being here is very comforting to her."

"Banger runs between your tent and ours. Elmer Bailey has taken a liking to the dog. He lost his dog in the explosion. How about you, Jen? We've talked about the others but not you."

"Oh, I'm alright. I'm concerned about the future as everyone is. Let me know what Phil says. Thanks for checking on us."

She turned and went back into her tent

CHAPTER 46

7:00 a.m. the following morning. The headquarters of General Elliot Arnold, the commander of Fort Kelly.

"Good morning, Sergeant. Contact Major Lenhart, Captain Edwards and Lieutenant Anderson and tell them we're having a staff meeting at 0900."

"Yes, sir. Right away, sir."

Major Joseph Lenhart, Captain Phillip Edwards and Lieutenant Bradley Anderson gathered at the General's office promptly at 0900.

"Gentlemen, be seated. I've called this meeting to address some of the issues and problems we are going to face in the near future. Since the influx of the people from Jerseyville Cavern our supplies are going to expire quickly. We must find ways to replenish them. You gentlemen are to compile a list of all the people you are responsible for and determine what skills, attributes or expertise they have and how best we can utilize it. Major Lenhart, compile a list of all activities that need be addressed and identify individuals to assign to those tasks. Captain Edwards, interview the people from Jerseyville. Lieutenant Anderson, you interview the military personnel and all residents other than Jerseyville. I need you to compile this information no later than 0900 the day after tomorrow. Thank you, gentlemen. Get busy."

The officers left and went to the mess hall to strategize over breakfast. Each of them had two hundred or three hundred people to interview. They decided Major Lenhart's military personnel would be best used to handle the camp functions and as guards for residents who were foraging outside the camp.

Edwards said; "The residents would have to have guards. We had three incidents with Felix Murchison and his gang of criminals before we got here. They probably followed us here so we can expect more trouble."

"Murchison's a dangerous character. He and his band of stragglers. I'm sure there are some nice stragglers out there. People who were unable to go to one of the shelters or did not know of them. They have struggled tremendously not knowing exactly what has happened, why it has been so dark and so cold and if this is a permanent condition."

"You're right. It must be horrible for them. Not to mention the criminal gangs like Murchison's who want to take everything they have."

"We better get busy as the General said. Let's meet here tomorrow at 0800 to check our progress."

They left to go to their separate areas to get busy on their reports.

CHAPTER 47

Edwards went to talk to Jeff, Jen and Amanda, especially Amanda.

"General Arnold wants a list of all the residents and what skills they may have that will help us survive. I was hoping I could rely on you guys to help me."

"Sure, Phil, we'll help any way we can."

"I'd like to split up into teams to canvass all the residents. We would need to get their names, their ages and their occupation as well as any special skills they have."

"When do you want to start?"

"Now. The General wants the report at 9:00 a.m. day after tomorrow. The teams need to be a man and a woman as the tents are gender separated."

Jeff said; "I'll go with Jen and you could go with Amanda. I may be able to get Elmer Bailey and Cassandra to help. I don't think her husband Boris would be a help. He seems to have an aversion to work."

"It's a plan. I'll have Sergeant Riley compile the info. Maybe Amos and Tom could help him. Amos is still on crutches."

"If you think we need a fourth team, maybe Annabelle and Billy Bailey would help"

"We may need them. We have three hundred residents to interview. I'll get some paper and pens. Amanda, you and Jen talk to Cassandra. Jeff, get Elmer, Tom and Amos on board."

Jen and Amanda went to get Cassandra. They told her what they wanted and asked if she would help.

"Sure, I'll be glad to help. How are we going to do this?"

"Here, I'll show you. First we put tent number. Ours is number 12. Then we put the name, Cassandra…. Oh, I don't know your last name."

"It's Holwitz. H-O-L-W-I-T-Z"

"Then we put your age."

"I'm 48. Why do you need that?"

"Some tasks can't be done by the old or the young. What was your occupation?"

"I worked in the school cafeteria."

"Do you have any special skills or hobbies?"

"I like to sew."

"That's it Cass. That's what we need to do. Any questions or are you ready to go?"

"Let's go."

The teams assembled and each took a street in the tent city. All the residents were housed in tents as all permanent structures had been razed or badly damaged in the explosion. Some structures were being built using logs from all the trees felled in the explosion. The tents were minimal protection as most were decades old and crumbly. However there had been no rain since the explosion. The earth had been in the shadow of Venus for three weeks after the explosion. It was always dark and cold during that time. Thankfully the earth was moving out of the shadow and becoming warmer with the sunlight.

Jeff and Jen started down their street. The streets were just dirt strips between two rows of tents. Dust rose with every footfall and hung in the air. They explained to the residents what they were doing and got the necessary information. Most of the residents were happy to hear that steps were being taken to resolve some of the problems. They were also glad to do whatever they could to help.

Jeff and Jen had a chance to talk between interviews.

"Jeff, I'm wondering how long the supplies we have will last. It seems the meals are getting skimpier and water is being rationed. We can only shower once a week and we have to have a ticket to do that. Clean clothes are another problem."

"I know, Jen. That's why we're doing this. We have to get a handle on this quickly. I don't know what is being done about restoring electricity or water supply or even sewage disposal. Maybe Phil knows what's going on. I'll ask."

They continued going tent to tent getting the necessary information. They took a break at noon, rounded up the other info takers and went to the mess hall for lunch. They got their trays, went through the line and sat down.

Cass said; "These meals get smaller and smaller every day."

They each had a cup of soup, a package of crackers and a small bowl with three slices of canned peaches.

"That's why we're doing what we're doing." Phil said; "We have to find a way to replenish our supplies. We are going to establish foraging expeditions to find clothes, medicines, tools, fuel and everything else we need. We have to do it before the stragglers get it all or they would be in charge of our survival. Needless to say they don't care if we survive or not."

"But what about food, Phil? You didn't mention food." Cass chimed in. She was worried about how Boris would react.

Phil replied; "There will be foragers going to the fields to see if anything is salvageable. The explosion happened late summer so many things were ready to harvest. We have to hope that the extended cold acted as a refrigerator and they are still useable. If they froze we have an even bigger problem."

They fell silent contemplating their plight. They ate their meager lunch. After a short time, Jeff said sarcastically; "I'm full. Let's get back to work."

The teams worked through the afternoon. At the end of the day they had canvassed the entire tent city. They had found a very diverse group with numerous different occupations and skills. Periodically they had given results to Sergeant Riley and his helpers so they could get a head start on compiling their report. When the last tent had been canvassed Captain Edwards called the teams together. He gathered the last of their papers to take to Sergeant Riley and said; "Thanks to all of you. I'll get these to the Sergeant so he can complete the report. Amanda, will you go with me?"

"Of course I will if you want me."

When they arrived at Phil's headquarters tent he handed the remaining papers to the Sergeant and said; "Sergeant, why don't you guys take a break. You've been at it for hours."

"Thank you, sir. We'll head over to the mess hall. It's almost time to eat."

Riley, Amos and Tom headed to the mess hall. As soon as they left, Phil turned to Amanda and said; "I'm sorry I haven't been able to spend some time with you, Amanda. Lord knows I wanted to but since the Colonel's death I've been in command. There have been so many things to do with getting the men settled and familiarizing myself with this place. We had to improvise shelter for the men as there were no more tents. Thankfully we had enough tents for the women so they could have some privacy. And this afternoon I wanted to talk to you but we were constantly interrupted."

"Oh, Phil, you don't need to apologize. I'm glad we're in the same place. I know you have immense responsibilities. I'm here whenever you can be here."

"That means a lot to me, Amanda. How are things going for your bunch?"

"As well as can be expected under the circumstances. The tent is cramped with the six of us being there. Jen and I get along very well. Annabelle's a nice girl. Myra and Angie are better now. Angie doesn't cry as much anymore. She loves Banger. Cass seems much more relaxed. I think that's because she's away from Boris."

"I can understand that. He's a hard person to like. He seems to be very selfish." Phil said.

"You know I try to remain strong but then I'll think about my family and wonder what happened to them. And my friends and all the other people." She paused for a few moments; "Oh, Phil. It can be so depressing." She sobbed quietly and a tear trickled down her cheek.

Phil reached out and gently wrapped his arms around her. He lifted her head and using his finger wiped the tear from her cheek. She looked up wanly and gave him a small smile. He kissed her eyelid and said; "Don't cry, Amanda. It hurts me to see you cry."

He kissed her gently on the lips. She responded with a more meaningful kiss. And then another. And another. They were holding each other in a tight embrace forgetting the outside world. Their whole world at that instant was wrapped in each others arms. Their hands were exploring each others body and they were ready to explode with desire. Then they heard Sergeant Riley's voice saying good night to Tom and Amos. They backed away from each other and grinned guiltily like kids with their hand caught in the cookie jar.

"Oh Sergeant, you're back. Did you eat?"

"Yes, sir, I did. Thank you. I hope I wasn't gone too long."

"No, Sergeant, it was fine. I had better get Miss Burgess home. I'll be back shortly to wrap things up."

CHAPTER 48

The report was completed and the officers gathered at General Arnold's office at 0900. The General read the report and commented; "Thank you, gentlemen. Now comes the hard part. Using this information and assigning tasks to individuals confluent with their abilities and interests. Major Lenhart, have you determined the tasks necessary and earmarked individuals to accomplish them?"

"Yes, sir. I have conferred with the Captain and the Lieutenant and we have come up with a list. The primary needs of the Fort are food, electricity, building materials and clothing. We are establishing four different forager details. The first is the food group. They will check all farm fields, demolished grocery stores, etc. for edible items. The second group will sort through the remains of all retail stores for useable items. The third group will be the log and building materials group. The fourth group will be comprised of those people unable to do manual labor and they will be responsible for inventorying the items and repairing them so they are useable. A primary concern is fuel. We are very short on gasoline and diesel oil. We have to have gasoline for the electrical generators. That is our only power source. But that means we cannot use the gas for our few vehicles. We will have to rely on the battery powered electric carts as they can be re-charged. We will have to improvise trailers for those carts to carry anything we gather."

"That's a good start, Major, but how are you going to gather logs or other building materials?"

"We have a lot of manpower, sir. We will make log caddies and pull them with ropes if necessary. I don't think the electric carts would have enough power to pull them."

"How many teams will you have?"

"We only have eight of the carts, sir, so we're limited. The batteries last six hours at the most so we're limited on how far we can go. We also have to have enough battery life to return."

"So that means if you send them out in the morning they would be unavailable in the afternoon." The General interjected.

"That's right, sir. They would have to be re-charged in the afternoon."

"Are you planning to send out only four in the morning and have the remaining four for the afternoon?" The General said.

"That's a possibility or we could send all eight later in the day and have overnight to re-charge them."

"I don't think you should send all eight out at once." The General said. "You would not have any left in reserve in case of an emergency. Don't send more than six out. Reserve two."

"Yes, sir."

"Alright gentlemen, start immediately. We must get going or the stragglers will have it all. Give me a daily report of the activities and what we have gathered. Thank you. Dismissed."

The officers spent the remainder of the morning preparing a schedule of activities and a roster of individuals assigned to those activities. A copy was distributed to all residents and military personnel. The schedule covered the next three days.

CHAPTER 49

Jeff contacted Edwards and told him he was concerned about what Stan had told him.

"If you could arrange it, Phil, I would like to go to Dr. Blackmore's lab and talk to Stan. Maybe, Sergeant Emmons could drive if you don't have him doing other duty. He knows how to get there."

"I'll talk to the Major about it and see if anything is available. I'm not in charge here so it's not my call. I'll tell him what Stan is doing is very important."

"Thanks, Phil. I'll wait to here from you."

Jeff went back to his tent and told Tom and Amos that Edwards would see if he could get a vehicle to take him to see Stan.

Some hours later Edwards called to say that he got permission to use one of the electric carts the day after tomorrow. Emmons would drive.

Boris was lying on his cot listening intently.

The work detail list for the following day had Jeff and Tom assigned bus boy duties in the mess hall. Amos, being on crutches, had desk duty at headquarters. Elmer and Billy had maintenance duty. Boris was assigned to forage duty outside the Fort. The foragers were to scour the country side for any thing that may be usable as everything was in short supply.

CHAPTER 50

They picked up Boris for forage duty right after breakfast. A half-ton pick-up truck with a soldier as the driver and another resident. They all got into the cab, it was crowded.

They drove out of the Fort and into the rubble of the city. The driver said; "We look for building materials, motors, generators, anything that is usable. We've pumped and siphoned the fuel from the underground tanks. That is, any the stragglers have not gotten."

They found the remains of a hardware store and salvaged nails, screws, and some tools that were buried in the rubble. Boris complained that it was a lot of work for the few things they got. The driver looked disgustedly at him but said nothing. They drove further from the Fort and found a service station that looked like it hadn't been raided. The driver got out the hand pump and the gas cans, opened the fill cap, inserted the pump hose and started pumping. Success, there was still fuel in the tank. He pumped for a few minutes then turned to Boris and said; "Your turn."

Boris took over and after two minutes said; "I have to take a leak." He handed the pump handle to the driver, turned and walked into the woods. He walked for a while and then sat down on a fallen log. He thought he'd done enough of that stupid, dirty work.

The stragglers were watching the truck. They saw them pumping the gas and decided to wait until they finished to attack. Let them do the work, and then we'll take it all. They saw Boris walking toward them and thought that's one less defender.

The driver and the resident were finished pumping.

The driver said; "You get in the truck. I don't know where that bozo went."

Then the shot rang out and panged into the truck inches from the driver's head.

He exclaimed; "And I don't care. He should have stayed here."

He jumped into the truck, slammed it into gear and took off with tires squealing.

Boris heard the shot. He looked up to see what was happening and instead saw two stragglers approaching him with guns drawn.

"We got us one of 'em, Gus. Shall I kill him or do you want to."

"I might kill him with my bare hands. He don't look like he's worth a bullet."

Boris had not done what he said was his reason for going into the woods. Now you could tell by looking at the expanding wet spot on the front of his pants.

Boris said; "No, no don't kill me. I know stuff you guys can use."

"What kind of stuff."

"A machine, a very valuable machine."

"Whaddya think, Gus, should we kill him or take him to Felix."

"Let's take him to Felix. If he's lyin,' Felix can kill him."

They shoved Boris ahead of them as they took him to Felix's camp. Felix saw them approach and asked; "What is that and why did you bring it here?"

"He says he has a machine that we could use. We thought you may want to know about it so we brought him. We can kill him later."

Murchison snarled; “Talk to me fast, pisspants so I know I shouldn’t kill you now.”

Boris was trembling; “I..I..I know where there’s a rain making machine. Nobody has rain and it could be worth a lot to anyone.”

“Where is this rain making machine?”

“I don’t know exactly but the guy that does know will be going there tomorrow. He’ll have to come this way to get there. We could follow him.”

“Who is this guy and how do you know this?”

“His name is Jeff. We’re tent mates. I overheard them talking. He’ll be in one of those electric carts.”

“When is he coming this way?”

“Tomorrow morning. He’ll have some soldier driving. It can’t be too far or they wouldn’t be able to use one of those carts.”

“OK loser. You can stick around until morning and point him out to me. If you’re telling the truth I’ll let you go. If he doesn’t show up in the morning, you’ll be dead by the afternoon.”

CHAPTER 51

The driver and the resident arrived back at the Fort with the forage truck. They reported to the Officer-In-Charge that they had a run-in with some stragglers. They told the Officer that Boris had gone into the woods to relieve himself. Then shots were fired at them. So they got out of there ASAP.

"Who was the man you lost?"

"His name is Boris Holwitz. But the way he acts it should be half-wits."

"I'll report it to his Commanding Officer. You get this stuff over to the supply depot."

"Yes, sir. Right away, sir."

The OIC called Edwards; "Captain, the foraging crew came back and a man named Boris Holwitz is not with them. He went off in the woods and they were attacked. They quickly got out of there before they lost all the things they had gathered."

"Thank you, sir. I'll contact his wife and tell her he's M.I.A."

Edwards went to the ladies tent and asked for Cassandra. He told her that Boris was M.I.A. and did not come back with the truck.

"You mean he's dead?"

"We don't know that Cass. We only know there were shots fired and they were attacked."

"Well thanks for coming to tell me Captain. We can only hope."

She neglected to say what she was hoping for.

CHAPTER 52

Mr. Murphy had left. Stan approached Holly; "Holly, I noticed Mr. Murphy said "my government" instead of "the government" or "our government" I wonder why?"

"Just a slip of the tongue, Stan. Nothing for you to be concerned about."

"I just thought it rather strange. I called Jeff. He thought so too."

"Oh, you called Jeff?"

"Yes. He's been very involved with all of this and I thought he should know we're making progress."

"He's not coming here is he?"

"He didn't say that but I wouldn't be surprised if he did."

"I thought we would invite him as soon as we have the directional component operating. If he was here now it would just take away from the time working on it."

"It may be a good idea Holly to have someone else knowledgeable about how to operate it."

"Well I've been looking over your shoulder for that exact reason."

"I was thinking of someone younger. You and I have been at this kind of work a long time."

"Yes, Stan. A very long time." Holly turned and went into his office.

CHAPTER 53

Jen was insistent that she go with Jeff to see Stan. Jeff put up a mild argument that there were still stragglers out there; it could be dangerous, etc. He thought it would be a good time for them to talk and just be together for a while so it was a very mild argument.

Emmons picked them up in the morning. They sat in the second bench seat so Emmons couldn't hear their conversation. Since it was only fifteen miles to Holly's lab, the trip didn't last nearly long enough for Jeff to be with Jen is what he thought.

The Sergeant took the cart to the charging station. Jeff and Jen went to the door. Jeff knocked and Joan opened it and greeted them; "Oh, hello. We weren't expecting you. Come in. I'll get Dr. Blackmore."

She turned and left and they were left standing there. After a few minutes Holly appeared.

"Well look who's here. How are the two of you?"

"Hello, Holly. Stan called and said you got the SPA operational. That's just great. We had to come to see it."

"I know you're very interested in it. Everything's under control. Stan is working on it right now. I'll take you to him but please don't interrupt him too long. He's about finished with the directional component."

"We won't bother him too much. We wanted to see how he was fairing. Whether you give him time off for meals and sleep."

"Very funny." Holly said smiling weakly; "We do. We work him hard but not that hard."

They went down the tunnel and to the SPA. Stan was at the console.

"Look who came to visit you Stan."

Stan turned around and saw Jeff and Jen and broke out in a big grin.

"Hey you guys, it's great seeing you. Thank you for coming. How is everyone?'

They mounted the platform. Jeff shook Stan's hand and Jen gave him a hug.

"Everyone's doing alright, Stan. Amos leg is healing although he's still on crutches. Amanda and Tom are fine. The ladies and men are separated, so Cassandra is in with Jen and we guys have Boris in our tent."

"How's that going?"

"As well as you think it is."

"That bad, huh." Stan said. "We have been busy here. The basic function of the SPA is operational. Now I'm trying to figure out the directional component."

"That's what you said on the phone. How are you progressing? Are you close?"

"I think so. Maybe tomorrow or the next day. It's hard to tell. This has never been done before. Holly, do you think we could give them lunch before they go back?"

Jeff said; "We have Sergeant Emmons with us. He's recharging the cart."

"Oh I think we can give them something. Have him come in."

They left the tunnel, crossed the entryway and went into the break room. Jeff pushed Stan. Joan got food out for them and they sat down.

Jeff said; "Stan says you have someone from the government coming here to check your progress Holly."

"That's right, Jeff. Name's Michael Murphy."

"What Department is he in, Holly?"

"Uh, The Interior Department."

"I'm curious. So many departments could have an interest in the SPA. Defense. Homeland Security, National Weather Service, just to name some."

"I know, Jeff. I don't know why they sent someone from Interior."

"Like I said, just curious. The government does do strange things sometimes."

They ate the lunch. Jeff and Jen said goodbye to Stan. They said goodbye and thanks to Holly and Joan, got in the cart and left.

They had not gone a quarter mile when Jeff said; "I don't know what's going on there but something is. Holly did not seem overjoyed to see us. He had told Stan not to tell us of their success and he hesitated when I asked him which department Murphy was in."

"I thought the same thing Jeff."

"Good, Jen. Maybe I'm not being paranoid. I'll ask Edwards if he can check the Interior Department for this Michael Murphy."

CHAPTER 54

That morning Murchison, three of his men and Boris had concealed themselves behind some fallen trees and waited. They didn't know exactly what time Jeff would come by so they got there early. It was cold.

Murchison kept glaring at Boris; "This better happen or you'll never go one more foot from where you're sitting."

"He'll be here. He'll be here."

They waited. Then they waited some more. Murchison all the while caressing his pistol and glaring at Boris. Then they saw the electric cart approaching. They were surprised there were two passengers and the driver.

"That's him. That's him" Boris said; "Let me go now. See, I didn't lie. Let me go now."

"But I don't know if any such rain machine exists do I?" Murchison said. "You get to stay with us for a while. Doesn't that make you happy?"

"You said I could go if they came by."

"I changed my mind. Shut up. Let's see where they go."

Murchison and two of his men followed at a distance. They left Boris guarded by the other man. Murchison wanted him available if what he had told them was lies. The cart wasn't going very fast so they able to keep up with it. They arrived at Holly's lab.

They saw Emmons start recharging the batteries. He was armed and they didn't know if anyone else there was armed. And if so, how many were there. They waited and watched.

They were still there two hours later when Emmons, Jeff and Jen pulled away.

Murchison's man said; "Do you want Gus and me to take care of them so we can have their cart."

"No, idiot, others know they're here. I don't want any of them to know we're here. Let's get back to the camp. I'm not going to attack that place with just the two of you idiots."

CHAPTER 55

Jeff and Jen arrived back at the Fort without further incident. Jeff and Jen went to talk to Captain Edwards. Sergeant Riley said he wasn't there. He had to go tell some poor lady her husband was M.I.A. Some guy named Boris. Jeff and Jen looked at each other. Poor Cass, or maybe not. After ten minutes Edwards arrived.

"Hi, Captain, the Sergeant told us where you were. How's Cass doing?"

"Remarkably well. She's holding up fine. How can I help you?"

"I would like your opinion on something and also ask if you know anyone in the Interior Department." Jeff said.

"To answer the second part of your question "No, I do not know anyone in Interior, maybe the Major or the General do. The first part, I have to know what you want my opinion on."

Jeff told him of their conversations with Stan and about Michael Murphy; "Do you think we're being paranoid?"

"Maybe, maybe not. It won't hurt to check it out. I'll see what I can find out."

"Thanks, Phil, give me a call regardless of what you find."

They went back to tent city. Jen went to console Cassandra and Jeff went to tell Amos and Tom about Boris and their trip to see Stan.

Phil called about two hours later. He said; “The General has a friend in Interior. The General called me in to explain why I needed to know. I told him the whole story about Stan’s project. He immediately saw the importance of it and placed the call. He said his friend said they did have four Murphy’s in the Department. None are named Michael. He asked if I was sure it was Michael and not Mike or something. I told him that was the name given to me. Are you sure it’s Michael?”

“That’s the name I heard, Phil. Jen was there. I’ll ask her to confirm if that’s what she heard. Hold the line.”

He ran to Jen’s tent and asked her. She confirmed that was the name. He went back to the phone call.

“Phil, she confirmed it. The name was Michael. I’m going to call Stan first thing in the morning and have him ask Holly what’s going on. Thanks for your help.”

“Let me know what’s going on too, Jeff.”

CHAPTER 56

The next morning Jeff called Stan; "Stan, I had Phil Edwards inquire about Michael Murphy. General Arnold has a friend in the Interior Department who said they do not have a Michael Murphy employed there. You better ask Holly what's going on."

"Thanks, Jeff. I will ask him."

Stan went to Holly's office. He rolled in and pushed the door closed.

"What is it, Stan. How may I help you?"

"What's going on, Holly? Jeff checked and there is no Michael Murphy employed in the Interior Department."

"Maybe they got the name wrong. Maybe they got the wrong Department."

"I don't think so, Holly. They had General Arnold check it."

"Stan, old friend. You know I've been working here 35 years. In those 35 years no one has ever been here from the National Bureau. They expect me to do all their work and they take the glory. Well I'm tired of it. Four years ago Bert Hornsby came to me with an idea he had. That idea has become the SPA. I thought why should Bert and I present this idea to them. If they approve it for development they would take all the credit for its success or blame me if it failed. I had Bert start working on it. I did some accounting magic to fund it for these four years. Bert had it ready for testing when the explosion happened and he was killed. I was sad about his death and also that the project would not be finished. Then you called and said Bert had told you about it. You can see it made me think that perhaps the project could be completed."

"Holly, I'm not saying you were wrong to go ahead with the development on your own. Although I think using the funds for unintended reasons and without authorization could be trouble. But that doesn't answer the question about Michael Murphy. Who is he?"

"Stan, you were right when you said it could be trouble. I knew I couldn't just go to the Bureau now and tell them I've developed this. It would have caused a million questions. So I decided to look elsewhere for a customer. I contacted the embassy of several Middle-east countries. The desert regions. Bringing rain to those areas could have immense economic value to them. Mr. Murphy is the representative from one of them. As you could tell, they are very interested in purchasing it."

"But, Holly. That could be treason. And misappropriation of funds and probably some other felonies they would throw at you."

"I don't care, Stan. I'll sell the SPA for millions and retire someplace nice."

"Holly, you've been outside. There aren't any nice places left that I know of. Besides, can you trust those guys or are they going to come get the SPA and not pay you or worse."

"I'm tired of all this, Stan. I want out. I could get you set up with them too. They need someone to operate the SPA."

"No, Holly. I'm not going to do that. What I am going to do is tell the proper authorities. General Arnold already knows. I'm calling Jeff."

He picked up his phone to call Jeff and Holly reached into his desk and brought out a gun and pointed it at Stan.

"You're going to shoot me, Holly? You're going to add murder to treason? I'm making the call. He punched in the number."

There was a loud crash and a scream from outside the office. Holly rushed to the door just as it was flung open sending him crashing to the floor. He dropped the gun and the intruder picked it up. It was Murchison. Holly struggled to his feet. Murchison herded both of them into the lab. There were fifteen or twenty other stragglers there. Joan was cowering in the corner of the room. The other two employees were seated on the floor with their hands behind their heads.

"Where's this rain making machine I've heard about?" Murchison asked.

Holly said; "It's not working yet. We're still trying to get it to work."

"I heard you tested it and it works. Don't lie to me. I don't like lies."

While that exchange was going on, Jeff answered the phone.

Stan whispered; "Murchison's here."

"Did you say Murchison's there?"

Whispering; "Yes. He wants the SPA."

"Who're you talking to crip? Give me that phone." Murchison yelled.

He snatched the phone from Stan and said; "Who is this?" No answer. Jeff had hung up.

"Who were you talking to?"

"My wife." Stan lied.

Murchison turned the gun toward Holly; "Take me to that machine. Now."

They headed down the tunnel toward the SPA. Murchison left two men behind with Joan and the other two employees. As they approached the SPA Murchison said; "Why is it so big?" He thought it would be portable and they could easily transport it.

Holly, pushing Stan, said; "It has a lot of work to do."

"Show me how it works."

"We have to get it out of the tunnel." Stan said.

Murchison told his men to push it out of the tunnel. They pushed it out to the football field. The field was littered with chunks of concrete from the demolished walls.

"Not far enough." Stan said; "It has to be in the middle of the field."

They cleared a path and pushed it to the middle of the field.

Stan said; 'It only works if we can find a cloud. Do you see any clouds?"

"I think you're stalling. Get the thing working?"

"I can't do it from here." Stan said," I have to be at the console on the platform. I can't get up there without help because I'm a crip as you put it."

"Don't get smart-assed. You men, help him up."

Stan said; "I'll turn it on. It takes about a half-hour to warm up. Have you seen any clouds?"

"You turn it on. We'll look for clouds."

Stan sat at the console fooling with the knobs and switches. Stalling for time. Hoping Jeff would be able to get help, get it organized and travel the fifteen miles from the Fort before Murchison realized he didn't need Joan and the other men and eliminated them. And maybe Holly too.

CHAPTER 57

Jeff got Stan's call and immediately called Edwards. He told him Murchison was in Holly's lab. Murchison wants the SPA.

"We can't let him have it. You have to stop him, Phil. Emmons and Lolene know where the lab is."

Captain Edwards rousted two squads of men and Sergeant Emmons. He told Lolene to get Jeff and bring him to the lab. They headed to the lab, less than fifteen miles away. They knew Murchison was capable of any atrocity. Holly and Stan were in big trouble.

Lolene went for Jeff; "Edwards, Emmons and two squads are on their way to the lab. I'm to bring you."

Jen came out of her tent. "What's going on?"

"Murchison's at Holly's. Edwards is on his way. Lolene's taking me."

"Me too." Jen said and hopped in the vehicle.

Lolene turned the vehicle around and they headed to the lab.

CHAPTER 58

As Edwards got close to the lab they left the vehicles and went by foot. He didn't know if Murchison had left guards nor how many of them were there. They saw no one outside the lab as they moved down the ramp to the door. The door was open. They entered cautiously and encountered the two men guarding Joan and the others. The guards raised their guns but Edwards shot them down before they got them waist high.

Joan said; "They're in the tunnel. Through those doors."

Murchison heard the shots. He knew Stan had alerted some one. He and his men turned and looked down the long tunnel and saw Edwards's men coming through the doors. They immediately started firing. The troopers hit the deck and returned fire from the prone position. Bullets were ricocheting off the concrete walls. Chips of concrete were striking the prone soldiers on their helmets and bodies. They were not causing serious damage but caused them to keep their heads down limiting their ability to shoot.

Lolene arrived with Jeff and Jen just as all the shooting started.

Jeff said; "Jen, stay here until we see if it's OK."

He and Lolene ran down the ramp and to the door. Lolene with gun drawn.

Jeff saw Joan; "Where's Stan, Joan?"

"He's out there. Dr. Blackmore too." she said pointing to the doors.

Jeff immediately knew the danger they were in with all the shooting into and out of the tunnel.

Emmons told Edwards of the plaza level above the tunnel. They could go there, look over the demolished walls and shoot down at the stragglers.

Edwards said; "I'll take a squad and do that. You stay here and advance if you can." He called eight men and they ran out the door and up the ramp to the plaza level.

Murchison had jumped onto the SPA platform and took a position behind Stan, using Stan as a shield. He looked around, to see if there was any way out of there. All he saw were the remains of the grandstands of the stadium, littered with rubble, rising twenty feet above him. Keeping the mass of the SPA between himself and the sight line of the tunnel, he moved across the field and to the grandstand.

Edwards reached the plaza level and looked over the walls just in time to see Murchison heading toward the grandstand on the other side of the field. He was dodging in and out among the rubble. Never exposing himself long enough for Edwards to get a shot at him.

Murchison reached the top of the stands and ran around it toward the ramp leading to the tunnel. Edwards saw him and ran to intercept him.

Edwards's squad continued firing at the stragglers on the field who were now shooting up at them. The stragglers were able to hide behind the piles of rubble so they were not "ducks on a pond" even though they were caught in the cross-fire of the men in the tunnel and the men up above. They began to follow Murchison and go up the grandstand. That allowed the men in the tunnel to get up and pursue them.

When Murchison reached the start of the ramp he saw Jen still sitting in her cart. He rushed her and tried to throw her out and take the cart. She fought back and he hit her in the head with his gun. She fell unconscious onto the seat. He got into the cart and started to drive away just as Edwards got there. Edwards grabbed the cart. Murchison pointed his gun at him and pulled the trigger. Click, click, empty. Murchison used his foot to kick him off. Edwards rolled off onto the ground and immediately sprinted to his truck. He jumped in, threw it in gear and pursued Murchison. The truck quickly gained ground on the much slower electric cart.

Murchison, driving at top speed, the cart was swaying side to side in every bend in the road. They came to a particularly sharp bend and the cart slid off the road and turned on its side.

Edwards saw Jen's body slide out of the cart and saw Murchison jump out of the cart and run into the woods. As much as he wanted to pursue Murchison, Edwards knew he had to check on Jen first.

He reached her side. She was scratched but breathing. He shook her gently to waken her. She moaned and opened her eyes; "What happened? Ow, Ow my arm hurts."

Edwards said; "Murchison took you. You fell out of the cart. Lie still. I'll get help." He hoped Murchison had run off and wasn't hanging around. He hated to leave Jen to get help but didn't think he should move her.

He got in the truck and drove back to the lab. He called the Fort Infirmary on the way to get help for Jen and anyone that had been wounded. As he got back Jeff was frantically searching for Jen. When Phil exited the truck, Jeff said: "Have you seen Jen? We left her here with the cart and now they're gone."

"Murchison took her and the cart. She may have a broken arm but she's alright. I'll have Lolene take you to her. I'll tell you all about it later."

He went down the ramp into the lab. He gave Lolene instructions then went to see Emmons. The fighting was over. No wounded on their side but two dead and three wounded stragglers. The rest got away.

Edwards said; "So did Murchison."

Lolene took Jeff to Jen. The medics from the Fort had not arrived yet.

"Oh, Jen, Jen, I'm so sorry. It's all my fault. I shouldn't have left you up there alone. I'm so sorry." Jeff blubbered.

"You owe me big time buddy. I may forgive you, but I'll never forget. I'm going to hold this over your head for years."

"Oh, thank you, thank you. That makes me so happy to know that you think we're going to have years together." He smiled. She did too.

The medics arrived. They took care of Jen and then Lolene led them to the lab. Jeff rode with Jen. The medics treated the wounded stragglers who were under guard. The stragglers, still under guard, were loaded into the trucks for transport to the Fort. Jeff rode with Jen in the medics van on the trip to the infirmary.

Stan and Holly were brought in. They were very much relieved to be safe although still nervous from the ordeal.

Edwards approached them; "That could have been much worse. Luckily you were on the phone to Jeff when they broke in or else we wouldn't have known. Have you talked to him yet or do you still need to?"

Stan looked at Holly. Holly was pleading with his eyes. Stan replied;" No, I think we have everything worked out." Holly looked relieved.

They were all relieved. Murchison's attempt at the SPA had been an intense episode. They all rested until late afternoon. Stan came into the break room and Holly was there.

Stan said; "What are you going to tell Michael Murphy, Holly?"

"I'll tell him the SPA is not for sale. I'll call him."

Holly called Murphy and told him the SPA was not for sale. Murphy was upset. He said Holly had agreed to sell it to him and he had informed his superiors. His superiors did not like to be disappointed. Murphy, or whatever his name, was in big trouble.

CHAPTER 59

Dr. Linquist examined Jen. Luckily her arm was severely strained and not broken. He gave her some of his limited supply of pain pills and put her arm in a sling. She had given permission so Jeff could stay while she was being treated. The doctor called and got a ride for them to their area.

Jeff accompanied Jen to her tent. They gathered all her tent mates and Jeff got all of his so they could tell them what happened.

Jeff said; "Murchison and his gang invaded the lab and tried to get the SPA. We were able to have Phil and his men prevent it. There was a fight."

Amanda interrupted; "Was Phil hurt?"

"No, Phil wasn't, but through my fault Jen got taken by Murchison and her arm is strained. Not broken, but strained. Stan and Holly and his crew are OK."

"Did they get Murchison?" Tom asked.

"No, he got away. He had taken Jen but Phil pursued him and was able to rescue her."

"But Jen, he's supposed to be my hero not yours." Amanda said playfully.

"He can be yours next time, Amanda. I don't want to do that again."

They all laughed. It was a laugh they all needed as laughs were few and far between. With that they started to drift into their tents murmuring about the morning's events. It was only about noon.

Jeff lingered to talk to Jen; "I wish we had gotten Murchison. He escaped as well as did fifteen of his men. I know he'll try something else."

"I'm sure you're right." Jen said. "I'm concerned about Stan and Holly. What if he makes another attempt to get the SPA? We were lucky this time but next time we won't know until it's too late."

"Maybe I could ask Phil if he could assign a guard detail to them."

"We could ask but then they would have to transport the guards back and forth and fuel is in such short supply."

"And if they stationed some troops there they would have to supply them with food. Holly does not have enough that he could supply them." Jeff said.

Jen said; "How difficult would it be to move the SPA to here?"

"It would be difficult but not impossible. Remember, the SPA is at the football field level. We would have to raise it up twenty feet. How they could do that I don't know."

"Phil or some of his men may know. Perhaps one of the residents was an engineer and he would have an idea." Jen said.

Jeff said. "I'll ask him later. I'm sure he's very busy with the details from this morning's events. Anyway Jennifer, you're injured and you need to rest. Why don't you do that and we'll talk later."

"I'll do that, Jeff. Thanks for thinking of me."

"I do that constantly."

She smiled and went into her tent.

CHAPTER 60

Felix Murchison was wallowing in his usual mood. Anger. When he wrecked the cart, the one Jen slid out of, after the failure to get the SPA; he ran into the brush and waited. He knew Edwards was pursuing him and would stop to help Jen because that's the sort of do-gooder he was. Sure enough, Edwards stopped to help. Murchison smiled, a rare thing, raised his gun and took aim. Got you now Edwards he thought. He gleefully pulled the trigger and heard a click, click, click. He'd forgotten he was out of ammunition. Now, even angrier, he made his way back to his camp and the remainder of his men he had left at the camp. The men of his that had survived the fight at the lab started drifting back into the camp.

He had been surprised at the size of the SPA. He knew it could be very valuable to him since no one has had rain. But there were problems. How does it work? Is that crip the only one who knows how it works? I could rush the place and take over but how could I force him to tell me how to operate the machine? Torture? He's probably a stubborn old man and too weak to withstand much. Then I wouldn't know what he was doing and he could destroy the thing before he would let me have it. But he's not alone there. There's the woman, the big black guy and the other two guys. I don't think he'd be that stubborn if he saw them suffering. Then there's that Jeff guy and Edwards, they'll keep in contact with the lab so they'll know if we take over. But how do I move that thing and where do I put it? First though, I have to get it.

CHAPTER 61

The work assignments had been posted for the following three days. Jen had been excused until she had full use of her arm.

Elmer Bailey and his son Billy were assigned to a team to visit farms and fields to dig for vegetables. The electric cart arrived for them shortly after their meager breakfast the following morning. It was towing a two wheeled cart. A young uniformed soldier was driving. He had a rifle. The electric cart had a driver's seat up front and two bench seats behind it. A raised area beside the driver contained the batteries and motor. There were two men seated in the first bench seat so Elmer and Billy took the second. Banger, the dog, hopped up into the raised area next to the driver.

The driver said; "A dog! I didn't know we had any dogs."

"This is the only one I've seen." Elmer said; "His name's Banger. He's a good ol' dog. Reminds me of my Buster." Elmer turned to the other men in the cart. "Howdy, I'm Elmer Bailey. This here's my boy, Billy."

The other two men introduced themselves. They were holding two shovels and a rake. They passed a shovel back to Elmer and one of them said; "I don't know why they sent four of us out if they didn't have four tools?"

Elmer said; "We're prob'ly lucky they were able to find any tools. We wuz out there for a couple weeks and there ain't much left."

The driver said; "We're to go out eight or ten miles and up some of the secondary roads. Maybe we'll find some farms that haven't been picked over."

They rode in silence on the main road. They turned up a secondary road. Its surface was paved but it was crumbly and rutted. It appeared as though no maintenance had been done for years. After a mile they saw a farm to their left with the remains of a house and barn. The debris was 200 feet from the road. There were cultivated fields on both sides of it. The remains of the house were nestled at the start of a dense woods that extended to the hills they could see far in the background. They exited the vehicle. Elmer and Billy went into the field on the right and the others went to the left. Banger trotted along with Elmer and Billy.

They scoured the field and found some ears of corn. It had already been harvested when the explosion happened so there wasn't much. Nevertheless they kept going working their way up to the woods where the field ended.

Billy had worked his way to about 50 feet from the woods when Banger suddenly stopped, raised his hackles and growled.

Billy said; "What's the matter boy? Did you hear something?"

Billy heard a rustling in the underbrush. Banger barked. Billy looked up just in time to see a bear emerging from the woods. The bear reared up on its hind legs to a full seven foot height and roared. Banger barked louder. The bear roared again. The bear dropped to all fours and started running toward them. Banger sprang into action and ran to intercept him. Banger leaped at the bear. The bear stopped running and swiped him away with his huge paw. Undeterred Banger again attacked. This time the bear swiped with his paw and missed. Banger knew what was coming and avoided it. The bear was roaring. Banger was barking. The bear kept swiping at the dog.

One after another Banger attacked until one swipe hurled Banger aside

Billy saw Banger attacking the bear and started backing away. He tripped on a cornstalk and fell backwards just as the bear hurled Banger aside. The bear left the stunned dog and started toward Billy.

Elmer and the driver heard the dog bark and saw the bear emerge from the woods. They saw Banger's attacks and saw Billy trip and fall and the bear start toward him.

"Shoot him. Shoot the bear." Elmer shouted to the soldier.

The soldier shouldered his weapon and fired twice. Both shots missed.

"Give me that gun." Elmer said and took it away from him. Elmer fired twice. He didn't miss. The bear turned toward the sound of the shots and roared angrily. Billy was backing up. He was still on the ground using his hands and heels. He scrambled to his feet. Elmer fired twice more. The bear took two steps towards them and fell to the ground.

They approached the bear cautiously. Bears can run 100 feet with a bullet in their heart. When they were within 20 feet Elmer put a shot into the bear's head and handed the rifle back to the soldier.

"Well, it looks like we're finally going to have some meat for supper don't it." Elmer said grinning.

By that time the other men had joined them. Banger got up gingerly and limped over to them. He sniffed disdainfully at the bear and walked away. They all agreed that was enough foraging for one day. They loaded the bear into the cart along with the few items they had gathered. Banger tried to jump up to his seat in the cart but was unable. Elmer lifted the dog, which let out a yelp of pain, and put him in the cart. The men got in and they headed back to the Fort.

They arrived at the Fort and took the bear's carcass to the mess hall. Elmer sent Billy to find Captain Edwards and tell him what happened. Elmer went in the mess hall to find the chief cook, Sergeant Busch.

"Sergeant, I've got a bear outside in the cart. I need to skin it and cut it up so's you can cook it."

"A bear. Where did you get a bear?"

"He came out of the woods. I reckon a month or so ago when it got cold and dark he thought winter had come and he hibernated. The past few days it's gotten lighter and warmer and he thought spring was here. He came out of his cave and he was hungry. We wuz the first food he saw."

"I've never cooked a bear. How do you cook a bear? Are they edible?"

"This one's going to be edible. With our food shortage, we can't be fussy. The meat is prob'ly pretty tough. You'd have to boil it a long time."

"I think butchering it is going to be messy. I can have someone help you if you want. You'll have to do it outside."

"Billy and me can handle it. I will need some knives and a bucket or two to catch the blood."

"To catch the blood! You're going to use the blood?"

"Sure. If you've got some oats and raisins and spices we'll make some blood pudding. My daughter Annabelle knows how. She can help you."

By that time Captain Edwards and Jeff had joined them and were listening to the conversation.

Edwards addressed Sergeant Busch. "Sergeant, give Mr. Bailey any help he needs. We will have to share this with the other mess halls so contact them. Elmer, I need you to tell me what happened. We'll have to inform the foraging parties to be on the lookout. Others may not be as lucky as you."

"That's right Cap'n. They won't have Banger to alert them. Billy, you go get Annabelle. She can tell the Sergeant 'bout the blood puddin'. I want her to see the bear's hide. She may be able to tan it. She and gramma used to do that but nothin' as big as this bear. But it sure would be nice and warm for somebody to have a bearskin blanket."

The encounter with the bear soon became the talk of the camp. Some were even more nervous about venturing outside the Fort because of this new danger. Others thought that danger was minimal when compared to the possibility of encountering stragglers. All were happy to have some fresh, though tough, meat. The meat of that one bear did not go far with that many mouths to feed.

When Elmer and Billy returned to their tent, all the residents of the surrounding tents gathered there to hear a first hand account of the incident. Banger received many "Good boys" and "Atta boys" and concern over his injuries.

CHAPTER 62

While Elmer and Billy were having the encounter with the bear, Jeff had gone mid-morning to talk to Phil about Holly's lab and the SPA. He told him what he and Jen had discussed and made his requests.

Phil said; "First. How is Jen? Is she in much pain? Have you talked to her this morning? How did she sleep?"

"No, I've not talked to her this morning so I can't answer your other questions."

"Tell her we're thinking of her. Now, I understand your concern about Stan and Holly Jeff. I don't think General Arnold would approve a guard detail stationed there. I'll request it but I don't think they'll approve it. As far as getting the SPA here, I'll suggest that and see what they think. It would not be easy."

"Would you do that, Phil? You know as well as I do that Murchison has not gone away and it's just a matter of time before he tries something else."

"You're right, Jeff and I'm waiting for the opportunity. I still have a score to settle with him over Colonel Burden's death."

At that, Billy Bailey came rushing into the tent. "Cap'n Edwards. Pa said I should come get you as we kilt a bear."

"You killed a bear?"

"Yes sir. Pa's got him over at the mess hall right now."

They left for the mess hall.

CHAPTER 63

After leaving Elmer, Billy and Jeff at the mess hall, Edwards went to find Major Lenhart and tell him of Jeff's concerns about the SPA and the personnel at the lab. They made an appointment to talk to the General. They explained the situation and the concerns to the General and asked about a guard detail.

The General said; "No, we can't assign a guard detail there for several reasons. The logistics to keep them supplied with meals and materiel are too great. Plus, all our personnel are assigned other duties trying to get this camp in shape. Since we have no definite idea of when or if Murchison would attack them again the guard detail could be there forever. No, that is not a viable plan. As far as getting this SPA here, we need to identify someone with the knowledge and expertise to accomplish that. Do you have anyone in mind for that?"

Edwards replied; "No sir. We wanted to get your opinion before we proceeded with those details."

"Very well, Captain, you and the Major see if anyone is qualified. Whoever it is must be informed of our limited amount of power and supplies. They will have to use ingenuity to raise that thing twenty feet and transport it the fifteen miles to here. Report back to me with what you find."

Lenhart and Edwards stood and saluted and said; "Thank you, sir."

They left the office and Lenhart said; "I have the results of that survey we did about skills. I'll go through it and see if there is anyone who may have the expertise we need."

Edwards said; "Good, I'll contact the people at the lab and see if the SPA can be dismantled somewhat for removal and transportation."

Although Edwards was serious about contacting the lab, going to the residents tent city gave him a reason to see Amanda. When he arrived there he called out Jeff, Jen and Amanda and asked them to meet with him in his headquarters tent.

They all arrived and Phil said; "Sergeant Riley why don't you take a break?"

"Thank you, sir. I'll do that. I'll be back in a half hour."

The women took seats. The men stood. There were only two chairs, the steel folding kind. Phil told them of his meeting with the General.

He asked; "Do you know if the SPA can be dismantled?"

They all replied negatively.

"Jeff, will you call Stan and see if he knows. It would have to be dismantled, transported and re-assembled."

"I'll go call him right now. Are you coming, Jen?"

"Sure." They left. Phil and Amanda were alone.

She said; "Imagine that. We're alone. Why I almost believe you planned it this way Captain."

"Do you think I am that devious?"

"No, I think you're that smart. And I love you for it. I've not seen you for way too long."

"I feel the same, honey. I had to do something to get some Amanda time. You have a narcotic effect on me. Too much abstinence and I climb the walls."

She stood. "I'm here now. What do you want to do?"

He didn't answer. Words were unnecessary. He took her in his arms and kissed her ravenously. He could feel the warmth of her body and it aroused in him a deep longing, a longing to have her. To have her physically, spiritually and mentally. To have her now and forever. To have her be a part of him. A part of his life.

Her arms were around his neck. Her hand reached up and she ran her fingers through his hair. Not gently but passionately. She felt the arousal of him as they clung closer and closer to each other. She felt herself responding. He was what she wanted. She reached down with her other hand and pulled down his zipper. She fumbled with his underwear in anxiety. Her hand closed around him and she stroked him back and forth. That was not enough for her. She wanted him inside her.

Phil was lost in emotion. He felt her hand upon him and his hand slid down her back and around her. He unbuttoned her and slid his hand under her panties to a mound of curly hair. His finger probed her as he fought his rising emotions. His other hand and arm reached around her waist and he picked her up and laid her on the dirt floor. He grabbed her pants and pulled them down. She kicked one foot out and spread her legs. A quick glance to admire her beautiful body and he was on her and in her.

Months of tension, frustration, helplessness and depression were wiped away in a few moments. Their need for each other was equal and manifested itself in their mutual climax. They lie there a few minutes sated with happiness. Then they both scrambled to their feet realizing that they were in a tent with a dirt floor and no locked doors. Anyone could come in at any time. That realization was worrisome for a moment but then they felt as if they had fought the nastiness in the world and beaten it.

He put his arms around her and said; "That was wonderful and you are wonderful."

CHAPTER 64

Jeff and Jen left Phil and Amanda and went to Jen's tent. Myra and Angie were just leaving to take Banger for a walk.

Jeff called Stan; "Stan, we've had some discussions about getting you guys here. We think Murchison will try again and we won't be as lucky as last time. One of the big problems is moving the SPA because of its size. Do you know if it can be disassembled and then reassembled?"

"No, I don't Jeff. It was assembled here and I'm sure one, if not all, of Holly's crew helped Bert assemble it. They may know how to take it apart. I'll ask and get back to you."

"OK Stan. See what you can find out."

They sat on Jen's cot. Cassandra was at the repair shop sewing clothes. Annabelle was at the mess hall with Sergeant Busch. They were alone.

"This is unusual." Jeff said; "To be alone with you for a few minutes."

"Yes it is. It seems there are always people around."

"But not now," Jeff turned toward her and put his arm around her good shoulder and pulled her to him. He kissed her and said; "There are so many things I want to tell you. So many things I want to ask you. And yet in the few moments I'm with you all I can think of is holding you. Kissing you. Making love to you. I've never felt as close to anyone as I feel with you even when we're apart."

"I know Jeff. I feel somewhat the same. I think we've established a bond of friendship."

"To me it's more than friendship. My feelings toward you are way beyond friendship. My feelings are more like…" At that moment Banger barked. Myra and Angie were back.

They stood just as mother and daughter entered the tent. Banger followed them in. Jen reached down and petted the dog and said. "Did you go for a walk.?" He barked yes.

Jeff, trying to hide his frustration, said. "I'll let you know what I hear from Stan. To be continued." He left the tent.

Jen knew what he meant.

CHAPTER 65

Stan called Jeff the morning after their previous conversation; "I think we know how to take the SPA apart Jeff. There will still be some very large pieces. We can't dismantle the large dish. It's about fifteen feet in diameter. The rest of it is not too bad, even though the carriage is eight feet wide and twenty feet long."

"Thanks, Stan. I'll see what I can do on this end."

Jeff called Phil Edwards and told him of his conversation with Stan.

Phil said; "We found some engineers but the ones we found are in different fields than what we need. From what you told me, maybe we need a rigger, someone who was in the business of moving large pieces of machinery or moving houses or dealt with large cranes. I'll see if we have anyone to fit those requirements. I'll call you."

Phil called back a little while later; "Jeff, there is a guy that may be able to help. His name is Dominic Manzia. He's in tent number 41. Do you want to talk to him or wait for me and we'll both go?"

"I'll go for now, Phil. If he's interested then you can talk to him. I think he'll have to take a look at the SPA anyway."

Phil agreed and Jeff headed to tent number 41 and Mr. Manzia. He stuck his head in the tent flap and said; "I'm looking for Dominic Manzia."

An elderly man reclining on a cot said; “He ain’t here. He’s on timber duty today.”

“Thanks. When will he be back?”

“Supper time I’d say.”

Jeff left and called Phil; “Phil, Manzia’s on timber duty today. What’s that?”

“I’ve mentioned we are using fallen logs to build new structures. The guys on timber duty go out and get them. It’s very hard work. Maybe he’d like a break from that.”

“When do they come back? Could you intercept him and find out if he’s interested?”

“I’ll do that. I’ll call and maybe you can come.”

Phil waited until he thought the timber crew would be returning. He went to the staging area where they delivered the logs. They were just returning. There were six men on the crew.

He spoke to one of them; “I’m looking for Dominic Manzia.”

“See that big guy giving orders. That’s him. Hey Dom. This guy wants to talk to you.”

“Yeah, yeah. When I’m finished with these little pieces of wood.”

Phil called Jeff; “Manzia’s here at the staging area. I’m waiting for him to finish wrestling these logs into place. Can you come?”

“I’ll leave now.”

While he was waiting Phil sized up Manzia. Six feet two or three, Two hundred forty or two hundred and fifty pounds. I wonder what he was when food was not scarce? Middle to late forties he thought. Top two buttons of his shirt open. Curly gray hair protruding. Weather-beaten face. Stubble of a beard. He was barking orders at the other men but not in an angry way. Just authoritatively because he was sure of what he was doing.

Manzia said; to his men; "That's it guys. Good job. We're on again day after tomorrow."

He left the men and the log pile just as Jeff arrived. He ambled over to Edwards and said; "You wanted to see me, Captain?"

"You're Dominic Manzia aren't you?"

"Yeah, I am. And?" Knowing there was more to be told.

"I'm Captain Philip Edwards and this is Jeff Lawrence."

They shook hands. Not surprisingly his were very rough. He had a firm grip.

Phil continued; "We may need your help for a big important project we're involved in. Do you have a few minutes we can talk? We can go over to the mess hall."

While walking to the mess hall Phil inquired about his background.

They got some almost coffee and sat down. Manzia said; "You ask a lot of questions. What's going on?"

Phil and Jeff explained the SPA to him. They told him it was in a lab about fifteen miles away. They needed to get it here before Murchison made another attempt to get it. They asked if he would be interested in overseeing the transportation.

He thought for a moment and said; "Yeah, I'd be interested. I need to see it."

"When would you like to go?"

"I'm off timber duty tomorrow. How about then?"

Phil said; "Let me arrange it. I'll let you know as soon as possible. Now I'll make a call and get you guys a ride back to tent city."

Phil made the call and a few minutes later Lolene pulled up in her cart. Jeff and Manzia got in and she took them to their tents. Jeff told Manzia he would be in touch. Jeff called Stan as Lolene was driving him to his tent.

"Stan, we found a guy that we think has the know-how and experience to move the SPA. We are going to come to your place tomorrow so he can look at it. Phil Edwards is arranging transport so I don't know exactly what time, but we'll be there."

"Very good, Jeff. We're getting kind of nervous here not knowing when Murchison will try again."

No sooner had they disconnected than Phil called.

"Jeff, we have transportation at 0900 tomorrow. Emmons is driving. We'll get you and then get Manzia."

"Thanks, Phil. I called Stan and alerted him. I'll go tell Manzia."

The next morning Phil and Emmons picked up Jeff then went to get Manzia.

He said; "We need to go slow enough getting there so I can see if there are any obstructions to be concerned about."

Phil said; "Most of the trees have fallen. We'll have to look for overhead wires. The roadway is fairly clean. We've been back and forth on it several times"

Manzia never took his eyes off the surroundings throughout the trip.

CHAPTER 66

At 0900 in the morning there was a knock on the door of the lab.

Stan exclaimed; "Good, Jeff got here early. Will you let them in Joan?"

Joan went to the door, opened it and screamed. Murchison pushed it aside and strode in followed by several of his men.

He laughed wickedly and said; "I thought that would work. Just knock on the door and the fools will open it. Good morning. It is for me. It won't be for you."

He gathered Stan, Holly, Joan and the other two of Holly's crew and herded them into the break room. He stationed two of his men at the bottom of the ramp at the entrance.

Murchison looked at his captives and said; "I have a problem. You are going to solve it for me. You're thinking you're not going to help but you will. Yes you will."

"Captain Edwards and his men are on their way here right now Murchison. So you better leave." Stan said.

"Nice try but I don't believe you. Getting back to my problem. I need you to show me how to operate that rain making machine you have. You see, I have to move it out of here. If I don't move it I'm sure Edwards will. Though if I move it I won't know how to operate it. That's where you come in to help. Simple, huh."

"Why would you think I would teach you how to operate it?"

"Because I can make it very painful if you don't."

"I'd die before I'd teach you regardless of the pain." Stan said.

"Once again you don't understand. It's not your pain I'm talking about. It's hers." He pointed at Joan. He said to his men; "Tie her to that chair."

They tied Joan to a chair and Murchison continued; "I've always heard that women can stand more pain than men. Do you think that's true? Let's see if she's still alive by the time you tell me what I want to know."

Stan knew Murchison would do what he said. He decided to take him to the SPA and stall until maybe Edwards and Jeff got here. I hope it's soon he thought.

"Alright, Murchison, you win. Push me out to the SPA."

Murchison left two men with the other captives. The remainder went down the tunnel to the SPA. They lifted Stan on to the platform. Murchison followed. Stan sat at the console and pointed at the dials and switches one by one and told Murchison what they were. Sometimes he even told the truth.

CHAPTER 67

When Edwards got in sight of the lab he saw the two guards Murchison had posted.

He told Emmons; "Keep driving. Don't stop."

They drove by and stopped after a bend in the road. "Looks like Murchison's already there. I wonder how long he's been there. I hope we're not too late."

"How do you want to handle this, Captain." Emmons said.

"Do you remember how we got in the air intakes at Jerseyville after Murchison attacked?"

"Yes sir, silently."

"Well you and I are going to do the same here. Do you have your knife with you?"

"Always, sir."

"Jeff, you and Dom stay here until we come get you. Let's go, Sergeant."

They left the vehicle and took a round about route to get to the lab. They approached the ramp from the rear. They were on the plaza level several feet above the ramp entrance. The guards seemed rather nonchalant. The vehicle that had passed by on this very seldom traveled road did not alert them at all. That was a mistake. Edwards and Emmons leaped simultaneously, clasped their hands over the guards' mouths and drove their knives into their throats before they could make a sound. Just like Jerseyville.

They cautiously opened the door and looked in. No one was there. They heard voices and knew that there were people in the other room. The break room. The break room door had a small ten by ten window in it. Edwards cautiously peered in and saw the four captives and the two guards. He held up two fingers and made a motion as if to slit their throats. Emmons nodded. Shots would have alerted the others. They had no idea of how many there were. Edwards nodded and they burst through the door and were on the guards before they could react. They dispatched them and Edwards held his finger to his mouth in the universal sign for quiet. Emmons untied Joan.

Edwards whispered; "Where's Stan?"

Holly said; "SPA. Murchison and four others."

Edwards nodded and said; "All of you leave. We have a vehicle just down the road past here. Go, but be quiet."

They left. Edwards and Emmons went to the double doors. They put their knives away and got out their handguns. Edwards held up three fingers. Emmons nodded. Edwards held up one finger, then two fingers and then three fingers. They burst through the doors and shot the first target they saw. The second targets were bringing their rifles around to firing position but they were too late. They fell. Murchison jumped down from the SPA platform and ran toward the tunnel exit. Edwards and Emmons fired at him but missed. Then he was out of the tunnel and gone again. They walked down the tunnel to Stan.

"That was scary. I didn't know what time you'd get here and what you could do after you did." Stan said.

They helped him down from the SPA and wheeled him into the lab.

"Where are the others?'

"We had them go down the road to our vehicle and wait. Will you get them Sergeant?"

"Yes sir."

Edwards had Stan tell him the details of the morning's events. By the time he finished the rest of them were back. They introduced Stan and Holly to Dominic Manzia. They went through the double doors and down the tunnel to the SPA stepping over the bodies of the dead stragglers.

Dom said; "You guys have been busy since you left."

"Just a bit Dom. Just a bit."

Manzia walked around the SPA carriage. He knelt down and looked under it on both sides. He mounted the platform and looked. He got down and went to the tunnel exit. He walked out several steps and looked up at the grandstand. He turned 360 degrees examining all of it.

He came back into the tunnel and said; "How much of this comes apart?"

Stan told him the four small discs could be removed and the console unplugged.

"Captain, do you have a vehicle that could tow this slowly if we leave it on its carriage?"

"Yes Dom, I think we have one that would work. But isn't it too wide?"

"Yes if we leave it as you see it. But we're going to stand it up. If we stand it vertically it shouldn't be a problem. I didn't see any low hanging wires on the way here."

"That should work. When do you think we can do this?"

"I'm scheduled for timber duty tomorrow."

"I'll get you excused from that. Can we do it tomorrow?"

"Sure. I'll want to get here early to get it upright and ready to travel."

"Good. Holly, can you have your guys start dismantling it."

"We'll start right away."

"Is there anything else you need, Dom."

“I’ll need some rope or chains and some planks. I’ll also need some pulley wheels. We’ll bring all that on the truck tomorrow.”

“The pulley wheels may be a problem.”

“Maybe we can rig some out of tire rims.”

“Okay. Let’s get back and arrange for that truck. I’ll have to talk to the Major and the General about where we’re putting it when we get it there.”

They shook hands and said; “See you tomorrow.” They went back to the Fort.

CHAPTER 68

Murchison had exited the tunnel and scrambled up the grandstands. He ran to his truck and hastily left not knowing if they were following him. He wondered how that mission had failed. The crippled guy was telling the truth when he said Edwards was on his way.

He went back to his camp. I should have taken a larger force he thought. I won't make that mistake again. I'll get them tomorrow. I'll take twenty men.

CHAPTER 69

Edwards had Emmons and Dom Manzia go to the supply depot and see what materials were available. He went to see Major Lenhart and told him what they were planning. Then they went to see General Arnold.

Edwards spoke; "Sir, we have made plans to move the SPA, the rain-making machine, tomorrow. We need to know where to put it. Overall it's fifteen feet wide and twenty feet long. It needs to be open to the sky and it needs electrical power."

"The open sky part is no problem, Captain. Talk to Mr. Velez about the electrical power. You and the Major need to ride around and earmark a spot. Then Velez will determine if we can get electric to it. As you know our electrical capacity is very limited. Perhaps you could find a spot where other things could be turned off when the SPA was turned on."

"Thank you, sir. We'll investigate and report back." They saluted and left.

"You know this place better than I do, Joe, where should we start?" Edwards asked.

"Let's look at the area just behind the construction area. We can put it behind the construction in those low foothills. Maybe we can run electric from the construction site that way we can operate the SPA whenever the crews are finished for the day."

"Sounds like a plan. Let's go take a look. Who's this Mr. Velez?"

Lenhart said; "That would be Roman Velez. He's an electrical engineer we discovered in our resident survey. The General's having him investigate the electrical distribution system. A lot of it is underground but getting a power source to it is a problem. I'll have him check on service to the SPA while you're gone."

Emmons and Manzia were pleasantly surprised at the amount of stuff they had at the supply depot. The foraging crews had been doing a remarkable job of salvaging all sorts of items. They found coils of rope and lengths of chain. There were some pulley wheels and some hooks. They gathered what they wanted and told the Quartermaster they would be back in the morning with a truck.

They went to the construction site and talked to the Sergeant in charge. They identified some boards, planks and timbers and asked if they could borrow them for a day. The Sergeant reluctantly agreed with their promise they would bring them back as they were hard to find.

Lenhart and Edwards reported to the General and he agreed with their selection of a site. They arranged for a truck. It was one of the ones they had used to come to Fort Kelly and had some bullet holes in it but no blood stains. It seemed they had everything set for a 0900 departure in the morning.

Edwards said; "Joe, just as a precaution and knowing Murchison, I'd like to take an armed squad with me."

The Major replied; "That's a good idea. Go ahead and arrange it."

Edwards took Emmons to get the truck at 0800. Then he picked up Dom Manzia and Jeff and they met Emmons at the supply depot to get the materials. They met the armed squad at the gate and they pulled out of Fort Kelly shortly after 0900. The trip to the lab was short and uneventful. When they got there, Jeff, Phil and Dom Manzia went into the lab and announced their arrival. They asked if there had been any trouble overnight. There had not.

Jeff asked Stan; "Did you take the SPA apart?"

"We got the four little dishes off but the big one is still attached."

Manzia said; "Leave it until we get it out of this hole." Then he said; "Captain can I use some of your men to help me clear the field of debris so we can get that thing out of the tunnel?"

"Of course, although I will leave two up top on guard duty."

Edwards went to give the order. He came back with six troopers. Manzia had them go with him to the SPA. They exited the tunnel and he told them the path he wanted cleared. They started moving chunks of concrete aside. Manzia went up top and they started unloading the timbers and planks. He went to the narrow end of the old football stadium and started to build a frame structure to attach his pulleys. When he was finished he went back to field level.

They pulled the SPA out of the tunnel and to the narrow end of the football field. He had four men go up and each bring back a plank about a foot wide and twelve feet long. He attached a hook to the SPA and a rope to the hook. He walked up the grandstand carrying the coil of rope. He ran the rope through his pulley system and pulled it taut. He went back to field level and told the men with the planks.

"I'm going up top and pull the rope. It's going to move this thing up to the top. You guys are going to use those planks to help. As it goes up you have to go along side it and put the planks under the wheels so it rolls on the planks. Do you understand?"

"Yes sir. We go along side and keep moving the planks up as it goes."

"Right, let's get started."

It was not easy getting it up the first couple of steps. The steps were the concrete seats of the stadium. They were fourteen inches high and thirty inches deep. The carriage was twenty feet long. Then it became a series of pull the rope, move the planks until they reached the top. They dismantled the pulley system. They detached the large dish from the carriage and built a frame to hold it vertical. They loaded the small dishes on the truck along with the planks and timbers. They hitched the SPA to the truck. The troopers got in their truck. They were ready to hit the road.

Manzia went to the lab and told them; "We're ready to go."

Phil said; "OK, Dom. We'll be up there in a couple of minutes."

Jeff said; "You're going with us aren't you, Stan?"

"Yes, I am. What about you guys, Holly? I don't think it's safe to stay here. Murchison's still out there."

"I hate to tell you this but I have to have permission for you to come to the Fort." Phil said. "It's at maximum occupancy and General Arnold has to approve all rescues."

Holly said; "I can understand that but I know Murchison would love to have this facility. I'm surprised he hasn't tried to get it yet."

"He most likely didn't know it was here." Phil said. "It is underground."

"But he knows now." Jeff said. "And if they stay here Phil, he may come back tonight. That could be murder."

"How about if I see if two of my men will volunteer to stay overnight?" Phil said. "That would give you some protection."

"And if he attacks with twenty men he'll have two more people to murder." Jeff said.

"You're right, Jeff. I'm going to take a chance and hope the General approves. They can come with us now although I don't know where we'll house them."

Five more people for Fort Kelly he thought. Five more mouths to feed.

They went up to the road level. Phil pushed Stan's wheel chair. Getting everyone on board was a minor problem. Holly and Joan rode in the truck with Emmons. The two men from the lab squeezed into the troopers's truck. They put Stan in the cart Phil was driving, along with Jeff and Dom.

They slowly headed to the Fort.

CHAPTER 70

Murchison had gathered his twenty men the following morning. They were on their way to the lab. He was sure that this attack would not fail. They were about to exit onto the road leading to the lab when they saw the convoy from Fort Kelly headed there. He withdrew his men until he could appraise the situation. He left most of his men and along with two others went to spy on the lab. They concealed themselves and observed.

They saw them disembark. They saw the armed personnel. They saw the removal of the SPA. They saw the preparations for transport.

Murchison saw all that. He saw they had no more than ten armed men. He had twenty. Here's an opportunity he thought. I can capture that machine and the crip. I can wipe out Edwards and the others. He went back to his men to prepare the ambush.

He said; "Don't shoot at the older guy in the cart. I need him. I don't care what happens to the others. Kill them all. Except the Captain. I want him."

They went searching for a good site for the ambush.

CHAPTER 71

Fifteen miles an hour. That's what they were going. That would put them at the Fort in about an hour. The SPA carriage had small tires and it was top heavy with the SPA vertical. They didn't want to dislodge it from its stand and have it fall.

They were about halfway to the Fort and passing an area of heavy underbrush when the ambush started. The first shots were deadly to two of the troopers and one of Holly's men. The rest scrambled out of the truck and took cover. They were going to return fire but the targets were hidden in the bushes. Emmons, Joan and Holly tumbled out of their truck and took cover. Emmons withdrew his gun and searched for targets.

At the sound of the shots Phil swerved the cart violently and headed toward the brush. He heard shots thudding into the cart and when he looked around Stan was lying on the ground. He had fallen out of the cart when Phil swerved. Stan was lying in the street helpless and an easy target for the ambushers. Phil, Jeff and Dom had taken cover in the brush. They looked at Stan lying in the roadway and then looked at each other. Without hesitation Dom stood up and ran to Stan. He gathered him in his arms and raced back towards cover. Bullets were striking the ground all around him and whizzing by his face. Phil and Jeff saw him lurch and stagger. He kept on coming, limping now. He made it back to the brush. He set Stan down and sat down himself. His leg was bleeding and Phil whipped off his belt to make a tourniquet.

They had to remain crouched in the brush as the firing was still intense. Phil had his gun out searching for targets. His troops were laying down intense fire into the brush with their semi-automatic weapons. All the ambushers were on one side of the road. The convoy members were on the other. They had some cover because the vehicles were between them and the attackers.

The intense firing subsided and shots were fired only when a target was available. Phil knew they were in a very precarious position. They were unable to move and he wondered when Murchison would try to outflank them. From the amount of firing he assumed Murchison had them outnumbered. It was less than ten miles to the Fort. He punched Major Lenhart's number into his phone.

"Joe, we're under attack and pinned down about eight miles out. We're outnumbered and they'll either flank us or charge us."

"I hear you loud and clear, Phil. I'll get a couple of squads to help ASAP."

The charge came before the flanking maneuver. They came charging out of the brush yelling and shooting. Fifteen or twenty of them. Murchison was behind them urging them on. As they came the troopers picked them off one by one. After losing five they gave up on the assault.

Murchison yelled at them; "Turn around you cowards. Get back in the fight."

A bullet went screaming past his head and he ducked back into the brush.

The charge didn't work. Phil thought they'd now try to outflank him. He crawled over to where his troops were .

The first two men he saw he said; "You two go out about fifty feet to make sure we are warned if they try to flank us."

They said yes sir and left. Phil crawled back towards the others. As he passed he asked Emmons; "Are you alright? No casualties."

"No casualties, sir."

Phil rejoined the cart occupants. Dom's leg was still bleeding and they were applying the tourniquet periodically. Phil said; "I'm going out about fifty feet to watch for flankers. If they charge again, give a shout. Hopefully the Major will get here soon."

There was sporadic firing as time passed. Then suddenly the attackers burst out of the bushes again. This time they used the vehicles for cover instead of a direct attack. It was difficult for the defenders to get a clear shot as the ambushers ducked behind the vehicles. They would raise up from the vehicle, shoot and duck down. It was effective. Two more troopers were hit and Joan got shot. Emmons knew her injury could be very serious if she didn't get medical treatment soon. She was bleeding profusely. Emmons did what he could with what he had but it may not be enough.

Phil heard the shots and looked up to see four men creeping through the brush. They were attacking on two fronts. He wondered about the other flank. He fired several shots at the creepers, hitting one and the others hit the dirt. He knew he couldn't leave his present position with the other three creepers there. He hoped the other cart occupants would be OK.

Jeff, Dom and Stan were as low as they could get in the brush. They had no weapons. Virtually helpless. Stan was handicapped. Dom was injured. Jeff was looking for a log or a rock or anything to use as a weapon. An attacker came around the side of the cart. Dom lurched to his feet. The attacker pointed his rifle at him ready to shoot. Jeff yelled; "Hey." The attacker turned his head slightly which was all Dom needed. He swung one of his ham-like fists and caught the attacker right on the jaw. Dom hit him with the other fist and knocked him out. He fell to the ground and Dom grabbed the rifle and clubbed the attacker unconscious. They were no longer weaponless. Dom grinned and looked out to see if he could find a target.

Phil moved to his left through the brush trying to outflank the flankers. When he thought he had gone far enough he headed towards what he thought was their position. He was trying to be quiet but the brush crackled and snapped as he moved through it. Maybe they wouldn't hear it over the gunfire. He saw them forty feet in front of him.

He said; "Throw down your weapons and get on the ground."

They turned. One dropped his weapon. Both the others raised their rifles. Phil shot twice. One for each of them was all it took. He advanced toward the other, picked up all three rifles, glanced at the other two and pushed his prisoner in front of him to where the others were.

Now they had two prisoners, Dom's and Phil's. They had no idea what they were going to do with them.

They heard the throaty roar of truck engines. The attackers looked down the street and saw trucks racing toward them. They deserted their positions behind the vehicles and ran into the brush from which they came. Major Lenhart and his troops had arrived. The trucks pulled up. Lenhart got out just as Phil was walking up to the truck.

"Did we miss all the fun Phil? Lenhart asked.

"You missed it. But it wasn't much fun Major." Phil said. "We have some casualties and I think three of them were fatal. I've been too busy to know if there are others."

"I'm sorry Phil. It's always hard to lose anyone."

"We have some injuries that need to be addressed immediately too."

"I brought a medic. He'll take care of them."

"I also have two prisoners I don't know what the hell to do with."

"We'll incarcerate them with the others we've captured, Phil."

The medic dressed the wounded paying particular attention to Joan. They inspected the vehicles and the SPA for damage. They got back in the vehicles and continued the slow journey to the Fort. Lenhart sent one truck with the wounded and fatalities ahead. Once again they would have to send a burial detail for the stragglers bodies.

Holly was agonizing over the loss of one of his employees and the injury to Joan. Phil had to face the dreadful chore of writing letters to the families of his fallen troopers. But in these chaotic times knowing where to send them and how to send them was difficult.

CHAPTER 72

Murchison's remaining men regrouped. They went back to their camp. Murchison was seething with rage. He was convinced in his mind that the ambush should have succeeded. Why did it fail? He ignored the fact that if he had stationed men on both sides of the road it had a much better chance of success. That would have been a fault of his. It was his opinion he had no faults. He was looking for someone to blame. He called for the survivors of his first frontal attack. The ones who retreated after five of them were lost.

He assembled them, there were ten of them, and said; "Which of you was the first to retreat?"

One of them said; "I don't know Felix. We kind of all quit at the same time."

"Is that so." Felix said. "Well, we're going to find out which one of you was the coward. Which one was the first to retreat. We're going to have a game."

The ten looked at each other. They knew Murchison's games could be fatal.

Murchison continued; "You are going to draw cards. The low card wins."

"Do you mean the guy that gets the lowest card is the first guy that retreated?"

"No, no, nothing that simple. The lowest card gets to go first in my game. I'll have a revolver with six chambers. I'll put a bullet in one of the chambers. I'll spin the cylinder and hand the gun to you. You put the gun to the side of your head and pull the trigger. If it doesn't kill you, the next highest card gets to play. We'll go up the deck until someone gets the bullet. Being the kind of nice guy I am, if after all ten have survived, I can blame all of you and decide if any other game is needed. I will be holding another pistol so if anyone doesn't want to play, I'll know who ran first."

He brought out a deck of cards and they all drew one.

One guy said; "Whooey, I got an ace." And he laughed.

Murchison said; "I think I forgot to tell you. Ace is low. You lucky guy. You get to go first."

"But that's not fair, Felix. Ace is always high."

"Not in blackjack or Felixjack. So you're first. Are you playing or not?" He lifted his pistol and pointed it toward him.

The man moved forward and took the revolver from Murchison. He nervously lifted it to the side of his head. He closed his eyes and pulled the trigger. Click. He gave the gun to Murchison and backed away, relief showing in his walk.

Murchison said; "Next." Another man stepped forward. He had a deuce. And it continued through the six. Lucky seven was not lucky.

CHAPTER 73

They arrived at the Fort with the SPA. Edwards led them to the site they had selected for setup. Stan, Holly, Emmons, Manzia and the troopers got busy unloading it even though their hearts weren't in it. Holly was mourning the loss of one of his men and the injury to Joan. The troopers had two of their buddies killed and two injured. They did not know the condition of Joan or the two injured troops.

Edwards took Jeff to his tent. He then went to his headquarters to have Sergeant Riley check on housing and meal tickets for the new arrivals.

Edwards left and went to arrange for electric for the SPA and to report to the General. When he arrived at the General's office, Major Lenhart was already there. They went in to report.

"Sir." Lenhart said; "We were able to transport the SPA here as we planned. A crew is setting it up now. I'll let Captain Edwards provide the details."

Edwards said; "We were ambushed by Murchison's men on the way. We lost two of our men and one civilian. Additionally two of ours and one civilian were injured. Major Lenhart was able to muster some reinforcements and get there in time to limit our losses to that extent."

"I'm sorry for your losses and I hope this sacrifice will be worth the cost. That is all."

They left his office. Lenhart said he was going to check on his men. Edwards went to the Infirmary to check on Joan and the two troopers.

He spoke to Dr. Linquist; "How serious are the injuries to the three Major Lenhart brought back?"

"The lady is in critical condition. She lost a lot of blood. She needs a transfusion but we have no blood supply."

"Maybe I can get a donor. What type is she?"

"A common one, O."

"How about the two men?"

"They are serious but not critical. They're awake if you want to see them."

Edwards went in to see the men, He thanked them and wished them a speedy recovery. He left to go check on the setup crew. He told them about Joan's condition but none of them had type O blood.

Dominic Manzia had been ignoring his injury. Now the SPA was back together and Phil took him to the Infirmary. He waited while the doctor dressed the wound and then took him to his tent. Phil thanked him effusively for his help.

Dom said; "My pleasure Captain. Let me know if you need anything else."

When Edwards had brought Jeff to his tent, Jeff gathered all his crew together to tell them about the trip.

Amanda said; "Phil dropped you off? He couldn't stay? Is he coming back?"

"I don't know, Amanda. I'm sure he wants to come back but he has a lot to do."

"I know it, Jeff. I'm being selfish I guess."

Jen was upset about the injury to Joan and the loss of Holly's man. She wondered if Phil would know Joan's condition.

It had been a long and traumatic day for Jeff. He asked Jen; "Have you eaten? I've had nothing. Let's go to the mess hall and see if they have anything."

"We went at our regular time but I'll be glad to go with you."

Sergeant Busch had a few leftovers he gave to Jeff after hearing why he was late. He started nibbling on the food.

"You know, Jen, even if we get the SPA operational; we still have a lot of problems. We've not heard the last of Murchison."

"I think you're right, Jeff, but we're much safer here than anywhere."

"Yes, of course we are."

Phil and Amanda walked into the mess hall. Amanda said; "Is it all right if we join you? Phil hasn't eaten either."

"Sure." Jeff said. "Pull up a bench and sit down."

Amanda went to see about food for Phil.

Jen said; "Have you heard anything about Joan's condition, Phil?"

"The doctor said she's critical. She needs a blood transfusion. Do either of you have type O blood?"

"Yes, I do." Jen said. "I'd be glad to donate."

"Great." Phil said. "Come on. I'll take you to the Infirmary." He grabbed a biscuit Amanda had brought and stood.

Amanda said. "Let's all go." The four of them went to the Infirmary.

They got to the Infirmary and told the nurse that Jen wanted to be a blood donor for Joan. The nurse said; "I'll get the doctor."

Dr. Linquist approached them; "The nurse told me you wanted to give blood for Joan. I'm sorry. Joan died about a half hour ago."

Shock registered on all their faces. Jen said; "If only I had known. I could have been here earlier."

Dr. Linquist said; "She had extreme blood loss and internal damage. Your being here earlier would not have saved her."

That was slight comfort to Jen. She knew Joan from their trips to the lab. Amanda had never met her.

Jeff said; “Thank you, Doctor. We’ll tell Dr. Blackmore. He’ll be very upset.”

They left to break the sad news to Holly. He and Stan were still setting up the SPA.

Jeff said; “I’ll tell him.”

Jeff got out of the cart and called him over.

“Dr. Blackmore, Holly, I’m sorry but I have to tell you Joan passed away about an hour ago. Her injuries were just too great. I’m sorry.”

Holly was stunned. He moaned and said; “Oh no, first Myron and now Joan. Oh no, no. And for what? This damned machine.” He wiped tears from his eyes.

Stan said; “I’m sorry, Holly. You and Joan had been colleagues for several years. What a shame.”

After some time Holly wiped his eyes and composed himself. He and Stan resumed work on the SPA.

Phil said; “I’ll come back later and take you to your quarters. I have to get these people home now.”

Phil took Jeff and Jen to their tents. Although Amanda shared a tent with Jen, they were not surprised when she didn’t exit the cart. Jeff and Jen stood outside Jen’s tent.

Jeff took her hands in his. She winced from her still sore shoulder. Jeff said; “I wish I could offer you more comfort than I can. It seems to be one tragic thing after another.”

“Yes it does, Jeff. It’s how life is for us now.”

“Even though, Jen, it would be so much harder if you weren’t in my life.”

“I know, Jeff. I feel somewhat the same.”

“Somewhat the same?”

“Yes, I really like you but I don’t want to rush.”

"I'm sorry. I don't mean to rush you or make you uncomfortable. I thought we shared a bond stronger than just friendship."

"I think so too, Jeff. I just don't want to rush into a relationship and then be hurt."

"I don't want to hurt you, Jen, just the opposite." He paused. "You've been hurt before haven't you?"

"Yes, I was led to believe things that were not true. He was a liar. He made promises he had no intention of keeping."

"Oh, Jen, I'm so sorry. What can I say? I can tell you that I would never hurt you but you would not believe it."

"You're right. Give me some time. Please."

"I'll give you a lifetime if you want it."

"Thanks, Jeff." She looked up into his eyes. He leaned forward and kissed her. She wanted that. She kissed him, turned around and went into her tent.

CHAPTER 74

Murchison had been obsessed with one thought that had been in the back of his disturbed mind since he didn't capture the convoy leaving Jerseyville Cavern. He wanted to capture Fort Kelly. His force was increasing all the time. He thought that soon it would be large enough to attack the Fort.

Until then, he had another plan.

The main area of Fort Kelly was situated on a plot of level ground at the foot of some low hills. There were fallen trees from a wooded area behind the low hills and large craggy hills behind that.

Murchison knew that the complement of men, even with the addition of the troops from Jerseyville Cavern, was insufficient to patrol the entire Fort. That presented an opportunity that Murchison was going to take advantage of.

He called his two best marksmen and said; "Do you want to have some fun?"

The men warily said; "Sure." You never knew what Murchison meant by fun.

He told them what he wanted them to do and sent them on their way.

CHAPTER 75

The SPA was reassembled. Stan and Holly had worked diligently to accomplish that task. They hoped it hadn't been damaged in the move. There was no way to tell until they tried it. Jeff came by to check on their progress and when told it was ready said; "I wonder if General Arnold would like to see it in action?"

He called Phil Edwards and said the SPA was ready and should we invite the General to see it operational? The General said yes he would and he would bring Major Lenhart and Lieutenant Anderson. They set the time at 1400 hours.

Lolene picked up the General, Lenhart and Anderson and drove them to the SPA site.

Edwards was already there. He introduced them to Dr. Blackmore and Stan Patterson.

Stan said; "We're hopeful it wasn't damaged. We need some wispy clouds to try it. The only ones I see are over by those hills so I'm going to direct it that way."

He sat at his console and turned the directional knobs until the Spa was pointed at the clouds. He turned it on and after a few minutes the thin wispy clouds began to roll and expand. They became increasingly dark as they rolled and expanded. After a few minutes there was a flash of lightning followed by a clap of thunder. It appeared that it was raining over there.

General Arnold said; "Most impressive gentlemen. Do you think it actually rained over there?"

"Yes, sir. We do."

The General said; "Lieutenant Anderson, take a squad of men over there to investigate. It appears to be a mile or so. I would like your opinion of how much rain fell."

"Yes, sir. I'll get them and be right back, while it's still wet."

Stan turned off the SPA and said; "We are limited to what we can see in our horizon. I am working on a directional component but don't have it yet."

The General said; "Perhaps we can make it mobile. Haul it on trucks."

"Yes, sir, if we had a generator." Stan said.

The General thanked them for the demonstration. They went back to their offices except Lieutenant Anderson. He gathered a squad of men and they left for the foothills. They marched past the SPA and headed in the direction of the rainfall. The Lieutenant was in the lead. They had gone about a half mile when a shot rang out. A bullet grazed Anderson's arm but tore into the chest of the man behind him.

Anderson yelled. "Hit the deck. We have a sniper. Did you get a location?"

"Yes, sir. I saw smoke at eleven o'clock. 150 yards." A man said.

"Two men go around each way. Left and right. You." He pointed at a man. "See if you can help this man. He was hit."

"Yes, sir. But you were hit too."

"It just grazed me. Take care of him."

The flankers were headed out through the sparse brush. Suddenly there was another shot and one of the two on the right fell.

"We have another sniper on the right. About two o'clock."

Anderson got on his phone to headquarters; "We're under attack by two snipers. One left and one right. I have two men down. Snipers about 150 yards away at two o'clock and eleven o'clock. I need help."

Major Lenhart got the call. He rousted two squads and left immediately to help Anderson. When they reached the SPA he had one squad go left and the other go right. He called Anderson; "Brad, I have two squads, one left and one right. How far out are you?"

"We're a half mile out. Snipers 150 yards more than that."

"Copy that. We're going to try to flank them."

Lenhart heard a shot followed by the chatter of an automatic weapon.

"What was that, Brad? Did anyone get hit?"

"No casualties. We sprayed the brush where we thought they were."

"We'll be there in a few minutes."

They got to where they thought the snipers were but no one was there. They had the squads search for them to no avail.

They called for medics who treated the two wounded and took them to the Infirmary.

They headed back to headquarters. If there had been rain it would have evaporated by now. Now they had an additional problem. Snipers.

CHAPTER 76

The work assignments had been posted. Jen and Amanda were scheduled to go on a foraging detail the next morning. Jen's arm felt much better and she wanted to do her part to sustain life in the camp. She agreed to go even though Amanda tried to talk her out of it. They were to find clothing and household items. The absence of rain since the explosion would help in limiting the amount of mildew in the clothing.

The electric cart arrived in the morning. It was towing a two-wheeled wagon. Lolene was driving. Lolene had a handgun holstered at her side.

Jen said; "Lolene, what have they had you doing the past couple of days?"

"Most of the time I've been driving the officers around. It's a large camp and they have so many things they must investigate to see if they're repairable. I was taken outside the Fort once to go on one of these foraging expeditions."

"So how are things outside the Fort? What can we expect?"

"We had no trouble when I was out there. However, there were four of us and we were well armed. We are going to the remains of the city this morning. It's about ten miles from here. These foraging expeditions have been going on since the Fort was re-established after the explosion. Most of what we now have was stored in a cave similar to Jerseyville Cavern. The previous expeditions were to the places closest to the Fort. Consequently we have to go farther and farther away from the

Fort to find anything worthwhile. You will be rummaging through the wreckage of what used to be a department store. It's dirty, dusty work. It's my job to watch for trouble while you're working. If I tell you to get in the cart, drop what you're doing and get in the cart."

They drove down the dusty street and picked up two more residents. Jen and Amanda introduced themselves to Karen Masters and Julie Brehm. Karen said to Amanda; "You were here with the Captain the other day."

"That's right. I thought you looked familiar. Lolene told us we're going to a department store. Lolene's the driver." Lolene nodded to them. "I don't think it's going to be a shopping trip to enjoy." Amanda said.

Lolene said; "No, it won't be. But if I tell you get in the cart, do it immediately."

They made small talk while exiting the Fort and traversing the ten miles to the store. All around them were piles of rubble. There was a very narrow path through the debris in the streets. All of it looked the same to the passengers but Lolene seemed to know where she was going. Lolene pulled up to a demolished building that, to the passengers looked like all the others.

"This is it." Lolene said. "Grab those bags there and a pair of work gloves. Be careful where you're walking and stepping. You don't want to twist an ankle or step on a nail. Happy hunting."

Lolene stayed with the cart while the women made their way into what was left of the building. They started their search for anything that looked salvageable. It was not easy. Concrete chunks. Steel reinforcing rods. Splintered wood, Shards of glass. All covered with dust. It seemed they were in what was the clothing department of the store. They pulled articles out of the debris, shook the dust off of them and put them in their bags. The dust hung in the air for a long time. When their bag was full they took it to the wagon they were towing, grabbed another bag and continued. Even though the weather was still cool, after a short time moving debris and pulling dirty clothes out of the rubble they were sweating profusely.

"Have you found anything you just can't live with out." Amanda said to no one in particular; "You know, like we did before all this happened?"

Julie replied; "Right now I'd be happy with just about anything that was clean and would fit."

Karen said; "I feel sorry for my tent mates. As much as I'm sweating and my shower time isn't for another three days."

Julie asked Lolene; "What do they do with this stuff?"

"They've set up a repair and distribution center."

Jen said; "Yes, that's right. Our tent mate Cassandra is assigned there. She said she likes to sew so they have her doing repairs."

"After the clothes are cleaned and repaired they are distributed as needed. They try to give people the correct size but a lot of times they don't have it." Lolene said.

The women trudged wearily back into the rubble. The wagon was about half full of what they had gathered. They knew it was to the benefit of all the residents to see how much they could get before it was time to leave. Lolene had kept track of the time since she had gotten the cart. The battery was only good for about six hours. She had to allow enough time to return to the Fort. She had rigged the motor so that the cart was still running. It normally died as soon as your foot was taken off the accelerator. Lolene tried to be prepared for any emergency. She hoped it was an unnecessary precaution but it could still be dangerous outside the confines of the Fort. There were still marauding bands of stragglers willing to kill for almost any reason. A cart full of salvaged goods would be a very good reason. Not to mention a bonus of five women to play with afterward. The games they would play would be disgusting and deplorable. Degradation, torture and rape and then killed for pleasure.

After another hour of gathering, Lolene called to the women that it was time to leave.

They came back to the cart dragging their bags behind them.

"Are we through? Can we quit now?" Jen said.

"Yes. We better leave now while the cart still has battery power. I don't think you're in any shape to push it back to the Fort."

"Hell no we're not. I feel like I need someone just to help me stand." Julie said.

"Well get in. Let's get going."

They got in the cart. Lolene headed back to the Fort. They had wended their way through the rubbled street for about a mile or two when Lolene saw four figures about 100 yards in front of them. Though unsure, she thought two were carrying rifles. She said; "Hold on ladies. This could be trouble." As the cart approached them, two of the figures moved to the center of the street and waved their arms. The other two positioned themselves on either side of the road. The cart was now 75 yards from them. Then 60 yards. Then 40. Then 25. Lolene floored the accelerator in an attempt to race past them before they could grab the cart and stop it. They sped as fast as the cart would go. Lolene gripping the steering wheel tightly and her passengers holding on to the seats trying to stay in the cart as it careened through the rubbled street. It hit chunks of concrete and brick as it jumped from side to side. The wagon in back was bouncing and losing some of the bags they had labored so hard to collect. The two in the middle of the street jumped out of the way just as the cart got to them. The others were trying to grab onto the cart as it went by. They were waving their rifles at them and shouting; "Stop. Stop. We need" and their voices faded as the cart sped past them.

Jen said; "They were shouting stop."

"I didn't want to stop" Karen said. "They had guns. They could have robbed us and taken the cart and what we've collected and who knows what else."

"I thought one of them was a woman. I heard a woman's voice" Jen said. "What if they're good stragglers? They know we have a cart so we must be in a safer place. They want to go there."

"I agree, but we couldn't stop. I'm the only one armed and we couldn't take the chance." Lolene said. "I'll report it when we get back to the Fort. They can send an armed patrol to see if they can find them."

She drove back to Fort Kelly and told the Officer-of-the-Day they had seen four stragglers about eight miles back. She said; "They may be OK and just need rescuing."

The O.D. asked her; "Were they armed?"

"Yes, sir, two of them had a rifle."

"If they didn't shoot at you they may be alright. I'll round up a patrol and have them investigate. Thank you, Corporal. Get this stuff you've collected to the supply depot."

"Yes, sir. Right away, sir."

CHAPTER 77

Lolene dropped the women off at their respective tents and then delivered the salvage items that were still in the wagon to the supply depot. She then drove to the motor pool to turn in her cart so it could be re-charged.

As she left she saw Captain Edwards. She saluted. He returned the salute and said; “How was your foraging trip?” He knew Amanda was part of it.

Lolene said; “It was fine, sir, until we were headed back. We encountered a bunch of stragglers that tried to get us to stop. Of course we didn’t. Jen Quigley thinks they wanted rescued. I told the O.D. He said he would send a patrol to investigate.”

“Thank you, Corporal. I’ll look into it.”

Edwards went to Amanda’s tent to get more details. She told him what happened and said that Jen heard a woman’s voice and thought they wanted rescued.

Edwards said; “I think I’ll volunteer to lead the patrol. Just in case it’s some ploy of Murchison’s to get into the Fort.”

“Oh Phil, please be careful. You’ve already had two bad experiences with him.”

“I doubt if it is him or his band. It’s probably what Jen thinks, a group of people who want rescued. Regardless, I’ll talk to Major Lenhart and see what he thinks. This camp is being strained to the max now with the amount of people we have.”

He left to talk to the Major. He found him at Headquarters and told him of the incident. Edwards said; "Sir, I would like to lead that patrol."

"I think it would be a good idea to have an officer in charge, Captain. But if there were four of them we don't know if there were others. Make arrangements to take two electric carts and six men plus the drivers. If you find them, bring the leader of their band here for interrogation. We have to know who they are, how they've survived and how many there are. I'll talk to General Arnold because we are already at capacity."

"Yes, sir, I'll make arrangements."

Edwards had completed the arrangements by the end of the day. The patrol was to leave at 0900 in the morning. The Major had assigned the six men and one of the drivers. Edwards got Sergeant Emmons to be the other driver. They were all going to be armed of course.

CHAPTER 78

Emmons pulled up to Edwards's quarters at 0850. There were two enlisted men seated on the rear bench seat. They drove to the Fort's entrance where the other cart with four men plus the driver met them. Captain Edwards explained to them what they doing. There were no questions. They exited the Fort and drove down the road the foraging trip had taken. They had traveled about eight miles when Edwards told them to stop.

He exited the cart and said; "We are now going to search for the stragglers camp or any evidence or clue as to where it may be. I will lead one group on this side of the road. Sergeant Emmons will lead a group on the other side. We will have the drivers stay with the carts. I need a volunteer to take Sergeant Emmons place as driver." One of the men held up his hand. "Good, you're the driver. The rest of us will spread out about 75 feet apart and go about a mile from the road. We will then move to the left or right, whichever direction is away from the Fort, and continue our search. If we're lucky and they are good stragglers, they will see us and try to contact us. However, we don't know what they are or how many there are so stay alert. Let's move."

They started moving away from the road. The area had been wooded on both sides of the road. Most stragglers camps were in what had been wooded areas. It provided some protection from view and also firewood for the camp. They walked a mile or so looking for remains of a camp fire, trash or any clue that was evidence of a camp. They tried to keep each other in sight but there was brush and fallen trees everywhere that they had to avoid. The branches lying on the ground acted as trip wires and if they did not look down repeatedly they would trip and fall. After the mile they moved to the side and started back towards the road. After reaching the road they moved to the side again. They continued their search going away from the road. Then back towards the road. Then away. Then back. Etc. They had been told the approximate location but it could have been a mile one way or the other.

The patrol had progressed almost a half mile. They were on their fourth trip into the woods with still no sign of any stragglers. They had almost reached a turn-around point when two shots rang out.

Edwards was immediately worried and shouted to his men; "Back to the road and the carts. Double time."

They started sprinting back to the road and the carts. Edwards only thought while he was running was chastising himself for only leaving the two drivers there. Two shots could mean that the drivers had been ambushed and killed and the stragglers had commandeered the carts.

They exited the brush and looked down the road. The carts were still there. So were the drivers. But the drivers had company. There were two men flanking each of them. They held a gun to their heads. Edwards and his men, now joined by Emmons and his men, trotted towards the carts. There was one man standing in front of the carts.

When they were within fifty feet of the carts the man said; "That's far enough. Who's in charge?"

Edwards called "Halt" to his troops and said; "I am. Captain Philip Edwards. Who are you and what do you want?"

"As you can see, Captain we have your drivers and your carts. I am Lyman Haskill. My little band and I were hoping you would come. We need help. We have been living in these woods for about two months."

"Well, Mr. Haskill, why did you ambush my drivers? Why didn't you just show yourselves when we were searching the woods for you?"

"You are already past our camp location. I didn't want you to think we were out of this area and give up the search."

"We were going to continue our search in the other direction after we had combed this area."

"I had no way of knowing that."

"No, you didn't, Mr. Haskill. How many of you are there?"

"There are thirteen of us. We started with twenty but we lost seven to the cold, the lack of food and shelter and all the harsh conditions we've endured. We were able to bury them this week since it got a bit warmer"

"This is what we're going to do, Mr. Haskill. You will take me to your camp where I can assess your situation. Your men are to stand down and not threaten my men. If you and your people are truly destitute and want rescue you're not going to harm them anyway."

"Fine, Captain, I'll be glad to do that. You have to turn your cart around to go to the camp."

"If I find everything is OK, I'll take you to see General Arnold. He's the Fort commander and the only one who can give you permission to move to the Fort"

Edwards told Sergeant Emmons that he was in charge of the men. Then he, Haskill and the volunteer driver got in the cart. The driver turned and said; "Where to, sir."

Edwards said; "Turn the cart around and head back down the road. Mr. Haskill will tell you where to go."

They drove down the road about a mile when Haskill told the driver to turn up a narrow, rutted dirt road to their left. They bounced along for 300 yards or so until they came to a patch of fallen timber. It was entangled in thick underbrush.

Edwards saw nothing that resembled a camp. He was immediately wary. Could this be some kind of trap?

"I don't see any camp, Haskill. What's going on?"

"We are very well hidden out of necessity, Captain.

With that statement he walked over to the brush pile and grabbed some and swung it aside. It revealed a dirt path leading through the brush and timber.

"If you'll follow me, Captain."

Edwards turned to the driver and said; "You stay with the vehicle. Are you armed?"

"Yes, sir. I have my rifle."

"Good. Be on the lookout for trouble. What's your name soldier?"

"It's Craig, sir. Private James Craig."

"If you hear shots where I'm going, don't try to be a hero. Go get Sergeant Emmons and the men. Understand?"

"Yes, sir, I do."

Edwards and Haskill headed down the path between the brush.

CHAPTER 79

Edwards told Haskill to lead the way. Edwards unholstered his gun and followed him. He was still wary and alert for any sign of trouble. This could be a trap but then why go to all this trouble. They headed down the dirt path. It was no more than three feet wide with impenetrable brush on both sides. It went straight for 12 or 15 feet then turned ninety degrees left for 6 or 8 feet then turned right for another ten feet.

Haskill said; "We put the bend in it so no one could look straight in and only one person at a time could exit in case we were attacked."

Edwards said; "Smart thinking." Although he was thinking that means it's more difficult for me to get out of here if there's trouble.

At the end of those ten feet they came to a clearing about 70 or 80 feet in both directions. In the center of the clearing was what must have been the basement of a house demolished by the explosion.

Haskill walked over to the foundation. Edwards followed. Edwards peered into the foundation. It was of concrete walls about eight feet deep. It had what appeared to be a concrete floor. It was about thirty feet square. There were piles of rags and cloth laid out along the walls. In the center of the foundation was a fire pit encircled by stones. A small fire was burning.

Edwards asked; "What is this?"

Haskill said; "This is where we live. Come on down. I'll introduce you."

With that he grabbed a ladder that was lying next to the foundation, positioned it into the basement and started to descend.

Edwards thought. "Wonder if this is a trap. Who's down there? How many are there? Once I go down there I've no way of getting out." Swallowing his fear he descended the ladder.

Haskill called out; "Hey, everybody. Come meet Captain Edwards."

The piles of rags and cloth started to move. One by one people started emerging from them. They were gaunt, emaciated people. They appeared to be sleep walking or totally unaware of their surroundings. Edwards saw two other figures sitting in the corners. They arose and walked toward Edwards. His handgun was still in his hand and he was alert to any aggressive action they may try.

Haskill said; "Relax, Captain. I want you to meet Bill Ayers and Sally Fleming. They are part of my control group. The other four members are with your men on the road."

"What do you mean your control group?"

"Well, Captain, you see all of us were in the lower level of Serenity Sanitarium when whatever happened, happened. We of course heard all the noise and eventually dug our way to the surface to find everything was gone."

"Why were you in the Sanitarium and how did you get here, Mr. Haskill?"

"I and what I call my control group were employees of the Sanitarium. We were in the basement because that is where the therapeutic baths are located. The people you see here, other than Bill and Sally, were patients. I had one more member but sadly he passed away along with six of the patients."

"Why didn't you stay at the Sanitarium instead if coming here?"

"We did stay for several days but no one came to help. We had no food and these poor people had very little clothing. They were in the basement because of the baths. You know how cold it got."

"But you're no better off here."

"We know that now. We were trying to find help. I went out several times to find help but couldn't. Then I saw a group of men attacking a man and woman. They tied him up and took turns raping his wife. Then they shot both of them. That's the last time I went out. When I saw those men and what they did I thought we should move somewhere else."

"And that's when you came here?"

"More or less. It was not easy. There were twenty one of us. When we started there were twelve patients and eight overseers. These people are not easy to control. They either do not comprehend or stubbornly refuse any commands. They wander off if they are not watched constantly. Eventually we came upon this place. When we found it, it was not surrounded by brush and trees like you see now. We did that as a precaution to prevent runaways. That is one of the reasons we live in the basement. They can't get out to wander away."

While they were talking the patients shuffled up to them. They stared at Edwards. Some tried to touch him or grab him. All had scraps of mismatched clothing, nothing more than rags, hanging on their body. Some babbled incoherently. Suddenly there was a loud cackling from the voice of a person still standing at the wall.

"Ah, hah, hah, hah. Leonard, you're back. Oh Leonard, I knew you'd come back. You look so nice in your uniform. I've missed you. Come kiss me hello."

She was a rag clad wraith with wild hair and even wilder eyes. She shuffled towards Edwards to collect that kiss.

Haskill intervened; “Miriam, stop. That’s not Leonard. That’s Captain Edwards.”

“No, no, that’s Leonard. Why are you lying to me? Why don’t you want me to be with Leonard?”

“No, Miriam, that’s not Leonard. Now why don’t you go back to your bed and finish that sweater you’re doing for when Leonard comes back?” He took her hand and led her back to the wall.

“Oh yes. Oh yes. I must finish that.”

“I’m sorry, Captain. Poor Miriam thinks he’ll come back but he won’t. Miriam is the worst of the six remaining. She is living in the past as so many with her condition do. The others are fairly quiet and docile. However, they will wander off if not supervised constantly.”

“Mr. Haskill, I’m going to be very up front with you. I will take you to see General Arnold to plead your case but I must tell you our facilities are stretched to the maximum now. We have no facilities to house these people. Our people are living in decades old tents as it is.

“I must try, Captain. There’s no hope of our surviving if we remain out here. There’s no food, my people are exhausted and there are still bands of thieves out here and we are virtually defenseless. Those two old rifles you saw when you came back to your carts are the only weapons we have. The only bullets we have are the ones that were in the guns when we found them. I have to try, Captain.”

“OK. We’ll give it a try. I see your problem and I’ll do all I can to help. Let’s get back to the cart.”

They walked back to their cart and rejoined Sergeant Emmons and the rest of the patrol. Edwards gave a brief update to the Sergeant. Edwards asked for two volunteers to accompany Haskill’s four men back to the camp and provide additional protection until he and Mr. Haskill returned.

Private Craig jumped out of the cart and said; “I’ll go, sir.”

"That's good. You know where it is." Edwards said.

Another man stepped forward and said he would go. He briefed them and then Edwards, the remainder of the men, and Mr. Haskill got in the carts to go back to the Fort.

CHAPTER 80

The two troopers that had volunteered, James Craig and the other, Noah Baldwin, and the four of Haskill's group started walking down the road toward Haskill's camp. Craig and Baldwin were surprised to discover one of the four was a woman.

Craig ambled over to her and said; "I'm James Craig." And held out his hand.

She shook it and said; "I'm Agnes Crum."

"Pleased to meet you Agnes. You know I normally introduce myself as; Craig, James Craig, but I think some other James has done something like that before. Some people think it's corny."

"I think its cute James Craig and so are you."

"Well thank you ma'am. So are you."

Agnes was about thirty-five. James was just over twenty-one. She looked as if she had endured a lot. Her face showed signs of extreme fatigue. Though she may have been slightly plump at one time, the lack of food and the harsh conditions had taken its toll. Her face was lined with exhaustion. They started talking about their situation. Agnes knew very little about what had happened and James filled her in with what he knew.

The other walkers were a step or two ahead of James and Agnes. They overheard snatches of the conversation and dropped back to glean more information. Noah Baldwin added what he knew about things.

James said; “That’s what we know about what happened and what’s being done. Of course there’s a million rumors out there so who knows what to believe.”

“That’s more information than we’ve had since we’ve been out here.” One of the men said.

They kept walking toward the camp. They came to the dirt road leading to the camp and Agnes said; “We’re almost there.”

James said; “Yeah, I know. I was here with the Captain.”

A hundred fifty yards away from them, concealed in the brush across the road, four stragglers, a patrol Murchison had sent to forage, watched them go up the dirt road.

One of them asked? “Do you think they have a camp up there?”

“They must. Why would they walk up that dirt road?”

“Should we take them?”

“No, I don’t think so. There are six of them and only four of us. And the soldiers are with them. Let’s wait a while and see what happens. Maybe we can get closer.”

CHAPTER 81

Edwards patrol arrived at the Fort. Edwards introduced Mr. Haskill to Major Lenhart. He told Lenhart very briefly of Haskill's situation and they needed to speak to the General. Lenhart called the General and made the request.

"Mr. Haskill, the General said he would see you but could not promise you anything."

"Thank you, Major. I have to try."

Edwards and Haskill went into the General's office.

Edwards saluted and said; "Sir, this is Mr. Lyman Haskill, He has a group of thirteen he wants to bring to the Fort. They are living in squalid conditions with no chance of improving their plight. I will let Mr. Haskill give you the details. Mr. Haskill, this is General Elliot Arnold."

They shook hands and Haskill said; "Thank you for seeing me, General Arnold. As the Captain said, my people are in desperate need of rescue. We are refugees from Serenity Sanitarium and have barely survived these past two or so months. I have already lost seven of my original group and it's just a matter of time until we are all lost."

"Mr. Haskill, you say you are from Serenity Sanitarium. Explain that."

"Yes sir. Seven of the surviving thirteen are care-givers. The other six were patients."

"Do you mean patients with mental disabilities?"

"Yes sir, in varying degrees. They do not display any inclination to violence. All except one are very docile."

"We are at maximum capacity now, Mr. Haskill. We have no additional quarters to house anyone, much less thirteen people, almost half of which have mental disabilities."

"I know, sir. Captain Edwards told me, but at the least if we were here we wouldn't have to worry about those roaming gangs. We are currently living in the basement of a demolished house. If you had something similar here we could occupy that. It also prevents the people from wandering."

"We also have demolished buildings. I don't know if any would be satisfactory for your requirements."

"Our requirements are very minimal. There is only one. Survival."

"Food is an additional problem. Our supplies are very limited."

"I realize that, sir. We have nothing we could immediately contribute but the seven of us who are not patients are willing to work for food."

"This is what I want you to do, you and Captain Edwards try to find a basement or something similar that would suffice as housing. Do that and then come back and we'll talk some more."

"Yes, sir. Thank you, sir. We'll see if we can find something and then come back. Thank you, sir."

They left the office. Haskill had a grin of hope on his face. He turned to Edwards and said; "Do you know of any place Captain? Can we ride around looking for some place?"

"I don't know of one so we'll have to ride around and see what we can find. Let's find Major Lenhart. He'll know where we should look."

They found Lenhart and told him what the General said. He said he would ride with them as there were still parts of the camp he needed to inspect. They got in the cart and started down the street. The streets in this area were paved and the debris from the explosion removed. There were men working on constructing buildings on the existing foundations of what had been Fort Kelly. Some buildings looked like log cabins. Some were made of plywood that had been salvaged.

Lenhart said; “We’re trying to make some quarters to house the men. Some of them are sleeping on the ground right now. That’s bad enough but blankets are in short supply too.”

They drove farther down the street and the further they drove the more rubble they encountered. They had to zig-zag around piles of debris. The construction area had ended. They saw the foundations of what used to be buildings which had now been reduced to trash.

They exited the cart to see if any would be suitable for Haskill’s people. They stepped carefully over the ground to get to the foundations. The ground was covered with wood, brick, concrete and broken glass. They went from foundation to foundation. All they saw were of concrete slab or crawl space foundations. After looking at six foundations and getting discouraged they decided to drive a bit farther. Maybe it would be better.

When they got in the cart and looked up the street they saw 300 feet directly ahead of them the remains of a building. The Major said; “That was the PX, the Post Exchange.”

Haskill asked; “What’s the PX?”

“It’s a store where the troops could buy sundries, magazines, clothing other than what was provided, that sort of thing.”

As they approached they saw the foundation protruded two feet above the ground level. A good indication it was deeper than what they had been seeing. They walked up and saw that parts of the floor structure were still intact. Peering into those parts without the floor they could see that indeed there was a basement.

“A basement. It has a basement.” Haskill exclaimed.

“This is a lot bigger than what you have now.” Edwards said.

They cautiously climbed onto the parts of the floor that remained. The structure was indeed bigger. Much bigger. It was about 35 feet by 80 feet. They saw there were stairs leading to the basement. Some of the treads were missing but they were able to carefully descend.

They gazed in amazement at what they had found. The basement had not been raided. There were shipping boxes labeled shirts, trousers, coats, gloves, and other clothing. There were boxes of soap, toothpaste, shaving cream and other sundries. As they wended their way through this bonanza they wondered why no one had thought to investigate it before. They walked through the basement weaving in and out amongst the boxes. One end of the building had a partition extending across it ten feet from the end wall. There were two desks, with chairs, four other chairs and file cabinets. They were not damaged as the floor above them remained.

"I'll have to report this." Lenhart said. "We'll have to inventory all of this. There are probably a hundred places that are in desperate need of these items."

"Can I at least have some for my people? If we hadn't come you wouldn't even know it was here." Haskill pleaded.

"That's up to the General. What do you think about this place for your people?"

"Oh, we can make it work just fine. We'll clean it up. The partitioned part is terrific. Maybe some privacy or separation could be had. We'll have to partition off the stairs to prevent wanderers. It's far enough away that we wouldn't bother the rest of the camp."

"Transportation and meals could be a problem." Edwards said.

"First things first." Lenhart said. "Let's report what we found to the General."

They climbed out of the basement, got in the cart and left. Lyman Haskill was grinning ear to ear. He had not had anything to smile about for a long time.

CHAPTER 82

The Major, Captain and Haskill arrived back at the General's office. They told him of the bonanza they had found. Haskill told the General the basement would be perfect for them.

The General said; "If I let you occupy that space it will be on a temporary basis. We may need it for other purposes later. Also, in due time I want you to find other quarters. We are not a sanitarium."

"Yes, sir, I understand, sir."

"Major Lenhart, contact the Quartermaster Sergeant and get some people there to take inventory. I want a report on what is there and the quantities."

"Yes, sir, I hope to have that for you by the end of the day tomorrow. It's getting rather late today."

"Captain Edwards, make arrangements to have a truck get Mr. Haskill and his people tomorrow morning and bring them here."

"Yes, sir."

Haskill said; "Thank you very much, sir. We will try to not cause any trouble for you. Thank you very much."

They left the General's office. Lenhart left to contact the Quartermaster Sergeant. Haskill thank him for all he'd done. They shook hands and he left.

Edwards said; "I'll take you back to your camp. You pack up and be ready to leave tomorrow. By the time I get the truck and get there it will be 9:30 or 10:00."

They got in the cart and left for the camp. When they arrived Haskill told his group that permission had been given and they were going to Fort Kelly in the morning. They were overcome with joy. Edwards told Craig and Baldwin to get in the cart for it was time to go.

Craig said; “Yes, sir. Right away, sir.” He walked over to Agnes and said; “Agnes, it was a pleasure to meet you. I’ll see you later at the Fort. He handed her his C-rations.”

She said; “Thank you, Craig, James Craig.”

They got in the cart and left.

Edwards said; “It seems as if you’ve made a friend, Private.”

“Yes, sir, she’s a nice person.”

The four stragglers had seen the cart go up the dirt road. Now they saw the cart coming back and the two soldiers were in it. They thought now it’s an even fight. Four of them and four of us. Now we have surprise on our side. It should be a fun morning.

CHAPTER 83

Edwards dropped off Craig and Baldwin. He told them to report in and then he went to see Amanda and Jen to tell them what he had found. Not only the clothing and supplies they had found at the PX but about Haskill and his people.

“Keep it quiet about all the stuff we found. Everyone’s in desperate need and I don’t need a clothing riot on my hands.”

“You’ve really had a full day, Phil. I bet you haven’t eaten. Are you hungry?” Amanda said.

“No, I haven’t had anything. Do you think the mess hall has anything left?”

“Let’s go find out. Some times they have one or two items left.” Amanda said.

They said goodbye to Jen and walked to the mess hall. Sergeant Busch saw Phil walk in and went to greet him. ”Hello, Captain, can I help you?”

“Hello, Sergeant. Do you have anything a poor, hungry, tired Officer could have?”

“I may be able to rustle up something, sir. Have a seat. You just made it. We were about ready to lock up.”

They sat on one of the benches. The mess halls had plank tables that seated ten and long bench seats. They fed two hundred and fifty to three hundred persons three times a day. There were three shifts each meal. Shifts lasted forty-five minutes. You had to eat and leave before the next shift started.

The sergeant arrived with some pemmican biscuits, raisins and water. “Sorry, sir. That’s it.”

“Thanks, Sergeant. This is fine.”

Phil turned to Amanda and said; “I don’t think I’m going to be much company for you this evening, honey. I‘ve told you about today. I still have to arrange for a truck and driver. Maybe Sergeant Riley would like to have a break from office work?”

“He probably would, Phil. Amos or Tom could cover for him. Amos is off crutches but limping so he’s still on light duty.”

“I’ll stop at their tent and ask before I leave.”

“I’ll walk over with you before we say goodnight, sweetheart.”

Phil finished the little food he had. They left and went to talk to Amos and Tom. Tom was already scheduled for the following day but Amos said he would be glad to cover for Riley. Phil walked Amanda to her tent to say goodnight. He kissed her goodnight. More than once, and reluctantly left. He went to his headquarters tent. Sergeant Riley was still there. He told him of the rescue mission he had to make and asked if he wanted to be the driver. Riley enthusiastically said yes. Phil told him to get the truck and pick him up at his billet in the morning.

CHAPTER 84

The morning was getting a bit lighter. It never got bright because they were still obscured somewhat by the shadow of Venus. The stragglers had spent a chilly night. They had not gone back to Murchison's camp. He would have been upset that they didn't bring anything back except themselves. They crossed the street and started up the dirt road. They got to the brush pile and were stymied. There was no gap in the brush pile. No entry.

One said quietly; "I know they're in there. There has to be a way in."

Another said; "Look! Foot prints in the dust here. Let's grab that brush and pull."

They pulled the brush aside and saw the narrow dirt path.

"Go on, Jake. Go on in. We'll be right behind you."

Jake moved onto the path and into the brush. He reached the left turn and hesitated. He saw another turn to the right. He turned right and saw the opening into the clearing. He crouched and approached the opening. When he got to the opening he saw a person sitting on a foundation wall.

Agnes was on guard duty. Bill Adler was scheduled to relieve her right then. Agnes was tired. She felt tired all the time anymore. It had been a long four hours. Dark and cold. She thought she had heard voices. No, she told herself. You're just tired. She looked up at the opening to the path and saw a man. That's not one of us she thought. She raised her antiquated rifle to fire but the man fired first. The bullet struck her hard in the chest. But she shot too. Her bullet smashed into her assailants kneecap and he fell.

Bill was on his way up the ladder to relieve her when he heard the shot. He reached the top just in time to see Agnes collapse onto the dirt. He ran to her. He saw the attacker's head still protruding out of the brush pile. He shot and the bullet creased the man's skull. The others pulled him back down the path. Bill called for help. Haskill heard the shot and was emerging from the basement. Another followed him.

Bill said; "Agnes's been shot. Can you get her down below?"

"Yes, we'll do that and then I'll come back up and help you. Take cover behind the foundation wall. They've no way in but that path."

They wrestled Agnes's limp form down to the basement. She was bleeding profusely. They stuffed a rag over her wound and applied pressure to try to stop the bleeding. Lyman came up and joined Bill behind the wall. They had their rifles trained on the path opening. Things were quiet for several minutes. Suddenly a man appeared in the opening. Bill and Lyman fired simultaneously. The man ducked back into the opening. Both shots had missed.

"I wonder how many there are," Bill said.

"I hope not too many. We don't have many bullets." Lyman replied.

Now it was a waiting game. Lyman and Bill had to wait and see what the attackers next move was. Were they going to rush them and overpower them? What if they kept teasing them by appearing in the opening to draw their fire until they were out of ammo? A waiting game.

The wait had now been about an hour. There had been no activity. Are they gone? Have they left? Were they discouraged? Bill and Lyman didn't know.

Lyman called down into the basement; “How’s Agnes?”

Sally answered; “She’s not good, Lyman. She’s laboring to breathe. Gasping for breath. I don’t have any way I can help her.”

“I know you don’t, Sally. Just stay with her. Your presence will be a comfort.”

”Oh, Lyman I don’t know if she is even aware I’m here.” Sally was almost crying.

Lyman and Bill were helpless to do anything. Then a voice called out to them.

“You people in there. You’ve got two minutes to come out and we’ll let you go.”

“I don’t believe you. Come and get us.” Lyman assumed they didn’t know how many people were in there.

“We’re not going to do that but we are going to get you out of there. You think it’s cold this morning. We’re going to turn up the heat for you.”

Bill said; “What’s that mean, Lyman?”

“I think they’re going to try to burn us out of here. Burn down all the brush and leave us exposed.”

He said that and looked up to see a thin wisp of smoke rising above the brush. As he watched, the smoke got heavier all the time. Now he could see flames above the brush. That brush is so dry it won’t take long to burn through.

“How many bullets do you have, Bill?”

“I only have two left, Lyman. What about you?”

“The same, two.”

“Should we surrender? Maybe it’s our only chance to live.”

“From what I’ve seen and heard about these gangs it’s a very slim chance. The patients would have no chance at all. As soon as they saw their condition they’d kill them all. Then they’d kill us because we saw it.”

They watched the flames grow higher. Lyman called down to Sally and the others and told them about the flames and how precarious their situation was. So they waited.

Edwards and Sergeant Riley were coming down the street toward Haskill's. Edwards looked up and saw the smoke to the right of the street.

"That's about where Haskill's is. Step on it, Sergeant."

Riley floored the accelerator. As they got closer Edwards could tell it was coming from Haskill's camp. They made a screaming right turn and bounced up the bumpy dirt road. The flames were shooting higher and higher as they approached. Edwards saw four men standing outside the flames.

"Head right for those guys, Sergeant. And get out your weapon."

The attackers heard the truck approaching. They turned and raised their rifles to shoot. The truck was bouncing back and forth on the dirt road. Edwards had his window down and was firing at them like in an old western movie. As the truck left the road and bore down on them they tried to run before it got to them. One limped two steps, tripped and fell and was run over before Riley could swerve. At least that's what he said sometime later. One stepped aside just as the truck got there. He raised his rifle to shoot Edwards as the truck went past but Edwards shot him first. The third was hit dead center by the truck and was pushed backwards into the flames they had set. He screamed in pain as his clothes caught on fire, picked himself up and ran screaming for a short distance before he fell to the ground. The last one ran like the devil away from there. Edwards raised his weapon to shoot him but then lowered it and let him escape. He was anxious to check on Haskill and his people. The brush was still burning but that part where the path was almost was burnt through to the clearing. He had Riley drive the truck through it quickly then reverse and through it again. A dangerous move to try to clear a path to the basement. He wanted to check on the people.

He called out; "Haskill, are you guys alright."

"Captain Edwards, is that you? We have one casualty, Agnes. She was on guard when it started and she was shot. She's in critical condition."

"I'll call the Fort and have them send the medics. Hopefully by the time they get here we'll be able to get through the flames."

"Thanks, Captain. You guys got here just in time. We were about out of ammo and the flames were getting dangerously close."

Edwards called for the medics. He told them to get Private James Craig to go with them as he knew the location. They were then helpless to do anything except wait for the flames to subside. It took twenty minutes for the medics to arrive. Craig was with them. He was stunned to hear that it was Agnes who had been shot.

The flames had subsided but there were hot embers still on the ground. There were a couple of small logs still smoldering. They pushed them out of the way with the truck as they drove into the clearing. The medics van right behind them. The medics immediately went to Agnes. Haskill and Bill Adler thanked Phil again.

Edwards said; "Are you ready to move? Can you get your people ready while the medics are working?"

Haskill called down and told them to pack up and get in the truck.

Craig said to Edwards; "Captain, may I ride with the medics to the Infirmary. Agnes knows me and it may be comforting for her?"

"You'll have to ask Mr. Haskill and the medics too. It's alright with me."

Craig approached Haskill; "Mr. Haskill, sir, is it alright with you if I ride with the medics to the Infirmary. Were you going to? Or maybe one of your people?"

"I would like to have all my people to help with the patients. So yes, you're welcome to go if the medics say it's OK."

"Thank you, sir."

They loaded everything they were taking. The medics brought Agnes up on a stretcher. She was barely breathing. They put her in their van, Craig got in and they left. Haskill and his group brought up the patients one by one and got them settled.

Miriam was the last they brought up. She was yelling in their faces; "What are you doing to me? Where are you taking me, sonny? I don't want to go. Wait until Leonard hears of this. You'll be in trouble. Let me go." Haskill got her calmed down and seated in the truck by telling her Leonard would meet her there. She wouldn't remember that anyway he said. They left for the Fort.

CHAPTER 85

The morning Edwards went to pick up Haskill's group, Stan and Holly went to the SPA site. They were still trying to get the directional component operational. Holly helped Stan onto the platform and bent over him observing while Stan was at the control console. They had worked until mid morning when Holly stood upright to stretch. There was the sound of a distant gunshot and Holly said; "Ugh." and crumpled to the floor. Stan turned and saw him fall and cried out; "Holly, Holly. Oh my god. He's been shot."

Stan was on the SPA platform. He was in his wheelchair, unable to bend over to help Holly and unable to get off the platform.

He started shouting; "Help, help. A man's been shot. Somebody help us. Help, help."

There were men working at the construction sites 200 feet away. The noise of their tools drowned out Stan's voice. He kept shouting. He was helpless to do anything himself. Then the sound of their tools subsided and they heard him calling. They were unsure of the direction. They looked around and saw Stan in the distance waving his arms and shouting. Three of them ran to him. They saw Holly crumpled on the floor and two knelt down to him. They heard another distant shot and a bullet whizzed past the man still standing. He immediately crouched. One of the men at Holley's side said; "Go get help. Go get the medics.

Tell them to be careful. We have a sniper and if you're standing, you're a target." He ran to get help.

Stan said; "Thank God you heard me. Is he OK? Is he breathing?"

"Yeah, he's breathing. I think the shot grazed his head. Enough to knock him out but I don't think it penetrated."

They did as much for Holly as they could. They staunched the flow of blood using the shirt one had taken off. They formed a pillow with another shirt. Then they waited for the medics.

The medics arrived and ran to the SPA in a crouch. They had been warned. They roused Holly somewhat, put him on a stretcher and left for the Infirmary.

The construction men went back to their site and told the other men there that some guy had been shot by a sniper.

Someone said; "That's only a couple of hundred feet from here. If he can shoot that far he can shoot this far. I don't know if it's safe for us to be here any longer."

"You're right. A sniper rifle with a telescopic site would have no problem adjusting for another 200 feet."

"I don't think we need to work here until they get rid of the sniper. I'm going to talk to the superintendent. You guys better take cover."

He talked to the super, the super talked to Lieutenant Anderson, Anderson talked to Major Lenhart, Major Lenhart called the General and was told to take two squads and search for and eliminate the snipers. It went up the chain of command.

Lenhart told Anderson to take two squads to search and destroy the sniper.

Anderson said; "There may be two snipers, sir. There were the last time."

"Then search and destroy both, Lieutenant." He said exasperatedly.

Anderson rousted two squads and marched into the area they had been previously. They spread out in a skirmishers formation, fifty feet apart, and advanced through the brush. This was not the heavy brush of the former woodlands. This was light brush allowing minimum cover. They nervously kept advancing expecting any moment to be shot by the sniper. They advanced a mile before Anderson told them to halt. He didn't think the sniper could accurately shoot any farther. He divided his two squads and had one go left and one go right for a half mile and then return. He knew the sniper had taken the shot and left after instilling fear and terror in everyone. That was the object of snipers. They dejectedly headed back to camp.

Doctor Linquist treated Holly's wound. He wrapped his head in gauze and said to him; "Dr. Blackmore you were extremely lucky. One inch closer and you would not be here."

Holly said; "I know. First Myron was killed. Then Joan died. Now this. That damned machine causes too much trouble."

"The machine does not cause trouble Doctor. It was designed to be beneficial. It's man that causes the trouble." Linquist said. "Get some rest now."

A nurse interrupted and said; "Doctor, they just brought in a lady named Agnes. She's been shot. You better come. It's a Code Blue."

Doctor Linquist hurried out

CHAPTER 86

The truck carrying Haskill's group arrived at the Fort and made its way up the rubble strewn street to the old PX site. Edwards was curious as to why no one was working on the construction sites. Edwards, Haskill and two of his staff went to investigate the PX premises and develop a plan for using it. They looked into the basement level and discovered the Quartermaster Sergeant and his crew had been busy that morning. All the boxes had been removed so they were able to plan to use the space as they saw fit. They had also repaired the stairs.

Haskill started to get the patients out of the truck and into their new quarters. The attendants led them down the stairs one by one. When Miriam got down from the truck she said; "Where's Leonard sonny. You told me Leonard would be here. Where is he?" She had not forgotten.

"He'll be here later, Miriam." Haskill said and led her down to the basement.

When the last of them had been removed, Haskill thanked Edwards and Riley. Haskill asked Edwards if they could take him to the Infirmary so he could check on Agnes. The three got in the truck and headed to headquarters. As they passed the construction sites Edwards said; "I wonder why no one's working on the construction Riley."

"That is strange, Captain. They've been working everyday."

They dropped Haskill off at the Infirmary. He went in and James Craig was there.

Haskill asked; “How’s Crummy, Private?”

“You mean Agnes, sir? She’s holding her own. The Doctor said to keep my hopes up.”

“We can only hope and pray.”

“You called her Crummy, sir, not Aggie or Agnes.”

“She hates the name Aggie, Private. And for some reason loves to be called Crummy.”

Edwards and Riley turned in the truck to the motor pool and got an electric cart.

Edwards said to Riley; “Before I take you to our HQ I want to check in here.”

They entered Headquarters. Major Lenhart was there. He said; “Did you get the refugees here OK?”

“Yes, sir, we did. They’re getting settled now. I noticed no one was working the construction sites.”

“You just got back didn’t you, Captain. You don’t know.”

“Don’t know what, sir?”

“There was another sniper attack at the SPA site. Dr. Blackmore was hit.”

“Blackmore was hit! Is he OK? How bad is it? He wasn’t killed was he?”

“No, he wasn’t killed, but it was close. He’s in the Infirmary.”

“Was Stan Patterson shot too?”

“No, he wasn’t. The construction crew heard Stan shouting and helped. They took him to see Blackmore. I guess he’s still there. The construction guys won’t work until the sniper is eliminated. Anderson’s out there now with two squads trying to find him.”

“Thanks, Major. That’s more bad news than I needed. Has anyone told Stan’s crew?”

“I don’t know, Captain.”

"I have to take Sergeant Riley there. I'll tell them."

They turned to leave and Lieutenant Anderson came into the office.

Lenhart said; "Any luck, Lieutenant? Did you find him and eliminate him?"

"No, sir. We searched a two mile area but no sign of the sniper."

"Be prepared to continue your search tomorrow. You can start earlier and hopefully be more successful."

"Yes, sir. I'll arrange it." He saluted and left.

Edwards said; "Let me know if I can help. Come on Riley, let's go."

They drove to their HQ. Riley went in and relieved Amos who had been there all day. Amos and Edwards went to the men's tent.

Edwards called Jeff out and said; "Get the women, Jeff. I have something to tell you."

They came and all gathered around Phil who said; "Dr. Blackmore was shot by the sniper. He's in the Infirmary. Stan's OK. He's with Holly. Lieutenant Anderson led a search for the sniper but did not find him."

"How did he get shot, Phil?"

"It was at the SPA. I guess he and Stan were working."

Jeff said; "Will you take me to see him?"

Phil nodded yes and Jen said; "Me too."

"They won't be able to work on the SPA until the sniper is eliminated." Jeff said.

Jeff and Jen got in the cart for the ride to the Infirmary. Amanda got in too although she didn't know Holly. When they got there they were taken to Holly's room. Stan was there. Holly's head was bandaged. He was awake. They expressed their concern and elicited the few details Stan and Holly knew of what happened. They asked Stan if he wanted a ride. He said yes he would so Holly could rest. It was crowded in the cart. Jen and Amanda took the front bench seat and Jeff, Stan and Stan's wheelchair were in the other. They took Stan to his building. He and Holly had been put in one of the newly constructed ones. Jeff went in to get him settled.

They drove to their tent area. Their tent mates were still gathered there talking, except for Boris. He stayed in his tent.

Elmer Bailey said; "How are your friends?"

Jeff said; "They're OK. Stan can't do any work on the SPA until they get the sniper. The construction crews can't work either."

"How long do you think it will be before they get him?"

Phil said; "They search for him but by the time they get there he's gone."

"Ain't there any signs as to where he's gone?" Elmer asked?

Phil replied; "I haven't heard of any."

"Well, gosh, they just don't know where to look. My boy Billy could track an ant across a flat rock and tell you when he zigged and when he zagged." Billy blushed.

"Maybe that's what we need, a tracker."

"Billy'd be happy to help if he could. Wouldn't you, Billy?"

Billy nodded yes.

Phil said; "I'll keep that in mind, thanks. Come on, Amanda, I'll walk you to your tent."

The others stayed behind. He was hoping they would.

CHAPTER 87

The following morning Phil Edwards went to the mess hall to talk to Sergeant Busch. He told him of Haskill's group of refugees. He asked him if it would be possible to gather up any scraps after all the authorized people had eaten and take them to Haskill's group. He said he would make a cart available for that purpose.

Busch said; "Sometimes we don't have any scraps, Captain."

"If you don't have any, you don't have any. But if you do?"

"Sure, sir, if we do."

"Thank you, Sergeant." He told him where Haskill was located.

He left the mess hall and was going to tell Haskill the arrangement. As he drove past the construction site he swerved to miss a piece of rubble and that saved him from the sniper's shot. He floored the cart and swerved left and right eluding any additional shots. He got on his phone to HQ.

"This is Captain Edwards. I just drove past the construction site and got shot at by the sniper. Has Lieutenant Anderson left yet on his search mission?"

"No, sir, not yet."

"Tell him to wait until I get there. I may have some help for him."

"Yes, sir, will do."

He drove to the men's tent and called Billy and Elmer out. He told them he had been shot at and wondered if Billy wanted to help find the sniper. Billy said he sure would and got in the cart. They drove to HQ. Anderson was waiting with a squad of men.

"Lieutenant Anderson, this is Billy Bailey. He's an excellent tracker and I want you to take him along."

"Glad to, sir. We need all the help we can get. Do you want a weapon, Billy?"

"Yes, sir."

They handed him an M16 and two magazines. He grinned with happiness. The patrol went to the construction site. Edwards showed them where he was when the shot came. They headed to the likely location of the shooter. They alertly marched in that direction. They didn't know if the sniper was still there. It was unlikely but possible.

After a quarter mile Billy said; "Why don't you guys stay here a spell, Lieutenant. I'll go on ahead and see if I can find anything."

"Alright, Billy, but be careful. The sniper may still be out there."

"Well if he is he better make his first shot count cuz he sure won't get a second."

Billy advanced about 500 feet and roamed carefully right and left through the brush. His eyes were always on the ground. He stopped a few times and bent over as if to examine something, then straightened up and continued his search. Then he stopped, bent to look at the ground, stood up and yelled; "Hey, Lieutenant. He went that-away." He pointed.

The patrol joined him and he led them in pursuit of the sniper. They traveled farther away from the center of the camp. They were into an area of denser brush and fallen trees. After a mile Billy called a halt.

Anderson said; "What's wrong, Billy? Did you lose the trail?"

"No, sir, not at all, sir. That fellow was joined by another. I reckon we've got two snipers now."

"Great news, Billy. The first time we were attacked there were two of them. Are they traveling together?"

"Appears so, Lieutenant. Let's go."

They followed the trail. It was easy for Billy. They had made no effort to conceal their path. After a quarter mile Billy turned to the Lieutenant.

"Sir, the signs are getting fresher. We better go silent."

They continued their pursuit as quietly as they could. Billy was ahead and turned and motioned for quiet. He waved the Lieutenant to come to him.

"Sir, I heard voices. I think they're just ahead in that brush."

"I'll have some men circle around. We'll give them a few minutes then we'll attack."

He went back and told the men. Four of them peeled off and left. He waited five minutes, then he and Billy and the other four men approached the suspected brush. They heard the voices distinctly now.

"I'll bet Felix will be happy with what we've done. This was a good idea of his to make 'em scared. Now maybe they'll be holed up and won't come out until it's too late."

"From what I heard Felix and all of them will be coming in about a quarter mile up. It's just about time so let's go join them."

Lieutenant Anderson had heard enough. Was Murchison planning to attack this morning? He wanted to know more detail from these two. He walked through the brush with his gun drawn. He said; "We have you surrounded. Throw down your weapons and surrender."

Instead of doing that they turned to fire. The bullets of the squad tore into them in multiple places. They staggered and reeled. Blood stained their shirts and pants. They fell to the ground without uttering a sound. The patrol gathered around them and stared silently.

Anderson called HQ; "Major Lenhart sir, we got the snipers thanks to Billy Bailey." A pause. "Yes, sir, both of them are dead. I heard them talking, sir. Something about Murchison attacking the Fort this morning."

"Thanks, Lieutenant, I'll muster the troops and be ready."

"Sir, we're about a mile and a half past the construction sites. I think that's where they're coming in."

"Copy that, Lieutenant, we'll head there. Out."

CHAPTER 88

Edwards left HQ after seeing Anderson, Billy and the squad leave on the sniper hunt. He resumed his trip to Haskill's group. He told Haskill about his arrangement with Sergeant Busch to deliver the leftover scraps. Haskill thanked him for what he had done for them.

Haskill asked; "Would you like to see what progress we've made?"

Edwards said; "Yes, I have a few minutes."

Haskill showed him around the basement. They had used the partitioned area to house the patients for control purposes. The patients were sitting around the walls on blankets they had been provided. All except Miriam. As soon as she saw Edwards in his uniform she said; 'Leonard, is that you, Leonard?"

Haskill said; "No, Miriam, that's Captain Edwards."

"Where's Leonard sonny? You said he'd be here." She still hadn't forgotten.

They left the patient area. The open area was office and attendant area. They ascended the stairs.

Edwards said; "All of you need to be aware that there is a sniper on the loose inside the Fort. We have a patrol searching for him now. If you see anyone approaching overland, not using the street, they are probably trouble."

"Thanks. We'll be on the alert."

Edwards said; "I'll call HQ and see if the patrol found the sniper."

He punched in the number and said; “Major, any report from Anderson yet?”

“Yes, Phil. They got the snipers but they overheard them talking about Murchison attacking this morning. Where are you?”

“I’m at the old PX with Haskill’s group.”

“From what Anderson told me that’s about where they’ll be coming in.”

“It’s quiet now, Joe.”

“I’ll call Anderson and have his patrol head your way. I’ve already mustered the troops here. We’re leaving now for your area.”

CHAPTER 89

Lenhart called Anderson; “Lieutenant, do you know where the old PX was?”

“Yes, sir, I do.”

“Captain Edwards is there. There are civilians there and they may be in a direct line of Murchison’s attack. Get your squad over there as fast as you can.”

“Yes, sir, will do.”

He gave the order and they double timed through the brush and fallen trees. They had gone a quarter mile when Anderson looked to his right and atop a low hill 200 yards away was a horde of thirty or forty men headed their direction. They saw each other at the same time and the stragglers fired at Anderson’s men. Anderson said; “Return fire.”

He turned to Billy and said; “Billy, you run over to the old PX, It’s over that way, and tell Captain Edwards we’re engaged in a fire fight and we’ll hold them off as long as we can.”

“I can shoot, Lieutenant.”

“I know you can, Billy, but I want you to go tell Edwards. That’s an order.”

Billy turned and said; “Yes, sir.” He took two quick shots. Two hits. He started running.

Anderson said to his men; “Fire and fall back. We may not be able to stop them but we sure as hell can delay them.”

He had four men fire and then fall back and alternate with the other four who'd fire and fall back. This kept a constant stream of fire at the stragglers and slowed their advance. However the stragglers were firing too. One of Anderson's men was hit, then another. The wounded men were helped to retreat by two others of their meager force. That left only four plus Anderson to hold off the charge. He had the four take cover behind fallen trees and had the others retreat toward the PX. Since they were behind cover and able to get more accurate shots, they inflicted considerable damage to their attackers. But there were too many. They kept coming. Anderson said; "Fall back and fire." They would retreat a few steps, turn and fire. Then retreat a few more steps, turn and fire.

CHAPTER 90

Edwards heard the shots off in the distance. He knew it could only mean Anderson's patrol had been engaged. He knew he was unable to help them. He called Lenhart; "Major, I hear shots. It must be Anderson's patrol."

"We're on our way, Phil. I hope they can delay them long enough for us to make it."

They disconnected. Edwards looked in the direction of the firing and saw someone running toward them. He drew his weapon and then realized it was Billy Bailey.

Billy stopped in front of him and said; "Captain, there's about forty stragglers attacking the Lieutenant. They're headed this way."

"Thanks, Billy. I've already talked to the Major and he's bringing reinforcements."

Wait. That's all they could do is wait. Wait for the patrol. Wait for the stragglers. Wait for the reinforcements. Ten minutes passed and Edwards looked up to see the two wounded and their support coming about a hundred yards away. They were staggering and weaving, not only the wounded but the support. They were no longer running just walking as fast as they could.

Edwards thought "Where are the others? Are the others dead? Is this all that's left of Anderson's patrol?"

He put those thoughts into words as soon as they arrived and was told the Lieutenant was engaged in a delaying tactic. He wanted to hold them off until reinforcements arrived. Edwards said to take the wounded down to the basement. Maybe they would be able to treat them.

Wait some more. Hurry up and wait. The story of the military. Ten more minutes passed and in the distance were five running men. They were being followed by about twenty running men. The twenty were firing. The five were not. My god, they're out of ammo, Edwards thought.

Edwards drew his weapon and said; "Billy, I think they're out of ammo. Lay down a cover fire for them."

The two who were the support for the wounded had come up from the basement and heard the order and started firing. Anderson's men were just feet from Edwards's group. The stragglers turned some of their fire toward Edwards's group. Suddenly there was a shrill yell.

"Leonard, where are you? I know you're up here with these other G.I.'s. Where are you?"

Miriam had followed the two soldiers up the stairs. Haskill was right behind her trying to corral her and get her down to the basement. She ran toward the soldiers. Toward the midst of the fighting. She had almost reached them when she staggered and fell. A bullet had hit her in the chest. A torrent of blood stained her dress. She moaned but did not speak. Her eyes closed. Haskill ran to her and knelt down; "Miriam." He sobbed. "Miriam, why didn't you stay downstairs? Oh Mother, why didn't you stay downstairs?"

Edwards saw this and heard him and went to him: "Lyman, I'm sorry. She was your mother?"

"Yes, and Leonard was my father. He was killed in the war and her mind could never accept that. All the casualties of war are not on the battlefield."

He picked up her lifeless body and took it down to the basement.

Anderson's patrol had reached Edwards group. Anderson's right arm was hanging limply at his side. Two of his men were bleeding through their jackets. They handed them ammo and the fight continued. The stragglers had not advanced any farther and were taking cover wherever they could find it. There were less of them now and they had lost their aggressiveness.

CHAPTER 91

The Major was on his way to reinforce Edwards and Anderson. He had a sizeable force with him. He was sure that Murchison would attack the Fort sometime. This was the time. He had told General Arnold of the attack and of his reinforcement column. The General was comfortable with that until the Officer-of-the-Day, who was a non-com, called him.

The O.D. said; "General, sir I have a large group of men, seventy, eighty or a hundred approaching the gate fast. They're in trucks and jeeps and humvees and they're going to…" and the line went dead.

The General ran out of his office and yelled at the Sergeant; "Sound the alarm. We're being invaded."

He ran outside to see vehicles careening down the street. They were carrying men who were shooting at anyone who showed their face. He went back inside before he too was shot.

He called Lenhart; "Major, where you are is a ploy. The main attack is here. We are under attack. There may be a hundred of them. Leave a token force there and get here immediately."

He had just hung up when he heard shots in the outer office. His door flew open and three men burst into his office. He found himself facing the barrel of a .45 and Felix Murchison.

"Good morning, General, or is it good afternoon? I don't know. Time flies when you're having fun. It will be fun for me but not for you."

"You won't get away with this Murchison."

"You know who I am. That's good. Now I don't have to introduce myself. My good name has preceded me."

"You haven't had a good name your whole life."

"That wasn't nice, General. It's the same name my father had. I don't like people saying my father did not have a good name." He drove his fist into the General's mid-section.

"I'm surprised you know who your father is Murchison."

He hit him again. The General grunted in pain.

"General, you will call an assembly of all your people. Military and civilian. The parade grounds. Twenty minutes. Then we will talk about your limited options."

"And if I don't call this assembly?"

"Then my men will go get them. If they refuse to come they won't have to. They won't have to because they'll be dead."

There is a loud speaker system in the camp used for bugle calls. The General picked up the microphone; "We have been invaded by Felix Murchison and his band of thieves. There will be an assembly of all personnel, military and civilian, in twenty minutes at the parade grounds."

"Pretty good, General, except the band of thieves comment. I prefer to think of us as liberators. We are going to liberate you from all your worldly goods." He laughed wickedly. "And maybe even your lives. Sit him down and tie him up." He said to his underlings. "I'm going outside and check our progress. I'll be back."

Murchison went out and saw that Aaron Strang and the other men of his who were prisoners had been freed.

Murchison said; "You didn't think I would let them keep you, did you?"

Strang said; "No, I didn't, but I wondered how much time they were going to let me have."

Murchison said; "And now they have to wonder how much time *I'm* going to let *them* have."

His men had gone to the Infirmary and hustled Dr. Linquist and his staff out to the parade ground.

Dr. Linquist said; "We can't leave these patients. Some of them are critical."

The troops who had been shot in the first hunt for the sniper were there as was Agnes Crum. Holly had been released a few minutes earlier that morning. Lolene had picked him up and took him to his billet. He and Stan shared it. It was one of the newly constructed buildings close to the SPA. That made it easier for Stan in his wheel chair.

As Lolene was delivering Holly the invasion started. They heard the gun fire of the invaders and then all was quiet for a little while.

Lolene said; "Will you be alright, Dr. Blackmore? I need to see what's going on."

"I'm alright. Thanks for the ride. You see if you can help. Stan and I will be OK. I have my pistol." It's the same pistol he had used to threaten Stan.

As he finished speaking the announcement came that all should report to the parade grounds in twenty minutes.

CHAPTER 92

The far-away shots of the fight at the PX were heard in tent city. The tent-mates in all the tents, turned to each other with curiosity, blended with fear, on their faces. Just like before the explosion, they were starting to call it E-day, gunshots meant trouble.

In the women's tent, Amanda said; "Gun shots. I'm so worried. Phil's out there somewhere."

Jen said; "I'm sure he's OK. Those shots could be Elmer getting another bear."

Amanda said; "Yeh, here in the middle of tent city. Not likely."

"Think positive thoughts, Amanda." Jen said.

Amanda said; "I am. I'm positive Phil's in trouble."

Jen turned away. She was scheduled for cafeteria duty for the evening meal and was going to rest a while.

The men were equally curious about the gunfire. They looked at each other.

Jeff was the first to speak; "I think that patrol hunting the sniper found him. That's what the gun fire was."

Elmer said; "With Billy trackin' them I'd bet your right."

Then the second round of shots came. These were closer, much louder. Now the mixture of curiosity and fear was replaced solely by fear. Something was wrong. They did not have to wait long before the announcement of the invasion and the order to assemble was heard. Now the fear was a palpable thing. They were all aware of Murchison. Aware of his psychotic behavior.

Jeff, Tom, Amos, Elmer and Boris went to the women's tent to accompany them to the parade grounds. They were joined by Jen, Amanda, Cass, Myra and Angie. Boris had stumbled wearily into the Fort two days after the first attack on the lab. Surprisingly Murchison had let him go. He wandered for two days before he found the Fort.

The residents streamed out of the tents and headed to the parade grounds. Men and women and children forming a mass of humanity shuffling down the dusty street. They passed the HQ tent and the mess hall. Sergeant Riley and Sergeant Busch and his workers joined the parade of worried walkers.

As the tent city residents approached the parade grounds, the military personnel started streaming in from the opposite direction. The troops didn't know what to do. Their officers were at the PX site. The General was the only officer left. He had just said to assemble in the parade grounds. That was the only order they had. They obeyed it.

Murchison's men encircled them when they had assembled. They milled around. They didn't know which way to face or what came next. Murchison came out of the Headquarters office. He had General Arnold with him. His underlings held the General on left and right.

Murchison said; "I'm sure you all know your ex-commander General Arnold."

He turned, raised his .45 and shot the General through the heart. Arnold's body was pushed back by the force of the shot. He had a stunned look momentarily before his eyes glazed over and he died. His body slumped supported only by the two holding him by the arms. They let go and let him fall to the floor.

The people were equally stunned. This is cold-blooded murder. This man is a monster. Oh my god. What's he going to do with us?

Murchison said; "Now you know why I said "ex-commander." He continued. "My men will now pass among you erstwhile citizens and relieve you of your excess baggage. Things that are too heavy for you to carry. Such as watches, rings, necklaces. You get the idea. Then you are free to leave. You will leave this Fort immediately. This Fort is mine now."

One man said; "But we'll have nothing. How can we survive?"

"I did." Murchison said. "So did my men. Now it's your turn. Of course if you don't want to go you don't have to. You will stay here forever but you won't know it."

They all understood the threat.

They separated the residents from the troops and started passing through the residents collecting booty. Boris passed in front of Murchison who recognized him from the attack on the SPA.

Murchison pointed at him and said; "You, pisspants. How did you get back here?"

Boris trembled and said; "Yes, sir. I made it back."

"And now you get to go out again."

"I don't want to go out again, Mr. Murchison."

"And I never wanted to see you again pisspants."

"But Mr. Murchison, I know things that could help you."

"Shut up, Boris." Cass said.

"What kind of things, pisspants?"

"If I tell you can I stay? My wife too?"

"You tell me and I'll decide."

"Don't tell him anything, Boris." Cass said.

"See that one. That one right there." He pointed at Amanda. "She's Edwards girlfriend."

"Well the Captain has good taste. You men, grab that girl and take her into the office."

"Boris you chicken shit asshole. You bastard. I hate you." Cass said.

"But Cass, I'm doing it for you. I said "my wife too."

Jeff and Jen and the rest glared at him. What a low-life.

Murchison's men went through the residents ranks. They took everything except their clothes. The thieves took gleeful pleasure in doing body searches of the women. When the husbands or boyfriends or just friends objected they were clubbed with a rifle. When they had finished confiscating the valuables they escorted them to the gate of the Fort and out into the devastated earth.

Jeff, Jen and the rest were pushed out of the Fort. Cass was with them. Boris stayed behind fawning over Murchison.

Jen said; "What's going to happen to Amanda?"

Jeff said; "I don't know. But I do know Phil is out there with his troops. He'll do something."

The amount of residents being pushed out increased. Soon there was a large group just out side the gate. They started complaining and grumbling. Their anger and frustration was evolving into rebellion. What they needed was someone to lead that revolution. Suddenly the booming voice of Dominic Manzia was heard; "Let's rush them. If we stay out here we don't have a chance."

Other voices joined Dom's; "Come on. Let's go. We'll rush them. Who's with us?"

Murchison heard the grumbling and discontent. He said to his men at the gate; "A short burst of your AK47 should discourage them. Do it."

The residents heard Murchison's order and ran away from the gate or fell to the ground. Except Dom Manzia who stood alone in defiance. The short burst of the AK47 hit him in three places. He staggered and fell. That took the impetus out of their rebellion.

Jeff, Tom and Amos rushed to help Dom. He was bleeding from wounds in both arms and his right leg. Cassandra rushed up and said; "We need to make tourniquets." She removed her scarf and tied it around Dom's arm. Jeff peeled off his shirt to make bandages. The two others did the same. They applied tourniquets and the bleeding stopped.

Dom was awake. He said; "Thanks guys for the help. You too, ma'am. I guess I owe you a scarf." He grimaced with pain and said; "I'm no match for an AK47."

Jeff said; "None of us are and they have all of them."

After confiscating what the residents had on their person, the horde of thieves had gotten into their trucks and drove to tent city. They ransacked all the tents and took everything of even minor value.

CHAPTER 93

Lolene knew Murchison's invasion had started. She decided to try to find out more. Lolene left Stan and Holly and cautiously made her way, on foot, to a concealed spot where she could see. The twenty minutes passed and all the residents and troops assembled. She saw Murchison bring the General out and murder him. She saw the residents being stripped of their possessions. She saw Boris infamy and Amanda being taken hostage. She had seen enough. She knew the Major and his troops had gone to the old PX site. She had to tell them what was happening. She went back to her cart and headed up the street to the PX. It was past the new construction and the foundations not yet being done.

CHAPTER 94

Lenhart got the General's call about the invasion and told Edwards. They did an about face with their troops. They left Lieutenant Anderson in charge at the PX. As they went they strategized about how they should attack. The General said there may be a hundred enemy.

They were unaware of the assembly of everyone on the parade grounds. They were concerned about the residents' safety. They could be caught in the crossfire of a battle. They wondered why they had heard such few shots. Had they been taken by surprise and unable to return fire? Too many unknowns.

Then Lolene came driving up the street in her cart. They called a halt to the troops and listened intently to Lolene's report.

Major Lenhart decided they would split their forces. Half of them would attack from the residents' area and half attack from the military area. Murchison's men would be in a cross fire.

Edwards was very concerned about Amanda being Murchison's hostage. He told Lenhart of his concern; "Joe, I think we have to get Amanda out of there. Murchison will use her life as a threat to get what he wants. We can't put her in that kind of danger."

"I know she's in danger, Phil, but she's being held in the General's office. How can we get her out?"

“An exchange. He really wants me. Suppose I go in under a white flag and offer myself instead of Amanda.”

“Would he even honor a white flag? He would shoot you on sight.”

“I don’t think so. He would want me to suffer first.”

“Supposing he does go for the exchange, how do you get out of there?”

“I haven’t figured that out yet. Something will come up.”

“OK, Phil, see what you can come up with while I get my force over to the military side. Let me know.”

CHAPTER 95

Lolene drove down the street at the parade grounds waving a white flag. Edwards was sitting in the first bench seat. The thieves didn't know what to do. That's the problem with having a boss with a violent temper. What if they do the wrong thing? It could be hell to pay. They let them drive on.

When the cart got within 200 feet of the HQ office it stopped. Edwards yelled; "Murchison. Come out here. I want to talk business."

A half minute passed and Murchison came out; "Captain Edwards, you've got guts coming in here. What do you want?"

"You're holding a friend of mine. I want to see her."

"And why would I let you?"

"Because I'm willing to have an exchange. Her for me. But I have to see her first."

Murchison said; "Bring the girl out."

Two men came out with Amanda between them.

"Amanda, are you alright?" She nodded yes.

"So that's the pretty lady's name, Amanda. I don't know whether I want to give her up Edwards."

"You get me instead, Murchison."

Amanda yelled; "Don't do this, Phil. He'll kill you."

"And if I don't, he'll kill you."

Murchison said; "It comes down to the value of the prize. Amanda could be a lot of fun. Then again, you could be too but in a different way Edwards. What to do. What to do. Some of these executive decisions are very difficult. Hmm. Very well, Edwards. It's a deal."

Edwards said; "You have your two men bring her out. I will meet them. When they release her, they take me."

Murchison said; "Take her out and get him."

They left. One man on each side of Amanda.

As they started Edwards stepped out of the cart. He slowly removed his gun belt and laid it on the shelf next to Lolene. The men and Amanda were closer now. He walked toward them slowly. When he was abreast of them he said; "Get in the cart, Amanda." They took his arms and tried to move him away. He shrugged them off and said; "Wait until she gets in the cart." They turned to see if she was in and he broke away from them. He ran to the cart. Amanda had made it to the cart and jumped in. Lolene drove toward Phil to pick him up. The two guards were drawing their guns. They had cleared their holsters and raised them to shoot when two shots rang out in rapid succession. They crumpled to the ground. Billy Bailey was not only an excellent tracker he was a superb marksman.

Murchison saw what was happening and shouted to his men; "Shoot them. Shoot them. Don't let them get away."

Lolene was going as fast as the cart could go, swerving left and right. Bullets whizzing by them. She was heading up the street they had left the troops.

Murchison yelled; "After them. Get your trucks and go after them."

His men scrambled to their trucks and started the pursuit. Even with the delay in getting in their trucks they were gaining fast on the little cart. The cart reached the construction area and continued up what became the rubble strewn street. It weaved in and out of the chunks of concrete and piles of debris. The trucks slowed to miss some of the debris.

The shooting started then. Not the trucks shooting at the cart but the troops hidden among the demolished buildings firing at the trucks. The trucks could not turn around and go back easily because of the rubble. They had to pull ahead a few feet, back up, then pull ahead to turn around. All the while they were being fired upon. Bullets were penetrating the cab, the body, the hood and the men. Some tried to return fire but the troops were well covered. The lead truck had stalled. The troops were pouring shots into it. One hit the fuel tank and the truck exploded into a burning, hulking mass. The occupants ran for their lives. Some made it. The other trucks eventually made it down the street and away from the shooting.

Lolene had stopped the cart when she saw the pursuit had stopped. Phil and Amanda jumped out of the cart and grabbed each other in a bone-crushing hug followed by a kiss of love and gratitude.

Amanda said; “That was a crazy thing to do and I love you for it.”

“I had to do something, honey. I couldn’t let you stay there.”

“You’re making it sound as if you’d do it for anybody.”

“No, honey, I’d only do it for your body.” Phil grinned.

He reluctantly released Amanda and called Sergeant Emmons over: “Have you heard from Major Lenhart?”

“Yes, sir, they are in position.”

“Good. Assemble the troops and I’ll explain the operation.”

“Yes, sir.”

Billy Bailey came trotting up.

Edwards said; “Good shooting, Billy.”

“It was only about two hundred yards, Captain. I can hit the eye of a squirrel at that distance. I know you told me not to shoot Murchison cause you wanted him, but I put a shot over his head just for fun. You shoulda seen him skedaddle back inside."

"I would have liked to have seen that, Billy."

CHAPTER 96

The truck carrying the thieves that had gone to tent city came back to the parade ground with their meager loot. They were disembarking from their trucks and the rest of the thieves ran up to see what they had brought. That's when the first hand grenade hit. Then the second. Then multiple grenades tearing into their ranks.

The ones not wounded or killed by the grenades looked up to see a mass of troops rushing towards them from two directions guns a'blazing. They tried to raise their weapons to return the fire but most of them were cut down before they could. The surprise attack had worked well.

Maybe Murchison didn't know that there was a force that had gone to the old PX. Maybe he thought that the ones they had assembled were all the military personnel. Arnold Strang was a prisoner and not a spy and couldn't tell him.

The troops that had been part of the ones assembled grabbed the rifles of the fallen thieves and joined the fight.

Murchison heard the explosion of the first grenade. He looked out the office window and saw that the fight was not going well for him. He ran outside and saw Boris cowering against the wall; "You, pisspants. Where's that crippled guy that runs the machine?"

"I…I…I think he's in one of the new buildings they built."

"Which building?"

"I don't know which building. One of them."

"You're no help." Murchison said and shot Boris in the head.

Murchison started easing his way out of the heart of the firefight and toward the new buildings. He knew that Stan was the only one who knew how to operate the SPA. If I can't have it no one will he thought.

Edwards was busy directing the troops. Giving orders and warning of dangers to his men. He looked up just in time to see Murchison go inside one of the new buildings. Now's my chance he thought. I've got him trapped inside that building. He disengaged himself from the fight and headed toward that building. He had taken two steps when Murchison exited the building and went to another. What's he doing? Then it dawned on him. He's after Stan. He started running.

CHAPTER 97

Murchison was getting angry and frustrated. No one in the first building and now no one in the second building. Was pisspants lying or just trying to save his worthless self? He won't be telling any more lies will he?

Murchison went to the third building. He opened the door and saw Holly Blackmore with a pistol pointed at him. Murchison lurched aside and Holly's shot missed him by inches. Murchison went to the window, the one in which Holly had seen him coming, and peered in. He didn't see Stan. Maybe they were in different buildings? Then he saw Stan wheel himself into the room.

Murchison went back to the door, flung it open and raised his gun to shoot Stan and Holly. Phil Edwards launched himself at Murchison and landed on his back just as he pulled the trigger. The shot went into the ceiling. Murchison had been knocked down by Phil's attack. He quickly turned around to see Phil picking himself up. He raised his gun and Phil kicked it out of his hand. It went clattering across the floor. Holly picked it up and tossed it to Phil. It didn't make it. Murchison caught it instead. He whirled around to shoot and Phil crashed into him. He forced him backwards into the wall. They thudded into the wall and Phil grabbed his arm that held the gun with both hands. Phil threw his arm against the wall trying to dislodge the gun. Again and again. Murchison held on. Murchison took his free arm and punched Phil's mid-section time after time. Phil let go of the arm with one hand and swung his fist into Murchison's face. Blood streamed out from his nose. They veered away from the wall and were whirling together. Both trying to gain an advantage. They crashed into the wall on the opposite side of the room barely missing a collision with Stan. They crashed into a window. The glass shattered and a piece cut Phil's hand. The slippery blood made it even more difficult to hold on to Murchison's arm. He was losing his grip. He swung at Murchison again and again with his free hand. Some punches to the face, some to the body. Blood began dripping onto the floor. Some from Phil. Some from Murchison. Phil's feet slipped on the bloody floor and he fell. He still had Murchison's arm so he fell too. The jarring movement of hitting the floor caused Phil to lose his grip on Murchison's arm. Murchison quickly jerked his arm away, stood up and swung the gun toward Phil. A look of utter surprise covered Murchison's face as he was shot by Holly's pistol. That surprise lasted long enough for Phil to unholster his own gun. When Murchison swung his gun toward Phil he was ready. Three quick shots to the torso and Felix Murchison fell face forward onto the bloody floor just missing Phil who was stall laying there. Phil stood and gasped for breath.

He said; "That's for Colonel Burden and General Arnold and all the other people you've murdered."

Phil looked at Stan and Holly and said; "Are you guys alright?"

Stan said; "Yes, but if you hadn't gotten here when you did we would both be dead."

CHAPTER 98

The battle had ended. The victorious combatants were policing the battlefield. They had some prisoners to lock-up. Major Lenhart was assuming command. He was the senior Officer after General Arnold's death.

The residents were filing back into camp. Jeff, Tom and Amos had taken Dom Manzia to the Infirmary. Jen, Amanda and Cass went along. They waited for Dr. Linquist report.

He came out and told them Dom had severe wounds but would recover. He turned to Jen and said; "You were here the other day volunteering to give blood to Joan."

Jen said; "Yes, I was, but she had expired."

"I have another lady here who requires type O. Her name is Agnes Crum. Would you be willing to donate?"

"I would be happy to." Jen said. "I'll be back soon."

"Thank you." The Doctor said; "Now, if you'll excuse me I have several wounded to attend to."

They were headed to the door when it opened and Phil Edwards came in. He had a cloth wrapped around his hand from the cut he had received. His clothes were covered with blood stains and sweat. His hair was mussed and he looked exhausted. They looked at him and wondered what happened. Why did he look like that? Except Amanda, she was overjoyed to see him alive. She rushed to him and threw her arms around his neck.

She said; “Oh Phil, Phil, I was so worried for you. Are you alright?”

“Thanks, honey, I’m tired but alright. I cut my hand.”

“You cut your hand. I’m so glad it’s nothing worse. How did you cut your hand?”

“During the fight with Murchison, Amanda.”

“You fought Murchison?”

“He went to Stan and Holly’s.” Phil said. “We fought. I won. He’s dead.”

“He’s dead? You killed him?”

“Yes, he’s dead.”

They collectively breathed a sigh of relief. They congratulated Phil and inquired about Stan and Holly. Phil said they were alright.

Jeff said; “You had better get that hand taken care of. Come on guys, let’s go.”

They left, except Amanda. She stayed with Phil.

When they left they saw Boris body where Murchison had murdered him. They paused for a moment. Cass said; “I’ll have to make some arrangements for him.” She shed one tear and then they moved on. Apparently she had too.

Jeff took Jen’s hand as they left the Infirmary. He walked slowly so the others were slightly ahead of them as they went back to their tents.

Jeff said; “Murchison dead. That’s one big problem eliminated.”

“Yes.” Jen said. “But we still have plenty of others.”

“Yes we do, Jen. I hope they’re not between us.”

“No, Jeff. They’re not us. I think we’re going to be good together for a long, long time.”

Jeff grinned happily and they walked down the dusty road hand in hand.

End of Parts 1 and 2

Epilogue:

Earth was moving out of Venus Shadow. They were getting longer periods of light as the sun made its appearance. It was also warming the earth and making the days much more pleasant.

What happens now? Jeff and Jen? Phil and Amanda? Will there be more than a scarf tying Dominic and Cass together? What of James and Agnes May/December relationship? Stan? Dr. Blackmore? Lyman Haskill can leave his colleagues now. Roman Velez? Lolene? Emmons? Riley? Dr. Linquist? The Baileys? Sergeant Busch? What happens now?

That was the thought of all of them. It had only been two and a half months since the explosion. They had neither been able to know the fate of their loved ones nor to mourn their loss. What will happen in the coming year? How are we going to get food and power and fuel and water and clothing? How will we? What happens now?

Printed in Great Britain
by Amazon